MERIGAN TALES

Stories from the World of *Star's Reach*

MERIGAN TALES

Stories from the World of *Star's Reach*

EDITED BY

JOHN MICHAEL GREER

FOUNDERS HOUSE
PUBLISHING

Merigan Tales: Stories from the World of *Star's Reach*

Copyright © 2016 John Michael Greer

All rights reserved.

All stories are copyrighted to their respective authors, and used here with their permission.

Published 2016 by Founders House Publishing, LLC
www.foundershousepublishing.com

Cover art © 2016 Grandfailure/Dreamstime.com
Cover and interior design © 2016 Founders House Publishing, LLC
Paperback Edition: March 2016
ISBN-13: 978-1-945810-00-8
ISBN-10: 1-945810-00-9

Printed in the United States of America

CONTENTS

MERIGAN TALES

Stories from the World of *Star's Reach*

FOREWORD

JOHN MICHAEL GREER

It seems like a very long time now since the day I sat down in front of my keyboard, gave the blank screen in front of me an equally blank look, and finally started typing: *One wet day on the road that runs alongside the Hiyo River to Sisnaddi...* Once the words started, they came more easily than I'd expected—more easily than any other fiction project I've ever written. Trey sunna Gwen, the protagonist of my novel *Star's Reach*, had found his voice.

That was in the summer of 2009. A few weeks earlier, my wife Sara and I had bailed out on the west coast, where we'd spent all our lives up to that point, and moved to an old red brick mill town in the north central Appalachians. My writing career was at a crossroads, too, though I didn't really know that yet. For the previous three years I'd been writing a weekly blog on the future of industrial society, *The*

Archdruid Report, and the year before, I'd placed a book on the same subject with New Society Publishers; that would be the first of ten so far, but of course that was still in the future when I started work on *Star's Reach*. All I knew is that I had things to say that would no longer fit within the boundaries I'd staked out with my previous books on nature spirituality, and some of them might best be said through the medium of fiction.

I wrote *Star's Reach* an episode at a time over the course of more than three years, and posted them, one more or less each month, to an online blog I'd started for the purpose. It seemed like the most sensible approach, as I had no particular hope that publishers would be interested in a story that didn't fit into any of the established genres—a novel set four hundred years in the future that wasn't about spaceships and rayguns, and wasn't about the aftermath of apocalypse either.

It was a world that was still having to deal with the consequences of our civilization's frankly brainless maltreatment of the biosphere that keeps us all alive, as any realistic vision of the future has to be, and it was also a world still echoing with other legacies of our time, just as our time still echoes to events centuries in its own past. Through that world, Trey sunna Gwen, the young ruinman from the town we call Chattanooga and he called Shanuga, worked and wandered and fought and loved his way to a destination and a destiny I'd barely glimpsed when his first words appeared on my computer screen.

By the time he got to his goal, he had plenty of company, and that wasn't limited to characters in the story. To my great surprise, *Star's Reach* found an enthusiastic audience, and a publisher: Shaun Kilgore of Founders House Publishing approached me before the story was even finished and asked about bringing it out in a print edition, which duly appeared. Sales were quite respectable, and many of the notes and emails from readers shared a common theme: can we please have more stories set in the world of *Star's Reach*?

My own fiction had already headed in other directions by then, but there was a readily available answer. Through my main blog, I'd already hosted three contests for science fiction stories set in the kind of future we're actually likely to get—that is to say, not the hackneyed trope of humanity's supposedly invincible march to the stars, nor the equally dreary theme of overnight apocalypse, but a future in which individuals and societies have had to come to terms with the hard limits of a finite planet, and gone on to live their lives anyway. Those contests had resulted in four anthologies, also published by Founders House. Why not host a contest for stories set in Meriga—we pronounce that "America" these days—and the world around it, filling in some of the many blanks left by Trey's account of his wanderings?

The contest duly happened, the stories came in, and as usual, I had a very hard time sorting out a single anthology's worth from the many good tales that came over my virtual transom. I've arranged them in more or less chronological order, beginning a long time before Trey's lifetime and ending somewhat later. The tales ahead have many different themes and styles, but then that's one of the delights of any anthology written by many authors. As a little added bonus, I've included a glossary to the place names and other terminology found in *Star's Reach*, which some readers have found puzzling.

I would like to thank all the authors who submitted stories to the contest, and also Shaun Kilgore, whose enthusiasm for

Star's Reach and this project alike helped make both books a pleasure to bring to print. Most of all, though, I'm grateful to everyone who made room in their lives and their imaginations for Trey sunna Gwen and his journey. My thanks go with all.

THE SECOND COMING

AL SEVCIK

The cracks and splinters in the cart's plank floor pained Alex's knees. Mud and cow dung splattered the floor, the bars of the cage and Alex. Some who threw were recent friends, their faces now distorted in anger. Hands tied behind his back, Alex kneeled as low as he could and bent his head to protect himself. Blood trickled across his left cheek and dripped on the wagon floor.

The cart's metal-edged wheels dropped into the road's ruts then jolted upward on dry mud mounds rocking the wagon far to the side then down again. Two men in faded grey-green uniforms slouched on the front bench guiding a pair of reluctant mules. The wagon lurched past vegetable stands, two butcheries, the taverns, and the town's smithy. The storekeepers, the butchers, the town's trades people, wives, kids from small to tall, had gathered on both sides of the narrow road, their backs to the shops. Most watched silently but many hurled insults and trash. An elderly man shouted, "Why did you do this to us? You knew it was a lie." A woman in her mid 20's with tear-streaked cheeks yelled, "We wanted so much to believe you." She spat at Alex. "I'll hate you forever."

The crowd thinned as the cart left the shops, moving through a scattering of packed dirt yards and owner-built houses of rough-cut lumber. At the edge of his vision Alex glimpsed people whose names he knew, but mostly he crouched in the center of the wagon, eyes closed, chin against chest, frightened, enduring. He felt the sun's heat. He waited for this to pass.

The wagon stopped while two men struggled with a girl who had fought her way into the road in front of the mules. She broke free and ran to the wagon, grabbing the bars with both hands. "I don't care what you say. I believe him." She kicked at one of the men who stepped back. "You can't stop me. I'm going with him."

The men hesitated, looking at each other. One shrugged then called to the driver, "Might as well put her in the cage too."

"Can't do that. She's not charged with anything."

The driver prodded the mules and the wagon started moving again, the girl's right fist held onto a bar. The man called after the wagon, "We charge her with being stupid." Then, in a lower voice to his companion, "Just like the rest of us."

Alex lifted his head to look as the girl stumbled and grabbed at the cage with her other hand. He saw a plain dirt streaked face, unevenly cut short brown hair, and a long brown skirt. He didn't know her. He dropped his head again.

His horse, tied to the back of the wagon, snorted as a

thrown rock bruised her neck. Please, not my horse, he thought. I deserve your anger, but my horse is innocent.

The hecklers dispersed as the wagon, Alex, his horse and the stumbling girl passed through the collapsed remnants of what had once been a gate in an encircling stockade. The stockade's timbers had been repurposed decades earlier, but gateposts remained to mark the town's official edge. For the next half mile the countryside opened to planted fields but then the road came to brush at the edge of a forest. The wagon stopped. The driver's companion slid off the bench and jumped to the ground. He untied the rope to Alex's horse and then unlocked the cage, grabbed Alex's arm and jerked him out. Hands still tied behind him, Alex fell kneeling in the dirt. Pulling a knife from a scabbard at his waist, the guard cut Alex's wrists free. Then he pushed the girl away from the wagon so that she fell backwards onto grass. He climbed back on the wagon as the driver whipped the mules to make them turn and start back.

The driver spit in Alex's direction. The wagon rumbled away.

Alex sat up rubbing his hands to bring back circulation. He watched the girl who grimaced as she pushed up from the grass. She crawled through the grass to Alex then knelt to study his face. "Your forehead's a mess." She stood, looked around, and pointed to where the ground dropped out of sight. "There may be a stream over there. I'll need some water to wash off that blood." She took an unsteady step, paused for deep breaths, then disappeared into brush. She returned holding out the dripping edge of her skirt. Kneeling again, she washed his face then squeezed bloody water from the cloth. Brown eyes studied the wound. "You'll live." She rocked back on her heels. "If you're wondering, my name's

Nora."

Alex stared at her, trying to focus his mind. There was grass and bushes and a girl he didn't know. "I'm Alex." His fingers touched the soreness on his forehead. "I don't know what to do."

"I know you, Alex." She studied him for several seconds, then pushed up and stood in the road looking back the way they had come. Then she turned around and eyed the forest. She held her hand out and helped Alex to his feet. "Alex, it looks like there's only one way to go from here." She walked to where his horse was grazing. She patted the spotted gray flank and teased a tuft of white on her forehead. "What's her name?"

"She's Nellie. My horse."

Nora felt Nellie's lips nuzzling her hand. "Nellie's a work horse. She's strong enough to carry us both." Nora looked at the sun, half way down the western sky. "We better go."

Alex thought. "Are we both going to ride on Nellie?"

"Yes. I don't think Nellie will mind."

"Nora, where are we going?"

Nora patted Nellie's flank. "The folks here don't like us anymore. Let's you and I go find a place where the people are friendly."

"We'll have to ride bareback."

"Come on, Alex, help me up."

He cupped his hand for her foot as she grabbed the horse's mane and pulled herself up. He half-jumped half-pulled himself onto the broad back. He felt her hands on his waist. He jiggled a rope that was loosely tied around the horse's neck. Nellie snorted then stepped onto the road. In a few steps they were surrounded by brush, then the tree tops closed over them. Sunshine flickered through restless foliage.

Ahead the road was clear but they could see only a short ways though the brush covered forest floor on either side.

After about an hour Alex spoke into the air. "Why did you grab the bars of the cage?"

Nora's body sagged, she pressed her forehead against his back. "I had to. You need me."

* * *

To Nora, Alex had appeared magically in the morning three months ago although some said that he had walked into town overnight and others thought they saw him at sunrise jumping off a wagon that didn't stop. He was friendly and he offered his hand to everyone he passed. "Hi, my name's Alex. I want to tell you about the machines from the Old World and how we're going to get them back."

Some of the folks he spoke to said, "Not likely," "I don't think so," or "That's not possible." But others smiled and later said to their friends, "He's so positive and enthusiastic maybe he really has special knowledge. Anyway, his smile is nice, and he is likable." They found him a place to stay and saw that he had food and clothing. People came to hear him talk and then stayed to daydream about the wonderful machines. Many became believers. But then, after weeks passed and no machines appeared they became impatient, then angry. A delegation went to the mayor who charged Alex with disturbing the town and told the police to take him away.

Nora had been one of the first to see Alex the day he arrived, and through the following weeks and months she stayed within sight of him, but always from far in back, in the shadows. Where others saw a liar she saw a confused man struggling to understand voices and images from an ethereal realm. When the others turned on Alex and drove him from the town she knew what she had to do.

* * *

She felt his ribs sharp against her hands. "My friends tried to stop me from coming with you. I fought them," she whispered. "I'm a bad person."

The soft swish of Nellie's hooves on the dusty road blended with wind-rustled leaves and the subtle buzzes and chirps of forest life. After a time Alex stopped the horse and turned around. "You're my friend, Nora. I know you're not a bad person. So don't say that."

The only words Nora could think to say were, "Thanks Alex. That helps." She looked around at the long shadows and the darkening forest. "Alex, it will be dark soon. I think we should stop for the night."

Alex nodded.

Nora continued. "It's best to be off the road. Strangers and dark are a bad mix." She pointed into the brush. "Under that tree over there might be good."

"I'll go look." Alex jumped to the ground and held his hands up to Nora.

"I can do it." She descended in a controlled slide down Nellie's flank. The horse stepped to the road's edge and pulled at clumps of grass.

Alex led Nelly away from the road into the trees and brush for several hundred feet, stopping by a white barked tree. "You're right, Nora. We can stay here."

"Good," she said. "I saw some berries. I'll get our dinner."

Waiting for her return, Alex cleared the grass beneath the

tree, scraping away sticks and leaves. He kicked clumps of debris that might shield snakes. She came back holding her dress up cradling dark berries. He frowned at the harvest. "You're sure these are ok to eat?"

"We'll soon know," she said, scooping up a handful.

After a time he lay back on the grass. "It's not soft, but it's not too bad. I wish we had a cover, it could get cold."

She shrugged. "We'll lie against each other."

She woke once in the dark as Nellie shifted position, her hoof snapping a branch. An almost full moon flashed intermittently through twitching leaves. Beside her Alex breathed heavily. Then it was dawn.

She turned to Alex. He was awake. Tears channeled across his cheeks. She touched his face. "Alex..."

He sat up, his fingers smearing the wet. "The dream came back. It's so real." He searched her face. "I want them to leave me alone. I'm not smart enough to do what they want, Nora. You saw what a failure I was." He covered his eyes with both hands. "I was put in a cage and now the dream people are forcing me do it all over again."

She pulled him to her, his head against her breasts, feeling his heavy breathing. She whispered, "I'm eighteen, Alex. Younger than you but I can help, if you'll let me."

He sat back and looked at her, his cheeks red. "In the Old World they had machines that did everybody's work. The machines did everything. Everybody knows about that. It all went away a long time ago." He stood, hands loose at his sides. "But people, mostly old people, come to me in the night. They say I have to bring it all back so that everyone will have a good life again. Nora, I don't know how to do that."

"I don't understand you Alex, but I'm here to help you."

She held out a handful of berries. "Eat these. This is our breakfast."

They gulped the berries, then up onto Nellie's back and onto the road. As the sun climbed up the sky the forest shadows shortened, flowering bushes turned their leaves toward the intermittent light. Towards noon they met a wagon piled high with hay driven by a ruddy faced man and next to him a boy. Alex nodded, "Any problems on the road?"

"Me and the boy left the farm at sunup. All ok." He tousled the boy's hair. "Gonna sell some hay and show my kid the town." He studied Alex and Nora, obviously noting the absence of saddlebags or possessions. "May Gaia grant you an easy ride."

"Thanks," Nora said, "Good luck with your sale."

Alex let the rope slap Nelly's neck, telling her to go.

The forest thinned as they rode and then gave way to cultivated fields and distant farmhouses. Late in the afternoon they passed a dirt turnoff that led to a rough wood-sided house a quarter of a mile away. A nearby barn leaned uncertainly. Two young horses grazed by the barn. Nora poked Alex's back. "No one's around. Do you think we could take one?"

"That would be wrong, Nora. It's a poor farm. It would hurt these people to lose a horse."

Nora poked his back again. "It was a joke, Alex. I'm not a thief."

"Oh. I'm sorry, Nora."

"That's ok. But where are we riding to? It's getting late, I'm hungry and I'm tired of sitting on Nellie."

Alex looked at the farm, at the field beyond, and then up and down the road they were on. He frowned and pressed fingers against his temple. "I don't know. What do you think

20

we should do?"

Nora said, "Let's ride Nellie to that farmhouse and knock on the door." Alex jiggled Nellie's rope, she turned into the farm and stopped at the house. Together they stepped up onto the narrow porch, jumping when the front door opened inward revealing a large woman who filled the frame. Green eyes probed them and then their horse. Red-grey hair was restrained with a green ribbon. A home-spun shirt, faded blue, hung open across her chest and stomach, knotted at her waist. "What do you want?" Her voice held an edge of annoyance.

"I... We..." Alex stuttered.

Nora said, "We can work for food and a place to sleep tonight."

She eyed them distastefully. "I don't think so." She partly closed the door, then opened it again. "Wait. My husband will soon be coming from the field. He might be wanting for help." She stepped back. "Come in. Go to the table. Sit. Don't touch anything." She gave each a slice of buttered bread and poured two cups of milk. "Your names?"

"I'm Nora. This here is Alex."

"Ok, Nora and Alex. Stay right there. I'm going to find my man." She left the kitchen.

Eating silently they eyed the plank table and benches, dented pots scrubbed shiny, the cast iron griddle hanging on the wall, and the tin-lined sink with hand pump for well water.

"The bread is good," Nora said. Alex nodded.

The woman came back followed by a man larger than herself placing each of his steps with care. He had black hair streaked with white, narrowed eyes, an off-white mustache curled down around his lips. The muscles in his arms rippled as he moved. "You're too skinny to work." He said.

Alex stood. "Try me."

The woman turned to Nora. "Girl, can you do anything useful?"

"I never learned cookin', but I can scrub and clean."

Steadying himself with one hand on the table, the man sat at the far end. He put his hands behind him pushing at muscles in his back, lips pressed tight. He said, "I angered my back a few days ago. Can't lift. Can't carry. Can't do man's work. But I have a fence to build. Might use some help. Can you work?"

Alex said, "I don't know nothin' but work. Worked all my life."

"All your life." The man smiled briefly. What's that? Twenty, twenty-one years?"

"About that, I guess."

"Any schooling?

"I can write my name."

"Well now, y'all go with Mae. She'll help clean yourselves and your clothes. Then we'll have a real dinner. By the way, the name's John." Placing his hands flat on the table he pushed up and left the room.

* * *

Light from the kitchen window was fading when Mae lit two vegetable oil lamps. She set them at the ends of the table where they pushed the gathering dark into the corners. The four of them sat with Mae and John on one side facing Alex and Nora. Alex forked his sausage and buttered cornmeal. He spooned soft cheese from a crock and spread it on bread. "When the machines come again you won't have to worry about your back. The machines will dig the holes and stretch the wire. They'll build all the fences you want." He bit into his bread.

John stopped eating, his fork in the air. "And when is this going to happen, the second coming of the old technology?"

"Soon. After I see the boss."

"The boss of what?"

Alex looked at Nora. "I...I dunno exactly. They say I have to see somebody who's in charge. Somebody really important. I guess the boss of...of Texas." He looked into the space above Mae and John, at something beyond the kitchen. "I have to go to him, to tell him to release the machines. Thing is, I don't exactly know where he is."

John sat back. "Where he is? Son, do you have any idea where you are?"

"People always say Texas. I suppose Texas is pretty much everything."

Bert looked around the table. Mae and Nora were staring at Alex. "Well, Alex, if you go a few hundred miles east," he pointed to a kitchen wall, "You'll get to the country of Meriga. Bad place. A traveler told me it rains there months at a time." He pointed to the opposite wall. "There's mountains the other way, then desert. Go south and there's Meycan Mexico where folks are itching to grab part of Texas but Jennel Roberts won't let that happen. We are in Texas which is the biggest part of a country called the United States. If you're looking for a boss I suppose Texas Ranger Jennel Roberts would do. He heads the army and folks would say that he is the government in Texas. Most often he's in Dallas."

Alex chewed for awhile then spread cheese on another piece of bread. "I'm going to Dallas."

"One thing," John said, "Word is that the jennel is a mean son of a bitch. Might be best not to go."

Alex looked at Nora, at Mae and at John. He fingered the knife beside his plate. His fingers curled around it, making a fist. "John, this is what I have to do. I was told to. It's up to me to bring back the lost technology." His voice strengthened. "I'm the one and if anyone tries to stop me..." He stabbed the knife into the table. Then his muscles relaxed. He stared at the knife as if he hadn't seen it before, pulled it from the wood and lay it beside his plate. He sat back on the bench.

John cleared his throat. "Well, a person doesn't have to be totally sane to build a fence. I'm looking for you to help me tomorrow." He stood. "Breakfast is at sunrise. Mae, find them a place to sleep."

Mae said, "Alex, there's a rolled up straw mattress in the bedroom. It'll just fit on the floor of the pantry. You'll wake up when I come into the kitchen tomorrow. Nora, let's clean up now." Later, close to Nora, she whispered, "Are you sure you'll be safe? I mean, sleeping aside that man?"

Nora held Mae's hand. "Alex is good. I know he has a demon clawing at his insides, but who of us doesn't?"

* * *

The orange and yellow sky faded into sunrise as Alex followed John through dew wet grass across an open field. John stopped, selected a spot and pushed a stick into the ground. "We'll start here." He handed Alex a coil of lightweight rope. "Take this over towards that tree and stretch it tight. Then we'll mark where the posts go, every fifteen feet." They worked through the morning stretching rope, measuring,

24

marking, and Alex digging holes. When the sun was high Nora brought them pork sandwiches, cheese and a fresh jug of water. Alex and John ate sitting side by side on a grass covered mound. John broke off a grass seed stem and plucked at it absently. "Alex, tell me about the old world and all that stuff. The world that's coming back."

Alex let John's question hover unanswered until he felt it settle on him. He studied the water in his cup.

* * *

Years disappeared, he was looking through young eyes up at his uncle, acres of overalls then a beard and a permanently turned down mouth below heavy black eyebrows. Behind his uncle there were two boys about his age. They had books bound with straps and were walking away. His uncle's knuckles hit his head. "What you staring at boy? Get to shoveling. Damn kids going to school when there's lots of work right here. If it weren't for their mother..." He scowled at Alex. "Well, you ain't no kin of hers. She don't care nothin' about you so there'll be no wastin' your time with schoolin'. Your father was my brother but that don't make you special. Two years older than me, the family smart ass, all the time readin' then talking nonsense about something he'd read. Books even. What good came of that? He's dead."

At family meals Alex sat quiet. He listened to talk his cousins brought back from school, what visitors said, the churchman and the neighbors. He learned that he lived in Texas and that life didn't used to be endless physical labor. Long time ago, more than four hundred years, there had been machines that did all the work, plowed the fields, harvested, everything. Back then machines went on roads that were smooth. Once a visiting teacher said that what the long ago people had was technology. Technology made it possible to have the machines, even machines that could fly and space ship machines that went to the moon.

Over months and years this knowledge fermented in his brain. It was wrong. Unfair. Why did everyone who lived so long ago have technology but not today? Who took it all away? Why? Month after month as he pitch-forked hay into the manual bailer, as he guided the mule's plow, as he dug and cut and carried his anger gnawed. It wrapped itself around his brain, it clutched at his heart. The machines must have been hidden, long ago. Whatever the reason it must have long since gone away and now everything should be brought back. He rarely thought of anything else.

Then, six months ago in the dark time after midnight a hand shook him awake.

A man in farmer's clothing, his tanned face a web of sun dried wrinkles, bent over the bed. His face and his eyes were in shadow above a white beard which was trimmed below his chin. Alex tried to move but his muscles stuck. Tentacles of fear probed the edges of his brain. The farmer motioned for him to stand and he was able to move again. His bedroom wall disappeared. They were at the edge of a corn field. Alex reached for a tasseled corn ear but the figure stopped him with a raised hand.

A distant rumble coming closer and something dark, something larger than Alex, roared towards them through the field, passed them and was gone. In it's wake a row of minced stalks and sacks packed with corn. Alex's chest tightened. A machine, a real corn harvesting machine. But, he hadn't seen it clearly. As he turned to follow a cold hand gripped his arm. "What you saw. That's what could be." He

26

turned Alex around. "Look." A stooped white-haired lady was coming towards them carefully placing her cane at each step. The man squeezed Alex's arm. His voice was soft. "Life is so hard, Alex. A man and his woman get old too soon. You must help us." The farmer, his wife, the cornfield, disappeared.

He awoke with his uncle calling from downstairs. "Stupid kid. Staying in bed all day? Forget about breakfast. Get out to the field."

During the day his memory replayed the wonder of the harvesting machine. It was clear in his mind, but did it really happen? Were dreams real in a special kind of way? What troubled him was, if the specter was in some way real was his call for help also real? Must he do something?

As weeks passed Alex's concern became more obsessive. He stood puzzling the question one morning with his hand on the hayloft ladder when a rope snapped across his chest. Spots of blood colored his shirt. His eyes teared.

"Lazy kid. I don't feed you to stand around daydreaming. Move."

Weeks later the specter returned. This time the farmer was leaning on a cane. He looked older than before. Alex tried to get out of the bed but the farmer held up his hand. He motioned to someone Alex couldn't see. A young girl, maybe six or seven years old, stepped out of the shadows. She came to the edge of the bed and held the farmer's hand. She wore overalls over a roughly woven white cotton shirt. Her garments were clean but worn and patched. Shy brown eyes impassively regarded Alex. He smiled, but her expression didn't change.

"She's my granddaughter. Sick father, overworked mother, living with us to help with the farm." He looked hard at

Alex. "When I look at my granddaughter I despair for her future. Scratch the dirt, grow old, die." His thin wavering hand touched Alex's shoulder. "Alex, save my granddaughter, save all the children, all of us. Bring back the machines. You're the one. You do it. Go to the bosses, demand the machines back."

Then Alex was alone. Pressing hands to his head he tried to stop the headache, tried to stop shivering, tried to stop hearing the words over and over. He fell back on the bed.

When he woke at dawn his mind was calm. He had been given instructions. He knew what he had to do.

The next night he shoved a razor and some clothing into a cloth bag and walked away from his uncle's farm. He found a path that bypassed the nearest town but days later as the sun rose he came to another. He stopped, washed his face at a central fountain and then started talking. He didn't have to think, the words just came. He talked about the new world that was to be. He talked about the re-coming of technology which was waiting just beyond their view but blocked by the bosses. His voice was clear, his eyes glowed with certainty.

His words flowed easily and they had the persuasive strength of belief. As days passed, people gathered around. He was given food and shelter. People came, first a few and the few grew into crowds. But it hadn't ended well. The machines didn't appear. People misunderstood. They expected the machines to come immediately. They harassed him. They wanted the machines now. Adoration became disillusion then turned into hate. The barred wagon. Then he was in a cage, pulled through town crouching afraid, bleeding. He had failed.

* * *

Alex fingered the cup in his hand. He turned it upside down, pouring the water on the grass. He looked up. "I can't explain, John. A message was given to me. The words repeat over and over in my head. The old technology is waiting to be released again. I'm the one. I have to do it." He stood and wiped his hands on his pants. "John, I'll finish making the fence for you, then I have to go."

John studied Alex, then stood, pressing both hands against his back. "Who knows? Alex, you might..." He stopped. "Come on, you haven't got us the machines yet so we have to finish this job ourselves."

"John. A question."

"What?"

"Where is Dallas?"

* * *

Two mornings later Alex and Nora stood in the farmhouse doorway with bundles at their feet. A waterproof cloth was wrapped around a change of clothes, another bag held bread, dried meat and fruit. John squeezed Alex's shoulder then Mae gave him a hug. When she pulled Nora close Mae whispered, "Girl, if bad trouble ever finds you come back to us. Anytime. John and I would be content to have a grown up daughter in the house."

Nora's eyes watered, she nodded at Alex and they walked to Nellie. Alex positioned the bundles, helped Nora up and then pulled himself onto Nellie. When they reached the highway they looked back at the cottage and waved. Then they started trekking to Dallas.

From time to time they met other travelers and for several

hours they rode alongside a family on their way to market three pigs. Always, when travelers met on the road they kept a wary distance from each other until apprehensions subsided.

In mid-afternoon they found themselves alone and a darkening sky. When lightning danced across distant hills Nora poked Alex's back. "We need to find shelter." Then rain spattered the road. A thickening mist obscured their surroundings. They turned toward the only house they could see. A thin, sad-faced woman holding an infant let them into the barn. Later, still with the baby, she came by and handed them four hardboiled eggs. The little one reached out and touched Nellie. The woman said, "That's a good and patient horse. Where are y'all going?"

Nora said, "Thank you for the eggs. We're on our way to Dallas."

"My, you must have important business."

Alex said, "We do. We're going to bring back the lost machinery of the Old World."

The woman's eyes widened. "Really? Can you do that?" She almost threw the baby to Nora, ran to Alex and hugged him. "Oh I wish you could. That would be so wonderful. I want to believe that you can." She released Alex and backed away, embarrassed. Her expression became wistful. "My man and I...It's so hard, you know, just getting by. But I suppose that's the way it is most everywhere." She took back the baby and pushed the barn door open. "You can stay until after the rain. I'll bring you some soup later."

Standing in the open door Alex watched her go then stood absently watching the puddles grow. "Nora, the old farmer who comes at night with his granddaughter wants me to help this woman. The voices do too. That's why they want

30

me to go to Dallas, so she'll have machines to plow her land, to light her house, even to milk her cow." His hands gripped Nora's shoulders. He stared hard into her face, then over her head into the dark of the barn. His grip tightened painfully but she didn't move. "Am I doing the right thing? Sometimes I'm a little scared." Dropping his hands he turned away. "Jennel Roberts will understand."

* * *

They passed towns crouched down within stockades, further on the stockades had gaps, and as they neared Dallas houses and shops were without stockade protection at all. The roads had been improved, the humps shoveled down, the ruts filled in. They met more travelers with carts of farm produce. They passed concrete slabs imbedded in the ground, broken off concrete walls, occasionally a lone concrete pillar. At noon they stopped near a group beside the spectral remnants of buildings that had once bordered a paved area. A man in the group said, "I heard that over in Meriga they have people called ruinmen to take this stuff away. I could crack the concrete myself to get the reinforcing rods, but I don't care to answer to Jennel Roberts."

Further along the road there were more buildings. Homes, taverns and businesses. Pushcart vendors sold vegetables, clothing, and house wares. The country road became a city street. Alex stopped the horse. "Look, Nora. The shops are all the way to the end of the block and on both sides of the road." Dismounting, he walked Nellie past stands offering vegetables and even meat. At one shop the proprietor, a middle-aged man with a ruddy face, wearing a stained apron, stood at the road's edge. Alex stopped. "Morning mister. Are these from your farm?"

The man studied Alex, then eyed Nora and the horse. "From my farm, mostly. Some I traded for. Why are you asking?"

"With a gardening machine you could grow five times as much, easy, with less work."

"A gardening machine?"

"Everybody had them way back in the old days. But you know what? They're coming back again." Alex's voice became stronger. "That's why I'm here. I've come to Dallas to tell Jennel Roberts to bring everything back, all the machines." He grabbed a cabbage from the display. "You'll easily grow all of these you can sell."

The proprietor took back his cabbage. "Well sir, sometimes a crazy man does a wondrous thing. Remember me when you're passing out those gardening machines." He turned away.

Alex remounted Nellie. "One thing, sir. Where do I find Jennel Roberts?"

A pause. "Easily done, if you're sure you want to do that. Keep on this street until you come to the white building." He scratched the back of his neck. "Take care. I've heard the jennel isn't an easy man."

The street soon became crowded with horses, carriages, carts and pedestrians. Alex's mouth hung open as he looked from side to side. "I didn't know you could have so many people in one place." Then the shops stopped and the street split to the right and left before a city block that was paved with black marble. Eye-squinting bright in the noon sun, the marble appeared as shimmering water. At the far side of the black expanse there was a single-story white building that crawled across the stones. Four white columns stood apart from the building, marking the entrance. A dozen men dressed in grey pants and dark blue shirts stood near the columns, each holding a rifle against his chest.

Nora squeezed Alex's ribs. "I'm frightened." She poked his back. "Alex, let's think about this, we need to have a plan. Turn Nellie around. Let's go back and find a place to stay." They went back past the markets, the vegetable stands and the city businesses until the crowds thinned and again there was open land between buildings. Alex turned Nellie to a side road that ended at an undisciplined group of structures intersected by the remnants of a stone wall.

"Stop here Alex." He paused the horse before a tavern with a carved wood sign, "Bert's Place." Alex pulled open the door to a dim interior where a muscular bald headed man, arms tattooed from wrist to elbows, wiped tables, his sleeveless shirt wet with sweat. Nora said, "Are you Bert?"

The man grunted.

"My husband and I are from the country. We are hard workers. We need food and a place to bed."

Bert continued wiping the table and then the next. He stopped and gave her a long look. "You seem decent enough. Weather's warming. Could use help. You'll clean the place and wait tables. No pay. Tips only. No messin' with the men." He aimed a finger at Alex. "You'll do kitchen work. Put your horse around back and take your stuff upstairs. The room isn't much but it'll do for you."

Next morning he handed Alex a woven reed basket. "Go that way." He nodded his head. "Look for Pete's stand. Tell Pete to give you my usual. Here's money. Any change he gives you bring all of it back."

Pete, an elderly white-bearded man, leaned on a cane behind a display of fresh produce. An apron shielded him from neck to feet. "So, you're Bert's new man." Pete filled the basket with vegetables and then handed Alex a wrapped package of meat. "Tell Bert that I've spiced the sausage different."

"When we get the machines back you'll be able to talk to Bert yourself, right from here."

Pete repositioned his cane. He gave Alex a wary look. "When we get..."

"I know for a fact. The machines are coming again. Machines for planting, road machines for carrying stuff, even machines that fly." He pointed to a grassy space across the street. "Tomorrow morning this time I'll be standing right there and I'll tell you all about it. Bring others." Alex went to each of the dozen produce stands. He said, "What they had in the old world, it's all coming back again. The proprietors smiled and winked at each other, but the next morning when Alex handed the reed basket to Pete and stepped to the grass there were a dozen people waiting. He motioned to passersby to join the group.

"I know you're wondering who I am and why I'm standing here talking when I know you have your own work to get done." Alex looked at each person in the half-circle before him. Smiling, he lifted the dirt streaked hand of a middle-aged man in heavy work pants. "I see hands that know hard work, they work every day, hot or cold, whether this man is sick or well. Because the work has to be done and he has the calluses to prove it." Then Alex raised both his own hands, spreading them wide apart. "Sir, you probably have twenty years on me, but I'll match you callus for callus." He twisted his hands so everyone could see. "Look at these. This is who I am. I know work, how hard it is to work a farm. But I know more than that. I know that four hundred years ago folks like us all had something wonderful called technology that gave everyone machines to do the work. Machines that planted, harvested and carried produce. But sometime back then the machines were turned off, they were put away. I don't know why. But I know that it's time, now, to bring them back again. We need them now."

Someone said, "Amen."

A man waved his hat. "I was told the machines needed energy, more than we can get from the sun and the wind."

Alex thought for a moment. "Look down. Look what you're standing on. The earth. As far as you can see in every direction. And it's full of energy, all the energy we could want."

Another man spoke. "That's true. I've heard that there's dry country in the west of Texas where the folks long ago stuck thousands of pipes into the ground. They used the pipes to suck up the energy."

Alex said, "It was wrong to close the pipes. They must be opened again. I'm going to make them do that. I've been told what to do. I've been chosen to go to the boss, to Jennel Roberts. I'll tell him why he has to break away the plugs and gather the energy again. I've been given the words. I know it will happen. We'll have it all again." He walked back across the street and took his basket from Pete. "I'll tell you more about it tomorrow. Bring others."

Next day there were two dozen people waiting for him, more joined the group as he talked, including a blond haired man wearing the dark green of a minister of the Church of Gaia. He said, "If Mam Gaia wants us to have the machines she will bring them to us. Instead of talk about seeing Jennel Roberts you would do better to pray."

Alex thought for a moment. "With respect, Minister sir, I

know what I have been told. I don't know where the message came from. Every night I open my soul for guidance. Maybe Mam Gaia speaks to me. That's all I know. I know the words are true."

The third day a milling crowd of fifty was waiting, but when Alex stopped at Pete's stand the minister was there with Bert who stood with lips compressed, neck veins protruding, his hands in fists. He grabbed and shook Alex's arm. "You're making a fool of me with your stupid nonsense. Get your stuff. Get out of here."

Alex jerked his arm free. He turned and walked across the road to the people who had gathered and lifted his arms high. "Listen everyone." His voice was confident and strong. "We've talked enough. Now is the time for us to act. Today we will take back the machines that are ours. I promise. This afternoon. Meet me here. Together we will go to Dallas."

When Alex returned to their room in the tavern Nora listened and then fell to her knees on the straw mattress. "Alex, do you have any idea of what you are doing?" Without speaking, she gathered and wrapped their belongings. Alex tied the bundle onto Nellie. Then, leading Nellie, Nora followed Alex back to the marketplace.

A group of four dozen were waiting and with Alex and Nora leading they began the walk. As they moved into the city curiosity attracted others. Two hours later a group of two hundred stopped and stood uneasily at the edge of the black stone expanse. On the far side, beyond the mirage wetness, was the serpentine white building, the four columns and uniformed guards fingering their rifles. Alex stepped forward, onto the black.

"Wait." It was the minister from the Church of Mam Gaia. He came close to Alex then turned to the crowd. He lifted his hand for quiet. "More than anything, every person here wants to believe. We hope, wish, pray, that what you have told us is true." Facing Alex he raised his arms. "My son, may you have Gaia's blessing."

Alex walked from the silent group, step and then step again across the smooth stone. His stomach knotted, his leg muscles trembled, the black stones extended forever.

Nora broke away from the others. She ran after Alex and pulled his arm. Her cheeks were wet. "Alex, this isn't going to work. Don't do this. Let me help you. Please come back. Together we can..."

He looked at her, then eased her away. "I love you, Nora." He knew what he had to do. The world was depending on him. He continued walking. At last he came to the columns and the building's entrance.

Two guards crossed their rifles in front of him. In a strong voice Alex said, "I'm here to see Texas Ranger Jennel Roberts."

The guards traded glances. "What for?"

"I'm demanding that he bring back the old world's machines. They've been kept from us too long. We demand to have them now."

The guards studied him silently, then eyed the milling mob that was coming closer. With a shrug one of the guards turned and disappeared into the building.

Long minutes passed then a dozen soldiers came out holding rifles loose but ready in their hands. They positioned themselves across the front of the building. Flanked by two more soldiers, a tall man came out. He had short black hair and a dark mustache above compressed lips. He wore creased black trousers and a white shirt with gold emblems on the collar and gold trimmed cuffs. Alex stepped toward him, holding out his hand. The man stiffened. "Stop. Step back. Don't touch me."

Jennel Roberts studied the mob as it inched forward across the terrace. He turned to Alex. "Well. What is it?"

Alex's heart thumped, he held his breath. This was it. He would explain it to the jennel. He would tell the jennel why he had to unblock the flow of energy from the earth, tell him to loose the old technology. His fists clenched. "Jennel, give technology back to us. The machines, road machines, farming machines. The machines that fly..."

Jennel Roberts turned to a guard. "This again? You pulled me out here for another energy cult?" He pointed at Alex's followers. "Get that rabble away from here." To Alex he said, "You go home." He turned around and took a step back toward the entrance.

Alex panicked. "No Jennel! Wait! You can't..." Leaping forward he grabbed the jennel's arm.

Two quick shots. Alex dropped to his knees then fell onto the black stones. The jennel stopped, turned around, glanced at Alex, then continued through the entrance.

Nora raced across the black expanse. She dropped to Alex's side. She put her face close to his. "Alex. Please be ok. Please, please."

His shirt reddening, his face pale, he gasped for breath. His lips moved, she lowered her ear. " I failed them, Nora. The old man. His granddaughter."

"Alex, you're a good, kind man. Please stay alive. I'll help you. Together we'll..."

She strained to hear his words. "...next world. Will we... meet?"

She wanted to shake him. "You stupid fool, of course we will." She watched his eyes close. "Alex, listen to me. When it's my turn you must come for me. You must come in the fanciest road machine there is. I... I will be waiting for you at... the spaceport." She rubbed the wet off her cheeks.

His eyelids flickered. His lips relaxed. His breathing stopped.

Two medical men appeared. One laid his fingers on Alex's neck, then they lifted him onto a stretcher and pushed that into a covered wagon. Nora watched a horse pull it away. When I came to him he was in a wagon. Now a wagon is taking him away. We had such a tiny bit of time. She realized that one of the medical men was talking to her. "Girl, you have to move. What are you going to do?"

"Me?" She stood and looked around. The crowd was drifting away, the guards were back in their places, the afternoon sun reflected off the smooth black stone. She saw Nellie waiting in the street.

She said. "I'll be ok."

EIGHT STARS OF GOLD

GRANT CANTERBURY

Old Charley backs water, and the bow of the boat comes across the fetch of the waves. The plashing against the hull changes its note, the keel lifting and breasting in the swell as the line begins to draw taut; Nikolai shifts in his seat. The second boat rocks in the irregular cross-chop of the waves beside Agvik, as Andreas leans out to secure his line. Hikaru watches the movement of the water, bites into a wave with his paddle to brace the boat more steadily for him. Pretty well done for a chichak. Bright blood has speckled the sleeve of his coat.

Gray mist moves over the heaving water with the wind, disappears against the gray horizon. Gray water, gray sky— the only color a couple of orange-painted floats bobbing by Agvik's darkness. Above, a brighter spot in the enclouding marks the position of the sun, coming about toward the northwest on its long slide. Still many hours before darkness. Nikolai hears the yelping of brant on the move, somewhere back on the coast. Andreas, Ivan, and Hikaru bend to their oars and the other boat comes out toward them, Little Charley paying out the coiled line as the slack is drawn up.

Old Charley and Andreas call out to one another across the water, conferring. "We pull straight, but not too close to each other. And keep the pull matched up even."

Andreas says, "Oh, we'll keep it easy for you. Don't want to spend all day going in circles out here."

Old Charley laughs. "I'm saying, you all keep up! I know you got two chichak to our one."

"That's fine, I'll spot you one."

Ivan's English is still so-so, but he understands this okay. He swells and thumps his chest, maybe mocking affront for them, or maybe for real. "You think I'm a chichak? I'm Rosh! You watch, see how a real Rosh pulls."

Old Charley elbows Nikolai. "Well we're still even. We got our own Rosh fellow."

Nikolai mutters, "Half."

"We'll see then, eh?"

Nikolai draws out his compass on its chain—a relic of his father, with a tarnished brass housing and a makers mark engraved in Cyrillic lettering. He considers for a moment their last sighting of land before the fog, the set of the current, the angle of the sun, the substantial declination of the magnetic pole (this year drifting fast across Severnzemlya); raises one arm out straight to indicate the bearing for Port Tagera. Andreas nods and sculls a moment to shift direction.

"All ready?" Old Charley reaches out and taps Isaac and Selden. Both are travellers themselves. Isaac's a gray-haired sardo from up river in the Laska back country (down here at the coast visiting his daughter, who's married to Little Charley—there's a grandkid on the way any day). The other one's a world-wanderer, claiming to hail from the country of the Nihonjin, and before that from distant Merica.

"Put your back in then... hut!" The men heave, and eddies spiral backwards from their oars. Agvik rolls in the swell, shifting not at all. Twice and again, and slowly the black bulk turns, the waves beginning to lap it at a different angle. There is nothing like a wake, but one float and a second begin to drift trailing astern.

"Slow and steady. Hell to get it moving again if we stop to rest, hey? Just keep on going slow." They settle in for a long pull, muscles working, with the promise of aches to come branching out through their shoulders, arms, thighs, calves. Old Charley mutters to himself, "Yeah, wishing now we'd waited on that third boat." Behind their backs the slow, irregular clang of the gong buoy over Hope, ventriloquial in the fog. Before their faces, the dark island-like mass of Agvik, slowly drawn to follow them by the lines fixed to his lip. A spreading fan of black baleen juts from his half-open mouth; his flukes sway loosely in the swell. The oily smell of his blood is brought to them on the wind.

None of them is weak on his oar, Old Charley's jibes notwithstanding. But it's true Selden is not bred to handle boats like the others, and from time to time he misses the rhythm of the stroke, jerking high across a wave or biting too deep. Not too bad, and he's in good humor. Beside him Isaac gives a companionable jeer when he fumbles. Still, they may be drifting south of their best course.

Now a different bell begins to ring in the fog, distant, steady and high. It grows louder, approaching. In response Andreas whoops, blows sharp on a tin whistle. "Ahoy!" They

43

begin to hear voices calling over the water. "Give way," in Rosh. Some ship out of Murmansk or the Lena.

Nikolai shouts back, "Give way yourselves, we're tethered!" The Rosh vessel appears—triple masted, moving under moderate sail on the starboard tack—and ghosts toward them in the fog. Going slow, yet too close for comfort; they can see the sailors working the rigging, the metal cladding of the ship's hull scratched by a thousand growlers from each passage of the northern ocean. Leaving it a bit late, the helmsman turns the wheel and angles away from them. The bow wave rocks them a moment later. Sailors wave, point at Agvik, call out to them from the ship's stern as it settles back onto its course, toward the straits and the Pacific.

Ivan has pulled his hood up, bent forward so as to watch the ship without showing his face much. His chance of being taken up is not great, to be sure, but no doubt Nikolai would have done the same. "See any old shipmates of yours?" Nikolai calls over to ask him, still in Rosh.

"No. Not anymore."

"Neither did I. Of course it has been a long time since I sailed with my father."

They pull harder for a while, hoping to come out of the sea lanes soon. Nikolai remembers those childhood journeys on the *Davidov*, now twenty years gone. Baffin Island, Helsinki, Vrangelya. Cruising off Greenland, hearing the perpetual roar of the water-torrents and the thunder of ice-mountains crashing into the sea. Pondering the mysteries of the sea-charts, the interplay of cosines and tangents, the use of the sextant. The slow synchronous dance of the moons of Jupiter, seen through telescopic glass. Lying out on the deck at night, watching Polaris poised at the zenith.

The gong buoy is ringing louder to starboard. Nikolai

tosses out the lead for a sounding, and suddenly they are at four fathoms. This is the tough spot to judge. They are out over the old spit now, most likely, and the deepest crossing is a bit north of Hope; but the bottom is unconsolidated, still shifting under the changing currents. And they may have veered too close in. This would be no danger for the boats themselves, but even with the floats Agvik must draw at least two fathoms. Worriedly Nikolai makes another sounding— three and a half now. A few grains of beach sand adhere in the seal-grease on the lead. He looks at Old Charley, who shrugs, gestures to port. They change their course a couple points, and pull.

Three and a half fathoms. The tide, weak as it is in the northern ocean, is now falling; if they ground they cannot count on it to float them free. Three and three quarters. Three and *one* quarter. Four, and smiles appear on the men's faces. But they hear or feel a scraping, transmitted to them across the taut lines, vibrating through the water and hull into their feet. Their motion slows. Yet it does not stop. Andreas calls, "I don't think that was a gravel strike." Old Charley nods. Maybe Agvik has brushed against a structure. The framing of an old military installation, or the remnant walls of a house from the drowned village of Point Hope.

The next sounding shows four and a quarter. If the bottom is flat here, okay. Maybe they are past the village. Or maybe they are just over an old street...

At last the bottom drops solidly away, down to six and seven fathoms. Old Charley whistles, and they all draw in oars and allow themselves a rest. They munch on jerky and pilot bread as the boat rocks beneath them.

Nikolai passes round a canteen of fresh water, and they drink. He asks Selden, "Where is it you're from originally?"

"Minsota. The lake country."

"Is that over by New York?" Isaac asks.

"A bit farther inland, you might say."

"Long ways to come," Old Charley says. "What really brings you here?"

Isaac's laughter creaks. "He's here to collect fifty years of back taxes!"

"And I know you'd be good for it, man." Selden laughs, then looks downward into the belly of the boat. "No. But it's true, I am here because of..." He pronounces it deliberately. "America."

Old Charley cocks back his head at that, uncertain. Selden turns in his seat toward the others. "Listen. I don't care whether there's one president or fifteen. And we must be getting close to that. What have we got now? The good old United States. Minus the Southron Revival. Minus the big dust, minus Deseret, Cascadia, the Calforna fiasco. And Laska. We did get things patched up with the Newengl'ders, but I expect they'll be bidding us fare-thee-well again before long. They always know what's best, eh?"

"We always did see things different, right from the beginning. We came from different places round the world. It used to be one country just because we agreed it was. Maybe agreed after getting kicked in the ass, sure. But we all knew the same stories in those days. And not so hard for that to happen when someone could talk into a mike in New York and have a million people hear him in Georgia, Oregon, Maine. But the thing is, that was an artifice. What people heard talking was a machine. Not another person's real voice and breath. So when all that began to go away, those stories broke up like old plastic in the sun. And what was left was not so much the same everywhere any more. The country they had, it wasn't as real as they thought."

Isaac says, "Laska's real enough."

"That's why I travel. That's why I walked over the big dust. I've watched the hurricanes driving Florida under. I've seen the Sphinx in Vegas. I've had audience with the Empress of the Nihonjin in Seattle. I want to hear your stories in Laska. I want to bring them back home and tell them.

"It won't stop the fighting. Sometimes I hope it will. But probably not. Hell, my cousin, my uncle died in the Second Civil War. You bet I feel that, every day. I know that goes on, that will go on. But whether it's brothers fighting, or strangers, that's because of the stories you both know. Maybe if we do, we can be a country again someday. A real one."

He grins. "Hope that doesn't make you want to toss me out of this boat. If it does, well, in that case I'm just a simple trader who doesn't know a damn thing about Laska. That's true too."

Old Charley says, "I hear you. Don't worry, we're not tossing you out." He chews meditatively on a stick of jerky, stone-faced. Nikolai can see this one coming. "You still got to row."

So, after a bit, they do again, creeping onward in shifting fog with Agvik following them astern. They pull across the deeper water another hour or so, angling on a bearing toward the mouth of the Kukpok.

Andreas suddenly curses. Nikolai follows his gaze, sees nothing for a moment. A bulky movement and splashing back behind Agvik, obscured in the fog. Bearded seal? Then Isaac whistles. "That's a damn griz, way out here." A robust, water-slicked pale head bobs up, well back behind, and the bear regards them. "Oh, damn he's big. Christ. Biggest griz I've ever seen."

Old Charley says, "Probably you don't have slope griz up the Kobuk, Isaac. They got the blood of the ice. This guy's more than half nanook."

Andreas takes up the harpoon, though the range is much too great for a cast. Little Charley has their only gun – currently loaded with duckshot. The griz considers the boats, swims with little hurry back toward the rear of Agvik. It's a poor angle for any shot, low in the water and with considerable cover from the great body. The griz paddles against Agvik's side, braces with a clawed forepaw, and bites at the flank, wrenching away a mouthful of blubber.

Hikaru whoops, bangs his oar against the hull, to no great effect. Little Charley shrugs, raises the shotgun, and fires into the air. The report rings out sharp, dies away flat in the fog. The griz pauses, looks at them, lowers its head to take another bite. But the shot has made it uneasy, and its efforts to open a wider gash in the body are distracted by keeping an eye on the men. After swallowing a few more bites it growls and pushes back into the water. The men see it swimming away behind Agvik, glancing back at them now and again, head low in the troughs of the waves. Gone into the fog.

The encounter with the griz has slowed them, and they labor to bring Agvik back into motion. But they are closer now. The fog begins to clear, first in ragged gaps blowing past above that show glimpses of blue sky, then in an opening-out of the water horizon. A flock of cackling-geese passes, moving for the south.

Then they can see land to the east. Low clouds creep across the hills of Lisburn. Pale patches of tundra remain on the heights, but fresh dark forests clothe all the slopes. Spruce trees grow thick as hair on a dog. The line of the sky dips toward the valley where the Kukpok flows out of the hills. In many places along the shoreward water there are fields of fresh snags, where forest has briefly claimed the tundra only to be drowned.

It is none too soon to make it to land. They are all bone-tired now from their hours of pulling at the oars. And the sun is skating low toward the ocean horizon. Late August, so the night will be short enough. But a real one, a dark one, not like the brief twilights that punctuate the perpetual day of July.

The buildings of Port Tagera come into view by the Kukpok. Back toward the foothills some hay meadows show pale green swaths against the forest; a few hardy horses and cattle amble and graze at pasture. In the harbor, fishing boats with their sails furled; the moored hulk of an old Rosh ship; the Gennida trading vessel that has been in port a few weeks for repairs. A little farther out, a Laska coast guard cutter rides at anchor, the blue starry flag fluttering from its mainmast. Andreas fires a flare, and after a few minutes they see minute figures running toward the water; one ignites an answering red flash. Children climb on boulders, jump and wave to them.

Some folks come out in boats to greet them. There are cheers, congratulations, high fives mimed across the water. A girl in a kayak paddles round Agvik, trailing a hand on his black side.

A few more lines are set into Agvik, and the new boats help pull him into the shallows, by the gravel bar at the edge of town. Andreas and Old Charley cast loose, and they row the last few yards up to shore. Heavily they get out, boots sliding on the slick cobbles. The men stagger up-beach to sit on a driftwood log, exhausted; Little Charley lies down flat on his back in the gravel, arms out wide. Selden says, "I will be sore."

49

More onlookers are arriving from the village every minute. Port Tagera is a town of little wooden buildings, many salvaged and barged over from Point Hope and Kotz over the last few decades. There's been no point in setting down solid foundations; most of them are planted on skids. A team of Percherons has been working to haul one up a few more yards from the waterside; their owner unhitches them, lets them drink for a bit, leads them down toward the gravel bar.

Naoko, Hikaru's wife, comes flying up to them from town, cutting across the crowberries and cotton-grass, beaming. Halting, she speaks to him in bursts of rapid, excited Japanese with a few pauses for short breath, dances from one foot to another. Then she collects herself, bows. "Kujira-tori!" And promptly she whirls and dashes back.

Hikaru says, "She forgot to shut up the mercantile."

"Well tonight no one will be there, pretty sure," Andreas says. "I think we should make sure and tell her it was all down to you, eh?" Hikaru grins.

The sky and ocean flame red and gold as the sun slowly angles toward the horizon, skims the water, touches in the northwest and begins to sink. Cables have been looped around the flippers and stretched to shore. When the horse-team is hitched up, at a word they lean into the harness and heave. Their hooves punch sharp dark dents into the gravel bar. Agvik shifts, slides massively in toward shore behind them. Good enough, thought, after a few more tries the horses are let to rest. They may make another attempt, in a few hours, when they can pull best a bit better.

Old Charley rouses himself and wades out knee-deep, puts his hands on the black hide, looks into the great eye. For a moment he speaks, softly. He glances at Selden splashing up beside him, shrugs. "Thanking him."

The sun gone, the sky darkens toward blue-black; Venus begins to shine out bright. Children are running up and down the gravel beach, having been deputized to go gather sticks of driftwood. They bring them back, some working in pairs to haul the bigger awkward branches. Some folks have scraped out a quick fire-ring, and they pile up twigs to kindle a flame.

The men sit out on the log, watching the fire grow. Lots of people have come down to look, pacing off Agvik's length along the water's edge, the crowd-noise chattering louder. Someone sends a toy firework zipping into the sky. Isaac gropes about in his bag and pulls out a metal flask. He un-stoppers it and takes a quick drink, holds it out. "Hey, you want some? Good Sen Petersburg vodka."

Nikolai takes a sip. Alcoholic fire traces the shape of his throat. He coughs; beside him Little Charley stands up, glowering at Isaac. "You got nothing better to do than sit and drink? Don't you know any better than to bring out liquor?" He was "Little" when he was a kid; these days a head taller than Isaac, and disgusted mad. Isaac waves his hands to ease him, but Little Charley turns on his heel and walks away.

Isaac looks after him awkwardly. Old Charley says, "Yeah, he's not wrong. But I guess I'd have one swallow."

They pass the flask about. The fire's got a good blaze going now. Someone's picking out a tune on an old guitar; a few couples are dancing back in the shadows where the ground's more flat. On an old length of mast a Laska flag has been raised up. Fluttering above the firelight, the seven stars of the Big Dipper, with Polaris opposite.

Ivan scowls. "Dancing under their pirate flag," he mutters. Nikolai puts a warning hand to his elbow.

Andreas has overheard, unfortunately. "Watch your mouth there."

There's no big trouble with the Rosh these days. But it's not so long ago there were plenty of folks who might put out false lights on a foggy night; or take some small boats out in the dark to board a Rosh merchantman just passed through the strait. Most especially down near the Waikeh, the new shallow sea with its broad fields of eelgrass, its shoals shifting every month, its maze of deltas and distributaries from a hundred rivers, where no deep-draft ship could ever pursue. Andreas doesn't talk much about those days, but Nikolai's pretty sure he knows plenty.

Once word got out, it became the practice to form up in convoys with naval escort. It never quite got to what you would call a full war, but there were plenty of skirmishes at sea, before folks finally came to a settlement. And before the Waikeh finally went deep enough under. A few ships were sunk on the Laska side, a few on the Rosh. Including the *Davidov*, lost with all hands off of Sen Lawrence Island.

Ivan lurches up, goes sourly down to the fireside to warm his hands. Selden leans back against the driftwood log, looking up. "I think this is the first time it's been dark enough for me to see the stars since I've been up here. Never thought I'd see the North Star up so high. Right at the pole, eh?"

Nikolai says, "Almost at the pole, anyway. Really he does make a circle round the point of the pole every day like the other stars, but a tiny one. Just half a degree off. My father told me it was the year he was born the North Star came closest to the pole. Ever since then, been drifting away."

"But not fast, I guess," Selden says.

Nikolai laughs. "Not too fast. Come two thousand years, though, the pole will be over by... him." He points upward. "Alrai. Maybe we'll need a new flag then, eh?"

52

It's full dark now, no moon, and uncountable star-fields are speckling the sky. Great curving luminous shapes have begun to twist and glide above the ocean. Far-flung are the banners of the northern lights.

Selden says, "When our ship came in from Kodiag, the captain told us we were supposed to make Port Tagera on Friday, and I woke up Thursday morning, what I thought was Thursday morning, and here we are coming in to port. I was, what the hell?! Was I so seasick I slept away a day and a night?"

Andreas laughs. "Nobody told you we keep Rosh time here?"

"They told me nothing! I'm still not sure I got it right."

Andreas says, "There's a good story about that. So we used to have the line between today and tomorrow out on the strait. You saw the Dimee islands when you came through? Right between them. You could stand on one of them and look cross to tomorrow on the other one. So there was this fisherman Peter Corrin, he's still around, and he had the biggest fishing boat on the coast, he'd go out with his crew and chase pollock out on the Chokchi. A big wheel. And there was this woman he knew over in Provdenya, that's on the other side in Chukotka. On the Rosh side, but you know Chukotka folks aren't particularly Rosh any more than us, we all got relatives back and forth over the strait. Anyway the two of them had this long time thing, and what he'd do is stop by Provdenya on the way out, spend a warm night, go on out fishing next morning.

"Well she ended up getting married to another fellow, but she still did like Peter, so they carried on like before— she'd leave word for him when her husband was going to be out of town. Worked okay for a while, but then he got confused about the day, some say too much to drink the night before, I don't know, but for sure he came sliding in to bed right beside her husband. Got the hell beat out of him, came back to Nome with his tail between his legs, and this is actually true, he decided from now on, hell or high water, he was going to be on the Chukotka day of the calendar. Not only that, he made it stick with his crew, and pretty soon the other boats took it up, and within a couple years it was general all along the coast. You can ask Old Charley, he'll tell you it's true."

Selden says, "Hey, Old Charley. Tell me about Agvik now. What do the people say about him?"

Old Charley drinks a long swig of vodka from the flask, winces, passes it over. "Truth is, most of the real stories are gone. We lost them with the language. With the troubles with the Rosh. Now, with the water. Asking *me* about Agvik. I'm Yupik myself, mostly. I was born in Bethl, my brothers and me grew up fishing salmon and hunting geese. First time I even saw Agvik I was over forty. Well, we couldn't stay in the Waikeh once it went under, could we. But this here was all Inupia country once. Point Hope was Inupia. This place, Port Tagera, it wasn't even here when I was a kid, there was nothing—now look at it. And half the people here Yupik, half Rosh, half Nihonjin or Gennidan or whatnot. Too many halves, I guess. But you get me. That fellow over there, he's all the way from Zealand, his family had trouble with the Chinese and he lit out. Can't go much damn further than that, can you."

"So no wonder if we don't know who the hell we are. You're right, you know. But all those old stories are gone. Washed away…Down under the ocean with Agvik. But if we wait, hey? If we listen right. Agvik will bring them back to us."

Isaac has gone down to the crowd around the fire. He slaps Andreas and Hikaru on the back, hacks out a fierce laugh. Suddenly they hear his voice lifting up in song. "Eight stars of gold on a field of blue. Laska's flag may it mean to you." In fact, the old sardo has a surprisingly fine baritone.

Others have been drinking too. They sing along with him, plenty loud, more boisterous than in tune for sure. Ivan shakes his head, still annoyed, but Nikolai sees his lips following the words.

"The Bear! The Dipper! And shining high! The Great North Star with his steady light! Over land and sea a beacon bright!"

Nikolai stands, walks back over the cobbles into the darkness. Vodka burns in his belly. By the firelight he can see women clambering onto Agvik's back, loosening long strips of pink blubber with their knives. Up above, the curtains of the aurora ripple and glow green against the brilliant constellations. He cranes his head back, glances along the pointer stars to find Polaris. Still slowly spinning over the northern ocean, above Agvik's realm, suspended between Laska and Rosh for the balance of this age of the world.

He watches there, guiding all alike.

TINY'S LEGACY

TROY JONES III

I want to say upfront I regret that we couldn't do anything
for Mister Raff. I have known him all my life, and he was
just the sweetest, kindliest old man. He didn't deserve to get
caught up in any of this, and I am sorry we couldn't save
him. I am getting ahead of myself, I know, but I just wanted
to say that first.

So, that said, I suppose I should begin at the beginning.
The whole thing started when the fat dead man was brought
in to us, whose real name I still don't know even now. We
figured the fat man had probably been a man of means in life,
judging by his fancy clothes—pinstriped pants, leather shoes,
and a bright yellow oilcloth jacket, among other things. Usually when wealthy people die from foul play or go missing,
some other wealthy person will kick up a stink demanding
justice, or at least answers. In this case though, no one knew

who the fat man had been—or at least no one was willing to admit to knowing him—and there was no obvious clue as to his identity among his possessions. So when the sherf grumbled he had better things to do than try to figure out how this out-of-towner "had got himself reborn" while clearly "doing something he hadn't oughta," out on the outskirts of town, no one batted an eyelid. If anyone was concerned there was a throat-slasher running around town, they weren't concerned enough to complain too vocally about the sherf's apathy. The victim clearly had not been from around here, after all, so who knows what he was up to? Who can say whether he deserved his gruesome fate? You just never know with strangers.

And so it was that as soon as the requisite prayers had been said over his remains, the mystery man was released to us for burning. And since we weren't expecting any family or friends of the fat man to attend his cremation, Dad decided this would be a good opportunity for his awesome senior prentice—that would be me—to oversee prepping the corpse herself. He said I would have the opportunity to demonstrate the skills I had supposedly learned, and no one would care if I messed this guy up horribly. So I thanked Dad for his confidence in me and set to work.

The job of the burners is not as easy as it looks, you know; it is no small task to thoroughly but efficiently burn something that's mostly water. In addition, the bereaved prefer it when their loved one looks (and smells) much as they did in life, and it doesn't take too long after death for a corpse to start looking and smelling a bit off. There's a lot more to it than just chucking deaders in the furnace.

We have some tricks of the trade to make a corpse presentable for the last-chance viewing, but these are mostly guild secrets so I can't write them down here. You would probably find the details of what I did to Tiny (the nickname I came up for the fat man as I worked on him) terribly boring (or terribly horrifying) anyway. I will say—since this at least is widely known—that it involves stitching up obvious wounds and covering them with copious amounts of makeup to hopefully make them a bit less obvious. Tiny's jowly neck had been opened nearly from ear to ear; fixing that up good as new would be a challenge even for a Mister Burner. I was up for the challenge.

Not everyone was up for the challenge though. I had "help" in the form of Dad's junior prentice Jem. Jem is a cousin of mine on my mom's side so Dad was willing to keep him around, but he isn't really cut out for this line of work.

"Are you sure you can see what I'm doing from over there?" I asked him as I stitched up Tiny's neck.

Jem's back was pressed up against the corner of the room, as far away as he could position himself and still pretend to be watching. "I can see fine," he squeaked.

"If I were mean, I could make you hold his neck closed while I stitch it. Dad used to make me do that all the time. How do you think I learned these amazing skills?" I glanced back at him. "Wow, you're really turning green! I always thought that was just a figure of speech!"

He had no response to that.

After I'd tormented Jem enough, I sent him off to sort and clean Tiny's personal possessions while I worked on Tiny himself. Tiny would not be carrying anything with him into the next life, and had no known next of kin, so the things on his person when he died (including his clothes) would be used to offset his final expenses—if the blood could be cleaned off them, that is. After I closed up his neck I decided

59

he could use a shave and a fingernail-trimming. (Funny how that stuff seems to keep growing for a while after death, though Dad says that's an illusion caused by skin drying out and pulling away from fingernails and hair.)

Later, when I was done with Tiny but before Dad's final inspection of our work, I inspected Jem's progress on cleaning Tiny's things.

"Not too shabby." I picked up the dead man's folded shirt and rubbed the material between my fingers. "This fabric is really nice. Any idea what it is?"

"I believe it's silk," he said.

"Wow." I had never so much as touched a piece of silk before. I unfolded the shirt. There was quite a lot of it to unfold. "If they made tents out of silk we could sell this thing as a twenty-person pavilion."

Jem frowned. "We should be more respectful of the dead."

"If Tiny doesn't like it he can speak up." I examined the shirt more closely. "How did you get this so clean? This thing was completely soaked in blood before. Can hardly even see any discoloration now. I'm really impressed."

He shrugged and blushed. Jem is a blusher.

"Seriously, this is excellent work. Stellar. I think you may have a real future as a washerwoman." I grinned at my own wittiness. In fact I'm still smiling as I think back on it now. I am a terrible person, I know.

Jem sighed but didn't take the bait—he rarely does. "Where do you think he's from?"

"Memfis? People from Memfis dress like this. Stripes and checks and fancy fabrics."

"You ever met anyone from Memfis?"

"No, but everyone says that. Also everybody says the

food is really good in Memfis, which would explain his fatness. Mystery solved!"

I could tell Jem didn't approve of my jocularity in regards to the deceased, but I will say in my defense that Tiny never breathed a word of complaint during any of this. Or breathed at all in fact.

"Yeah. Well. There may be one more mystery for you to solve. This was in the deceased's bag." Jem directed my attention to a small wooden box on the table with Tiny's other things.

I picked it up. The box was about fifteen senamees long, with four bands around it, each about a senamee thick, also made of wood. It was unpainted, and aside from the bands, it was unornamented. There didn't seem to be any way to open it.

"I think it's a puzzle box," Jem said.

"A what?"

He took the box out of my hand and pulled off part of one of the bands. It came away from the box easily. "See where the little peg from this piece goes in that hole? I think the peg holds another piece in place. You have to remove or turn the pieces in the right order and it will open up. A puzzle box."

I took the box back and shook it. Something metallic rattled around inside-- several somethings. "Something in it," I said. "Were you able to get it open?"

Jem shook his head.

I twisted and tugged at each of the box's bands. The box remained stubbornly closed. I tried pushing in the ends of the box. Nothing. I looked more closely at it. It seemed to me I could see the seams where the box would open if only I could figure out the secret. I got as solid a grip as possible on Tiny's tiny box and pulled as hard as I could.

Jem scoffed as I strained at it. "I don't think you can open it that w-"

The box burst open. Broken bits of wood spilled out, along with a note and a few coins.

"Money!" I exclaimed. It's rare for a body to be brought to us with money still in its possession. Legally, the personal items of the indigent dead belong to us, but money always seems to find its way into a living person's pocket before a corpse is turned over to us. I guess in this case, whoever found the body decided a plain wooden box wasn't worth stealing. (I think more people should carry their money in puzzle boxes; we would certainly appreciate it.) I gathered up the coins as Jem looked on in horror. Sadly the coins were far less than one might expect for someone traipsing about in a silk shirt and an oilcloth jacket.

"You broke it," Jem observed unnecessarily. He picked up and unfolded the note. "Look at this," he said after reading it, and handed it over. I read.

To Whom It May Concern:

Congratulations, Sir or Mam, on solving the puzzle box! I am very sorry that I cannot congratulate you in person for your feat of brilliance, because if you are reading this, I am most likely dead. Either that or the puzzle box was stolen from me, but more likely I am dead, far away from home. (If there is any question, I am a rather portly fellow, usually fashionably attired). There are people who would want to be made aware of the fact of my unfortunate and untimely demise, but they would not wish to be contacted directly for various reasons. I'm sure you understand.

My final request is that the following classified ad be placed in the newsletter of the Memfis Weavers' Guild. Where blanks appear, please fill in details as appropriate.

The money in the box should cover the cost of having the ad placed.

"We regret to announce the death of Mister Mell sunna Eve, who passed away in _____ as a result of _____ this past _____. He is survived by his brother Mister Harmon."

Again, I thank you in advance for this small consideration.

Sincerely,

Your Late, Corpulent Friend

We both contemplated the note in silence for a while until Jem spoke up. "We should tell your dad," he said in hushed tones, as if we were involved in some conspiracy.

"Yeah. I wonder why he didn't sign his name Mister Mell?"

"Maybe that's not his real name. Maybe he's a spy...or a criminal or something."

I rolled my eyes. "A spy? Here? What would a spy want in Hunsul? Gonna sabotage the orange trees?"

"People used to make rockets here. You know, before the old world ended. The rockets that carried people to the moon were built right here in good old Hunsul, Bama."

I nodded slowly. "I had forgotten about that. But all that rocket stuff was broken down and carried away centuries ago. Why would a spy...Do you think they may have found something from the old world?"

Jem looked very solemn. "We should talk to your dad," he repeated. So we did.

* * *

Dad studied the note with a frown as I waited. Jem had been

sent away to sweep ashes out of the crematory. "The deceased had this on him?"

"Yes, sir."

He peered at me. "This isn't one of your jokes?"

I valiantly resisted saying anything sarcastic. "No, sir."

"Hm. Well, it's unusual, to say the least. But we are bound to honor last requests within reason, and this seems reasonable enough. We will place the ad. And by we, I mean you."

"I'm going to Memfis!?" I bearhugged my dad's neck and kissed him on the cheek.

"Calm yourself, girl," he said as he disentangled from me. "You're going down to the radio guild. They can make all the arrangements there, including transfering the money. Maybe you'll run into your sister there."

My sister is married to a radioman. "I don't think she hangs around the guild hall."

"Mm. Well. Wouldn't want you to be by yourself. You can bring Jem with you if you like."

I made a face. "Ugh. I... I'm sure he's needed here. Sir. I'll be fine by myself."

Dad grunted. "Mm." He paused thoughtfully and sighed. "You know, your mother and I had hoped you two would hit things off more than you have. He's a smart kid, and conscientious. I know he's your cousin, but you could definitely do worse than him for a husband..."

"Dad, Dad! No. Ew. Cousins or no, I'm not going to marry a guy I could pick up and break in half over my knee. Not happening."

"Danna, you're my daughter so you know I love you and think you're beautiful and amazing and et cetera, so don't take this the wrong way... but if you limit yourself to men you aren't capable of breaking in half, that would disqualify like a third of the men in the world."

"Only a third? You wound me, Pappy."

"Pappy? Are we hillbillies now?"

"Well, we are marrying cousins, apparently."

"Mm. You have me there." Dad sighed again. "Go. Radio guild. And come straight back."

"You don't want me to take the note to Sherf Ander? He might be interested to see this."

"Why, is there a voucher for a cask of Tucki bourbon on the back of that note?"

I stared at Dad blankly for a moment, then I wagged my finger in his face. "I will remember this day the next time you ask me where I get my jokiness from, Pappy."

He laughed. "Go on, get out of here, hillbilly." He shooed me out.

* * *

The radioman guildhall is on Chammin Mountain (which, in truth, is not much of a mountain), the nicest part of town. The burners' guildhall is down by the river (and, in truth, the Flint River isn't much of a river), with the lumbermen and other undesirables, arguably not in town at all, so I had a pretty long walk.

It was dark by the time I got there, but radio crews work around the clock so I wasn't worried there wouldn't be anyone there. I ducked my head in through the door (the world is not made for people as tall as me), and stepped inside. There was no one in the reception area so I rang the bell.

After a moment, a tall teenage prentice came out to meet me. He had blue eyes and a friendly smile, but the smile fled

65

from his face when he saw me and his eyes went wide. I can be a bit imposing at first sight, I have discovered, taller and broader of shoulder than nearly any man, and I suppose the hooded black burner's robe adds to the uncanny effect. I can see how an unexpected late night visit from the likes of me might be startling. I promise I'm a nice person though! I hardly ever break people in half.

"C- can I help you? Sir?" the prentice radioman stammered.

"Not 'sir'." I pulled back my hood. "I have an unusual request. A message and some money to send to the Memfis Weavers' Guild." I produced the note and coins from the folds of my robe.

The radioman recovered himself. "Terribly sorry, mam. Uh..."

"Don't have to call me mam, either. I'm a prentice, same as you. In fact, do you know Kev sunna Jin? He's my brother-in-law."

He took this in. "You... you're Lanna's sister? But you're, um..." He looked me up and down, clearly wanting but not willing to actually say, *so much bigger than she is.*

"So much better-looking than she is? So kind of you to say so." I favored him with a hopefully-not-terrifying smile.

He laughed. "Well, you do have her sense of humor at least. I mean... not that you're not good-looking too." He blushed and cleared his throat. "So, Memfis, you said?"

"Memfis! Yes."

We made the arrangements. The radioman, whose name I learned was Tom, thought it odd to place a newsletter ad instead of simply notifying the man's brother Mister Harmon, but that's what the note said to do, so that's what we had arranged to have done. In the morning, a prentice radioman in

66

Memfis would knock on the door of the weavers' guild hall and deliver the instructions and money to place the ad, less the radiomen's transfer fee. It was an odd last request, yes, but people from Memfis are odd (everyone says), so I didn't worry too much about it.

And so, everything handled, I made ready to go back.

"Would you, ah, like someone to walk you home?"

"Is 'someone' offering? And isn't 'someone' on duty here?"

"I'm senior prentice so I have some flexibility. And it could be dangerous out there. Murders and disappearances, you know."

"Disappearances?"

"Well, the one disappearance. Haven't you heard?"

I shook my head.

"Old Mister Raff the chemist disappeared just today. Went out to work in his garden, then just gone. His family was in the house too. No one saw anything. Broad daylight too! They've been radioing people all day, contacting anyone they can think of whom he might have suddenly decided to visit. No one knows anything though."

"Huh. That's bad. Mister Raff is one of the nicest people I know. And his accent is so fun to imitate. Think it might be related to Tiny's murder?"

"Tiny?"

"Mister Mell. If *that's* even his real name. Tiny is the nickname I came up for him while I was sewing what was left of his neck back together."

"I... see."

I suddenly feared Tom might be having second thoughts about his offer to walk me home, so I grabbed his arm before he could change his mind. "You're right, real dangerous out there, need a big strong man to walk me home." I more or less dragged him out the door.

* * *

A couple days went by. I can't say they were uneventful exactly, but I don't imagine events involving Tom would be of much interest to anyone but me. (Example: turns out Tom is an Old Believer. How about that! Christianity held no interest for me before but now seems like an endlessly fascinating subject.) There were no new murders or disappearances, however.

Then Mister Harmon showed up.

Somehow he'd made it all the way down from Memfis in time for burning day. (I figure everyone knows what burning day is, but if not: for the sake of efficiency, we only light up the oven once every few days so we can chuck several deaders in at once—respectfully, of course). We'd had a slow week for rebirths and only had Tiny and one other: an elderly old lady named Lissa whose family and friends had all preceded her into the next life, so we weren't really expecting anyone to show.

I was helping Dad warm up the crematory when Jem burst into the room. "Danna! Mister Mell's brother is here!" he reported breathlessly. So excitable. "He said he wants to talk to the person who prepared his body."

Dad and I looked at each other. "Can I trust you to handle this professionally?" he asked me. "If not—"

"Dad!" I was all wounded innocence. "When am I ever unprofessional?"

I could see Dad was not terribly keen on my sarcasm, but he made a gesture of dismissal. "Sit with the brother until it's time. Try to be professional. Jem can help me finish here."

So I went up front to talk to this Harmon. He was sitting in our tastefully-but-somberly appointed lobby. He stood as I entered.

"Sir and Mister Harmon?" I was determined to be as respectful as possible.

He gave an odd sort of smirk. Perhaps more of a sardonic half-smile. "You can call me that, I suppose."

He was a strange one, but I guess we all have different ways of dealing with grief. Plus he was from Memfis, so that probably explains it.

"I am terribly sorry for your loss, sir." I gestured. "Would you like to sit? It will be a while yet before we're ready. My name's Danna." We sat.

"Have you been to a burning before?" He looked middle-aged, so I figured he had. We always ask though. Tradition.

"Too many." He paused and peered at me thoughtfully. "You were the one who solved my...er, brother's puzzle box?"

"I..." *in a manner of speaking.* "I opened it, yes sir."

"Impressive. That devilish thing was a mother with babies to get open. Never could figure it out myself."

I nodded and decided to steer the conversation away from my abuse of Tiny's stuff. "Were you close to your brother?"

His sad sort-of smirk again. "I guess you could say that."

I wasn't sure how to respond to that so we sat in awkward silence a few moments.

Harmon spoke up. "How long had he been dead when he was found? In your professional estimation?"

"Perhaps half a day? Give or take."

He scratched his neck thoughtfully. "His message must have been one of the last things he did before he died," he mused, as if to himself. Grieving people sometimes seem to talk to themselves, I have noticed.

"Message?"

"Yeah, he sent for me just before he died. That's how I got here so quickly—I was already on the way."

"How did he do that? No one had seen him at the radio guild, I'm sure of that, and a letter would never have gotten to Memfis in time. Nor would a letter have met you en route, now that I think about it." My impertinence was perhaps crossing the line into unprofessionalism, but my curiosity was killing me, and Harmon was raising more questions than he was answering.

He shrugged. "We have alternative ways of conveying messages."

I thought about that. "'We'? You mean you and him? Or...are you part of something larger?"

His eyes twinkled as he smirked again, but he said nothing. I suddenly had the vague impression he was appraising me.

"If you're a member of some secret society or the illuminati or something, you can totally tell me. I promise I won't breathe a word of it to anyone." Professionalism forgotten.

He laughed. "Nothing so dramatic as all of that. We just...collect stories. We see that certain stories and other things are remembered, and at the right time, reintroduce them to society at large."

"Hm. I guess it must not be such a big secret if you're willing to tell little old me. The first rule of any proper secret society is to not talk about the secret society. And the second rule is the same as the first. Everyone knows that."

"Oh, but it is a big secret. This conversation could get me into some trouble with my colleagues."

"Then why...?"

"Why tell you? Selfishness, I suppose. I would like to have someone remember something about me when I'm gone, someone besides my anonymous colleagues. Besides that: you asked."

"Gone? Are you...sick?"

He shook his head. "No. But the way I figure it, decent odds I'll be reborn before the next sunrise."

That took me aback. "Are you serious?"

He shrugged and nodded. He was playing it nonchalantly, but I could plainly see he really was afraid of something.

My impetuousness got the better of me. "You think who-ever opened Tiny's neck will open yours?"

He raised his eyebrows. "Tiny?"

I winced. Dad would kill me. "I, uh...gave him that nick-name before I found out his real one."

Harmon chuckled. "Tiny. He would've laughed heartily at that. You and he would have gotten along famously, you know; your personality and his are very similar. Or were." The flash of amusement was gone as soon as it had come. "Mell wasn't his real name anyway, nor is Harmon my name, of course."

"I'm sorry I never knew him."

He nodded. "But to answer your question: yes. Whoever got to Tiny is still out there. Before he died, he arranged for a meeting between me, him, and a mutual friend of ours he had reason to suspect was in danger."

I went out on a limb. "Mister Raff?"

"How much do you know about Mister Raff?"

"I know he's kind and generous, and most everyone in town likes him a lot. I also know he's lived in Hunsul most of his life, but he came from somewhere out west originally.

Never lost his funny accent. Whenever anyone asks him what brought him here, he laughs and says he hoped to find some rockets to take him to the stars."

"He wasn't entirely joking about that. He escaped as a child from...from a place that belongs to the old world. Long ago, my predecessor helped him build a life in the new world in return for letting the old one stay buried for the time being."

I nodded solemnly. "Do you think he's dead? Mister Raff, I mean?"

"That I don't know, but it's a serious possibility. All I can do now is go to the meet and hope he's there, and alive, and that it's not a trap. It is equally possible that he's just laying low, waiting for me to rescue him, so I can't just cut and run either."

"Seems like a lot of cloak-and-dagger just for some story-rememberers."

"There are many who would stop at nothing, grasp at any straw, to bring the old world back. The old world is never coming back, but such people are dangerous nonetheless. We...often find ourselves at cross-purposes with them. Occasionally to the point of violence."

"So bring some muscle to the meet, just in case." I have read enough novels that I was not so naive as to suggest calling in the proper authorities. This was secret society business!

"I *am* the muscle that Tiny called in, and in this circumstance normally I would call for more myself, but we're spread very thin right now, and the nature of our organization is such that it's difficult gather large numbers on short notice. The meet is only a few hours away, and I find myself woefully short on additional muscle."

"You don't need large numbers, sir. Quality over quantity." I paused dramatically. "I volunteer."

Harmon shook his head. "That's kind of you, but I couldn't ask you to do that. This isn't your fight."

"You aren't asking—I'm offering. And justice is everyone's fight."

"How old are you? Nineteen? Eighteen?"

"Something like that."

"Not to mention you're...um..."

"A girl?"

He rubbed his eyes. "Look. This isn't some adventure novel. The good guys don't always win when it comes to real-world violence. This could be legitimately dangerous."

"I'm a legitimately dangerous girl."

"I admire your courage, Danna, but the answer is no."

"Hm. I know! I'll arm-wrestle you for it."

He laughed at that. "You are persistent; I'll give you that much."

"Come on. Afraid to be beat by a girl?"

I find that almost always works.

There are a couple of tricks to winning at arm-wrestling. One is to get your hand over on top of the other person's hand, giving you better leverage. The other trick is to be freakishly strong. And that's how it happened that Sir and Mister Harmon found himself rubbing his elbow, having agreed somehow to let some random kid come to his super-secret illuminati meeting and possible deathtrap.

Harmon, perhaps surprisingly, didn't tell on me to my dad. Instead, the final viewing went off as it normally does: Dad said a few words and then the remains were committed to the fire. I stood by Harmon and watched his face as he saw his...brother? Friend? Associate? For the very last time. He remained stoic and silent throughout the ceremony. Afterwards he thanked my dad and complimented me to him on my professionalism and kindness. Dad glanced at me suspiciously but gave no voice to his skepticism.

That done, we had a free afternoon—it would be many hours before the crematory would cool down enough to clean out, there were no bodies in need of prepping at the moment, and general housekeeping tasks at the guild hall had all been handled. (What a travesty it would have been if I had been kept away from my adventure by chores!) Before we went to the meet though, Mister Harmon wanted to send a radio message.

"I thought you all had alternative means of communication."

"We use a variety of methods."

Harmon thought to make that trip alone and meet back up later, but I knew better than to let him out of my sight. He would probably ditch me and go to the meet alone out of a misguided sense of chivalry. So we made the trek together up the mountain to the radio guild. When we got there I asked the person on reception duty if Tom was in. He was, and came out to meet us.

"Tom, this is Mister Harmon. Mister Harmon, Tom," I said. I stage whispered: "Tom will be super discreet sending your super secret message. He's the very best radioman I know."

Tom snorted derisively. One of these days I will make him blush! Not today though.

The message Harmon was sending was in code—gibberish letters and numbers to those like me without the key—and rather than sending it to Memfis, he was sending it to a particular person at the Cayder boatmans' guild.

74

"What's it say?" I asked.

"Updates and instructions in case things go bad. Beyond that, you don't need to know."

Tom was carefully going over the hand-written sheet of letters and numbers, double-checking that each was legible so that the code wouldn't have any errors introduced in transmission. At the mention of things going bad he looked up at me.

"Mister Harmon is part of a secret society," I explained. "Very cloak and dagger."

Tom blinked. "Sometimes it's hard to tell if you are joking or not."

I had hoped for a laugh. Oh well. "I get that a lot."

"Well. Not my business. Mister Harmon, I am very sorry about your brother, and we will see to this right away." Tom went into the back, leaving me with Harmon. I had hoped to recruit Tom for this grand adventure, but there he went, being all professional!

"For the future, I will have to ask you not to do that," Harmon said softly, but I could tell he was seriously angry.

"What? Why?"

"Because this is not a *game*." He leaned in and whispered fiercely. "You could very easily put lives in danger with loose talk, not least of which would be your own. I'm starting to think my initial instincts about you were wrong."

"But I don't even know anything! Tom thinks I'm joking anyway."

"What you do know could potentially compromise some people. And make no mistake, if I for a moment think you're putting my people in danger, I will not hesitate to kill you myself."

"Are you—"

75

"Threatening you? Yes. If that offends you, feel free to go back to the burners' guild and forget all about this fiasco." I looked at him levelly. "No. I want to do this. If Mister Raff needs help I want to help him." He gave me a searching look, not at all placated. "Then let's go. You will follow my instructions from now on." He turned on his heel and went out without waiting for an acknowledgment from me. I followed.

* * *

"This is the plan," Harmon was explaining. "No matter what, I will do all the talking. You stand there with your hood up and try to look huge and menacing."

"Yes, sir." Harmon had cooled off a bit during the long walk out of town, but I figured now was not the time for witty rejoinders about how easy it was for me to look huge and menacing.

"You're very...imposing. Especially with the hood. That can be useful. If it's just Raff there and he's just hiding out, your presence will be solid and reassuring to him, whether he recognizes you in the hood or not. Be strong and silent. I hope that's what the situation is. If it is, I would remind you not to repeat anything he or I say to anyone."

"Yes, sir. And if that's not what the situation is...?"

"If there is someone there who means harm, I will try to intimidate them. Again, a brawny freak of nature such as yourself will be useful in that regard, but for all your size, your voice is still very feminine and youthful. So, I will do all the talking. You just stand there and look intimidating."

"Yes, sir. And if they are not intimidated?"

Harmon was silent a long moment. "If it comes to violence, run immediately and don't look back. You won't be able to summon help in time to help me. If you get away, just... run back to town and go back to your normal life. And don't breathe a word of any of it to anyone."

"Yes, sir."

"It's not too late to change your mind and go back now."

"I'm not going back."

He sighed. "I would never have agreed to put you in this situation at all if not for the possibility that your presence might save lives. But there's an equal possibility that coming here could cost you your life. You sure you want to go through with this?"

"I'm sure." I can't really explain why I was so determined. Yes, Mister Raff was much beloved by the community, but he was no kin to me. And how could I trust Mister Harmon? I barely knew him. In fact, it would be fair to say I didn't know him at all. All I really knew about him was that Harmon wasn't his real name, that Tiny wasn't really his brother, and that he was no stranger to violence. Who's to say Harmon hadn't murdered Tiny and/or Raff himself? Who's to say he wasn't luring me out of town to the same fate? But I knew it wasn't like that. Sometimes you just know what the right thing to do is, and you just do it.

Still, I was quite unnerved by the time we got to the meeting place. And naturally, it was dark by the time we got there.

The meeting place was well outside of town, an old homesteader's cottage far off the beaten path that looked as if it had burned some number of years ago and stood abandoned ever since. The walls and roof were very much a ruin, but the chimney/fireplace—the sturdiest part of most buildings—was whole, and in fact there was a fire going.

The cottage door had burned or rotted away who knows how long ago, so we stepped through the empty frame without knocking. I had to duck my head, of course. The fire in the fireplace was burning pretty low, but there was just enough light to see by, and what I saw was two men standing by the fireplace, conversing in low tones as we entered. Mister Raff was seated. After a moment, I noticed Mister Raff was actually tied to his chair, like something out of a melodramatic adventure story. *Uh-oh.*

The men at the fireplace turned to greet us. They both had military-style haircuts. "Good of you to join us," said the shorter and older-looking one, addressing Harmon. "You must be the famous Mister Spengler, if you're still using that pseudonym. Rememberer extraordinaire, ha. I was beginning to fear you hadn't gotten your colleague's message." He noticed me then and his eyes traveled up…and up. "Well! And where did you find this specimen, Spengler?" He strolled over and walked all the way around me, looking me up and down and tapping his chin thoughtfully.

I stood motionless and silent, hood obscuring most of my face, willing myself to look as menacing as possible. Unfortunately, the talking man seemed more intrigued than intimidated.

"Amazing. I could definitely use a man like you," he said at last. "Yes. Whatever Spengler's paying you, I'll double it."

I said nothing.

"Sir and jennel," growled Harmon, or Spengler, or whatever on Mam Gaia's ample bosom his name really is. "You do not wish to make enemies of us."

Sir and jennel only laughed. "Haven't I already? Yet here I am, still breathing."

"For now."

The jennel grinned, cocky. "That sounds like a threat to me.

78

Does that sound like a threat to you?" he asked his henchman.

The henchman grinned, plainly delighted at the prospect of violence in the immediate future, and pulled out a revolver. "Yup. Want me to take care of 'em?" he asked, a little too eagerly. He levelled the gun at Harmon (or whoever) and sighted down the barrel, savoring the moment.

"Jennel, this is foolishness." Harmon didn't sound afraid, only tired. "Raff couldn't help you find what you're looking for even if he wanted to. He was a child when he left that place. I don't know where it is either—torture me all you like. And the only thing my brute here knows is how to twist heads off of shoulders."

The jennel and his henchman looked at each other. For the first time, a flash of uncertainty appeared there. The henchman shifted his gun to cover me instead of Harmon. Oh, great plan, this intimidation stuff. I did sign up for it though.

"Lies," declared sir and jennel. "*Someone* knows where Star's Reach is. It is the *key*, not just to the old world, but to Man's Destiny and The Future. I am close now—I can feel it. And we now have someone who was actually *there*. He says he doesn't remember, but excruciating pain can help clarify clouded memories, I've found. Or, failing that, the loss of loved ones."

Mister Raff went even paler than he was already. In fact, I noticed he seemed to be turning kind of gray.

"And if that doesn't work, I have *you*. *You* know, or if you don't know, you have the means of finding out. You and your damnable guild. So, let's make a deal. We're all reasonable people here. You know what I want. I know that you three want to continue breathing. I believe we can come to a mutually beneficial arrangement here."

"No. My damnable guild as you call it would sooner let me

die than let someone like you take Star's Reach."

The jennel scowled, gestured dismissively. "Then we're done here." He looked at his henchman. "Get rid of Spengler and his ogre."

"Ogre!?" Momentarily forgetting myself, I pulled back my hood and glared at the jennel. Looking back now, I can't imagine what I could have been thinking. Perhaps my terror was making me reckless.

The henchman sneered. "It's just a girl!" He switched his gun to his left hand and reached up to grab my upper arm with his right. "Come along, sweets." He let his gun point toward the floor as he tried to push me ahead of him.

He never saw my fist coming. A few of his teeth went flying as I crushed his jaw. He went down hard and stayed down, unmoving. The gun landed underneath him.

"*Ogre* will do fine, actually."

Sir and jennel stared at me mouth agape for a moment that, at once, seemed to stretch on and on, yet was over in an instant. Then he was lunging for his fallen comrade's gun. Harmon was across the room faster than I would have thought possible, also going for the gun, while I stood and stared like a great stupid oaf.

Harmon got the better of that struggle. He held the jennel at gunpoint.

"Turn around," he said.

The jennel turned around. "Going to order me to run off into the woods and never cross your path again? Is that it? I swear, you storytellers are such pathetic weak—"

Harmon blew his brains out.

* * *

I thought we had saved Mister Raff. He was still alive and uninjured after that ordeal, but too weak to walk. He looked really unwell, like...well, he looked like a corpse, and I know corpses all too well. Harmon and I had to resort to carrying him in a makeshift stretcher, but we hadn't been walking fifteen minutes before he made us stop and put him down.

"Mister Raff?" I said. "We need to keep moving. You don't look well—we need to get you back—"

"I'm not getting back, child," he croaked in his funny Western accent.

I felt tears welling up in my eyes. "*No*. Mister Raff—"

"No, don't interrupt me," he gasped. "I'm having a heart attack or something in the woods at least an hour from town, not to mention I'm ninety. I'm done. But I have something to say before I go to be reborn. To both of you."

We waited as he took a few ragged breaths.

"Danna. I know you like to joke that your sister got the brains while you got the brawn, but you are brilliant. Don't sell yourself short. I saw you back there—you were amazing."

"I didn't really d—"

"Don't interrupt me while I'm dying, girl. You." He gestured weakly at Harmon. "Mister Green or whatever your name is this week. You have a good eye for potential. This one here will be a fine addition to your group."

"I don't think she's r—"

"I said, don't interrupt me. Don't you people have any manners?" He held out his hand. I took it. His voice was getting weaker; I had to lean in to hear. "Tell my grandkids I love them and am proud of them." A tear rolled down his cheek. "And if anyone else wants to know about Star's Reach, you can tell them that that damned place can stay buried forever. Forever..."

He drifted off into unconsciousness.

* * *

The official story was that I went for a hike alone outside of town and found Mister Raff dead of a heart attack and carried him back. Mister Harmon meanwhile slipped back into the shadows. Those who had seen me walking around town with him probably assumed some kind of romantic tryst with the exotic out-of-towner. The truth, of course, was far stranger.

Before he disappeared though, Mister Harmon said he didn't entirely trust me not to tell anyone about my adventure, yet he wasn't prepared to kill me outright either (which I truly appreciate). He said the best thing to do would be to write it all down and commit the story to him and his order for safekeeping. It would be "out of my system" and therefore hopefully would not be straining to burst forth unbidden from my breast. And perhaps decades or centuries from now someone down the line will deem my story safe enough to be told openly, perhaps with some details altered. Or perhaps it will never see the light of day. Either way, won't be my problem. But that's what this is.

And speaking of Mister Harmon's order, despite what Mister Raff said, I have decided not to pursue becoming a full member of that mysterious group. I have a life of my own I like pretty well, and I think I've had my fill of adventure and harrowing danger for a while. But he and his people do have use for discreet allies willing to stand up for what's right. I would be prepared to help in that capacity.

I do not know if I will ever see Mister Harmon again after I turn over this manuscript.

But I hope to.

SILENT KEY

TONY F. WHELKS

I t was only when Marko's mutilated corpse washed up on the mudflats of Linsey's east coast that I understood the whole truth. Even then, I might have missed it, had it not been for the woman's body beside him. All the pieces of the puzzle fell into place almost before I was aware that there had even been a puzzle begging to be solved. I'd had my head in the clouds, that was the problem.

Marko Henders had been the First Operator at the Linsey Field Station for more than five years before I was posted there as his Second. Like every Second Operator in every field station, I was assigned to the night watch.

The evening radio watch was never exciting. The top and bottom of every hour were our regular sked times, and if there's traffic for us that's about as exciting as it gets. I would usually while away the rest of the evening scanning through the white noise and earwigging on other stations' traffic on our receiver. The First Operator was always badgering me to use the time keying on the practice oscillator to improve my fist, but I'll admit I tended to quit that as soon as he left the shack. And that's how I came to be tuning around when the strange signal struggled through the noise.

The voice that crackled in the back of the speaker took some deciphering. It was speaking English, after a fashion. I'm not sure if it was the heavy accent, or just the distortion caused by the fading and the static crashes of a distant thunderstorm, but I had to concentrate hard to make any sense of it.

I couldn't catch everything the voice was saying, it wasn't what you'd call readability five, but once my ears had picked out the first couple of clear words, they soon pricked up, like those of a startled fox hearing the hounds. 'Presden' was the first word that set the clangers ringing, then something that sounded like 'Cincinatti'. That sent a shiver down my spine, because there was no way I should be able to hear what I thought I was hearing, at least not if it was coming from where I thought it did.

The signal surged and faded for a few minutes, and I strained my ears and tried to tweak the tuning on the receiver. I jotted down what I was hearing, though it was really patchy and I had to piece it together the best I could.

"...yan cavalry offensive...repulsed but evacuation of...all non-guildsmen of military age are invited to volunt....the Hiyo Army under Jen...rebel forces have been pushed..."

That was all I got, with a few more words I didn't recognise, before it faded away back into the noise and lightning crashes. I sat back in my chair and stared at what I'd scribbled down and was still puzzling it over when I glanced at the clock and swore. It was five past the hour and I wasn't listening on our traffic frequency. Sure enough, as I hurriedly cranked the dial there were a string of Vs and our station call being hammered out in a familiar fist. It's funny the way Morse code can sound every bit as individual as a voice, and the rapid-fire dots and pounded dashes I was hearing sounded impatient to me, and for good reason, because the distant station had spent five minutes trying to raise a reply.

I grabbed the key and sent the all clear to let them know I'd heard and was ready to take traffic. As the message came in the furious tone of the sending returned to a more professional cadence and I transcribed it as I listened, though I could as easily read it in my head and jot it down later. However, that isn't good procedure, and our First Operator always insisted on live transcription.

GLNSI DE GZETL PSE CPI ES QSP FR JAMES BHEP. FR JAMES BHEP.

CFM RCPT SHIPMENT REF 10057 RPT 10057.

PSE ADVISE COLLECT OR FWD?

DE ZET TRANS CO. ZET TRANS CO.

GZETL BK

I keyed my confirmation back to the Zetland station, followed by a quick query for any further traffic, but there was nothing else to come yet, so I signed off and switched the transmitter to standby to conserve the batteries.

I imagine the message looks a bit gibberish if you're not a radioman, but is perfectly clear if you are. The best way I could put it in English is this: "Linsey Station this is Zetland Station, we need you to get this message to Brother James at the Eastport Brother House. The Zetland Trans-shipment Company has taken delivery of his consignment, reference number 10057, and they want to know whether he wants it sending on or will he arrange his own collection?"

Not as thrilling as reports of wars overseas, maybe, but it is our bread and butter. It was a bit late to send one of the apprentices over to Eastport seeing as the sun had not long set, so I slapped it on to the spike ready for the morning. The apprentices are taught all the abbreviations and procedurals long before we let them anywhere near Morse code. That way they can understand the message slips when we send them out to the recipients, and they're primed for what to listen for once they start on the code for real. The rest of the night was pretty quiet, and come sunrise there were still only three slips on the spike. Apart from Brother James's shipment we also had news from Umbra for one of the matrons of Sanjun Parish, who would be delighted to know that her daughter who was travelling with the trade mission was in good health and pleased to announce the arrival of the matron's first grandchild. Don't ask what the third slip contained because it was a series of five-digit blocks of numbers destined for the Portioners' Hall, and it would be one of the clerks there who had to crack out the code tables and extract the meaning.

— · · · — · —

The Old Man, that's the First Operator, didn't believe a word of what I told him the next morning. "I don't care what you think you heard," he grumbled, "it didn't come from America. The ionosphere is shot to pieces, and you'd know that if you paid more attention to your studies."

I could have pressed my case, but it would just come across as petulance. Anyway, I was up to date with my studies, I knew what the score was supposed to be and that's exactly why I wanted him to know. No one has been able to explain it yet, but there's plenty of ideas being discussed throughout the Radio Service. Some blame the climate, others go for sunspots. Some put it down to nukes that might have been used a couple of centuries ago, even though that's just a rumour. Then there are those who blame the effects of 'geo-engineering', whatever that's supposed to be.

The Old Man didn't particularly care why, he said, just accept it and live with it. Perhaps in the old times we could span the world with shortwave communications, but today nothing gets much beyond a few hundred kilometres. Either signals are not bouncing off the higher layers like they used to, or get absorbed lower down for some reason. Or then the ionised clouds just could be lower, so signals simply don't go so far. As I said, no-one knows for sure, everyone has their own speculations, and a few, like Marko, just don't care.

Despite the Old Man's lack of interest, I still had a mystery on my hands. Sure, there's no mystery about the fighting; there's been plenty of that any which way you might look. However, getting that weak burst from the American broadcaster was still sending a thrill through me. How could it be possible? Was this what it was like for the old-timers when they listened to their radios pulling in signals from all over the world? The Old Man might have been bit of a curmudgeon, but I couldn't deny that I was excited by my discovery, and was annoyed he didn't think it worth reporting to the Tower.

"Go get some breakfast, Denny," the curmudgeon growled as he dismissed me from the shack and settled down for his own watch period. "Then get these sent out," he added, passing the message slips back to me. I leant over towards the scratch pad and lifted the sheet with my scribbled war report before the Old Man could rip it out and throw it away, as I just knew he would.

— · · — · —

I was still in my first year at Linsey, barely a quarter of the way through the posting before I could head back to the Tower to take the exams for my full ticket, and it was taking some getting used to. Fish for breakfast, I ask you! Back home on the mainland I'd be tucking into bread and honey, or a plateful of eggs, that's a proper start to the day, but us radiomen don't get to pick and choose, especially a lowly Second Op like me. We're expected to follow the local habits wherever we're posted. And in Linsey Island, that means fish for breakfast. At least taking the night watch I could pretend it was supper, because I kipped down once the slips were sent out.

Rachel, one of the local apprentices, had my breakfast waiting for me in the living quarters, and I let her look over the slips whilst I ate.

"Ooh, can I take this one, Denny?" she asked.

"Which one's that?"

"The one for Goodwife Kirsten at Sanjun. I know her daughter, I'd love to give her the news. She'll be thrilled. The whole Parish will."

I couldn't resist her enthusiasm. It was quite a journey, but Rachel was doing well with her apprenticeship. I thought she could afford the time it would take, and it's always nice for the recipient of good news to hear it from a familiar face.

"Okay, but take the pony, though, I want you back in time for Morse class," I conceded, trying to hold a grave expression despite her infectious enthusiasm. "And you know the rules. No gossip on the way, the messages are private. Confidentiality is the core ethic of the Radio Service."

"I know, I know," she replied, still bubbling over with eagerness. "Mum's the word," she giggled.

I groaned at the pun, slowly shaking my head as she rushed off clutching the precious slip of paper, and she was out of the door before I realised she hadn't hung around to clean up the breakfast things. I washed up myself, still wondering about the strange voice I'd heard the previous evening, then went in search for another apprentice. I found Robyn in the workshop, stripping down some old equipment that had been salvaged from the ruined city at the head of the Serpent's Back. Neat piles of screws and nuts were lined up on the bench before him, and a few of the more recognisable electronic components were separated out, too, but the mysterious little black insect-like blocks that no longer had any use were pushed to one side for disposal. I was pleased to spot a little pile of the delicate ancient diodes that we could build up into crystal sets to sell.

Robyn was engrossed in his work, and he had the chassis pretty much cleared out. He glanced up when I dropped the message slip into the empty case.

"Morning, Denny. Did you have a good watch?"

"So-so," I replied, wondering whether to share my exciting discovery with the youngster. Maybe later, I decided. First a test. "Can you tackle this one?"

He scanned the note and I smiled as his lips moved whilst he read.

"Okay, it's for Brother James at Eastport. There's a package for him at Zetland, and does he want it sent on?"

"That's good enough. Can you run it over there now?

This chassis can wait."

"Sure, Denny. One thing, though. Why is 'Brother' abbreviated to 'FR'? It doesn't make sense."

He had me there, of course. "No idea," I admitted. "Just a tradition, I guess."

"You'd have thought it would be short for 'father'. That would make more sense, except it wouldn't, of course," Robyn joked. That was true. The Brothers and Sisters would never be fathers or mothers, and that's Linsey's answer to the nepotism that plagued the early years of their Portioning Council. As a visiting radioman, it wasn't my place to question my hosts' system of government, so I guided the conversation back to the business at hand.

"When you've delivered this, wait for Brother James's reply, and don't forget that there's no fee to collect. It will go on to the Brother House's account," I reminded him.

The final message, the encrypted one for the Portioners' Hall, I decided to take myself. I could use the walk after sitting in front of the receiver all night, and I was too fired up by the strange signal to get to sleep any time soon anyway. I had a lot to think about before turning in for sleep, so a gentle stroll through Westport and a blast of fresh air seemed ideal.

— · · — · —

Once a week I had to give the apprentices their Morse practice. Needless to say, it was the First Operator's duty, but his sending was as ropey as his handwriting, and he didn't want them learning his bad habits, or so he claimed. We had four apprentices in all, and they all gathered in the workshop with their pencils and paper, and I hammered out the practice texts. Now, there are ways and ways to teach the Code, some like to start real slow, and speed up over time but that has a problem—often as not the students hit a wall and can't get past it. So I prefer the Farnuth Method, as it's called. Each character is sent fast, but with long spaces between. Over time, the gaps can be shortened until you're going full whack, and all being well, there's no brick wall.

Our four apprentices were a mixed bag. Robyn, I felt really sorry for. He was a technical wizard, great with the gear, but had a tin ear. I couldn't see him ever making a good field operator. I might get him up to fives—that's five words a minute, basic proficiency – but he'll never make fifteens. When he goes to the Tower, they might be able to sort him out, but more likely they'll steer him towards the technician programme and he'll wind up with a posting to a broadcaster somewhere.

My star pupil was Rachel, and I guess it was her musical family that made the difference. She got it straight away. A lot of students struggle by counting dots and dashes and trying to remember the letters like they have to look it up every time, but Rachel just got the rhythm. She's going to be faster than me one day, but then I tend to melt down round about the twenties myself.

The other two apprentices, Matt and Freja, were competent. Neither as brilliant as Rachel nor as slow as Robyn. They were twins, and had started their apprenticeship quite young. In Linsey, large families are not favoured, and their parents had really struggled with the tithes they had to pay. It struck me as harsh because it's not the parents' fault if they drop twins, but that's the Portioners' affair and radiomen aren't supposed to get into that sort of thing. The eldest son stayed at home on their Holding and the twins were sent to us, and the family was better off without the extra tithes to pay.

We ran through a few pangrams, like the 'Quick brown fox...' and the 'Jackdaws love my sphinx...', then a random selection from the 'Lorem ipsum'. Then it was time to get them started on numbers, so I ran through zero to nine for them a few times, followed by a good chunk of digits of pi. As I expected, Rachel picked it up straight away, the twins struggled for a while, but soon caught up. After half an hour Robyn was still mixing up his seven with his eight, and his two with his three, and was visibly frustrated. By the time he started confusing his five and zero, too, I decided he'd had enough, and I called it a day.

"I'm never going to get this, Denny," Robyn confided after the others had left, "I'll never be a proper radioman."

"I know it's hard for you, Robyn, but you're not doing badly. You're about up to fives on letters, this was your first session with numbers. You'll get there. Just think what you have done. You've learnt to read and write. How many people in Linsey can say that? Just the Brothers and Sisters, and a few merchants who can afford private lessons."

"I suppose," he admitted, grudgingly.

"There's no 'suppose' about it. You're a smart young man. You might not be the best telegraphist in the Service, but your technical abilities will shame some back at the Tower. Once you get there, you'll see. Trust me, you're going to be a great radioman one day, so no more moping, okay?"

He nodded at this, but I could tell his confidence had taken a knock, nonetheless. I needed to restore it somehow.

"What have you been working on recently?" I asked.

"I'm still going through that last batch of salvage, seeing what we can use."

"And? Anything nice?" I asked, knowing full well what

had been brought in.

"I was going to start on all that wire next, strip it down to single strands."

"That's a good idea. I could find a use for that," I said, and then I told him what it was I needed, and he cheered up almost instantly with a new project to work on. "And whilst you're working on that, why don't you fire up the spare receiver there? Strap a dummy load across it, you'll be able to hear our outgoing traffic, and I can bring the scripts in later to see how much you've copied."

Strange as it sounds, some people find it easier to read Morse off-air, with all the noise and static, than they do from a practice oscillator in a quiet room, and I was willing to try anything that might help to clear Robyn's tin ear.

— · · · — · —

When I awoke later that afternoon I was eager to get back to the shack to see what else might come crawling out of the noise, bouncing off the high, thin clouds that shouldn't be there. The Old Man was tidying up at the end of his own shift, and we always had a short handover period to sort out any unfinished business and that's usually when we went over my studies and his 'teaching'. Let's just say he was not an inspired educator, and leave it at that.

Even though the Old Man had been sending out apprentices around town and further afield during the day, there was still quite the stack of slips on the spike, including a couple more encrypted ones for the Portioners' Hall. That adds up to a lot of diplomatic chatter, I thought, seeing as how we often went months without a single one. Three in a single day was unprecedented.

Although I could tell something was going on, it's hard to work out what it might be from the traffic, as encrypted messages are always sent with a generic callsign, and only the receiving station's call is sent in the open. I suppose it keeps nosey second ops from guessing too much if earwiggers can't tell who is speaking to who.

"Evening, Marko," I greeted the First Operator. "Good shift?"

"Busy," he grumbled.

I indicated the two encrypts. "Any idea what's going on? There's a lot of chatter today."

"Nope. I don't know, I don't need to know, and it's none of our business anyway. Confidentiality is the core ethic of the Radio Service, Denny." He glared at me reprovingly, as though I needed to be reminded of the little lecture I had given Rachel earlier.

Before leaving the shack, Marko pulled the stack of slips off the spike, and handed nearly half of the sheaf to me. "This is a verbatim. Do the fair copy, you know what my handwriting is like."

I looked at the papers. "That's a proper Warren piece," I grumbled. No-one remembers who this Warren was, but he must have been a famous windbag back in the old days to have got himself turned into a proverb.

A verbatim message has to be re-written for final delivery to the recipient, no abbreviations or procedurals left in, so they can read it themselves just as if it were a letter. It's an expensive service, so we don't get many, and they're usually for the well-to-do or folks in trade. Of course, the Old Man should have written it up himself, but I reckoned he wanted to keep me busy, another way of saying 'no earwigging'.

Resigned to the task, I started to turn Marko's ungainly

print into the best cursive I could manage. As soon as I heard the shack door shut behind me, I retuned the receiver to the spot where I'd heard the strange broadcast the night before, and kept one ear on the white noise and one eye on the clock as I scratched away at the fair copy. The core ethic might well be confidentiality, but another ethic is continual self-training, and whether or not the Old Man liked it, I convinced myself that hunting down more exotic signals counted as self-training.

The verbatim was long, a good five pages by the time I finished. It must have cost the sender a fortune, but clearly they could afford it, and it was going to cost the recipient another fortune on delivery the following morning. I hoped it was worth it, but the odd mix of family gossip and what looked like commodity prices suggested it was a report from one branch of a merchant family to another, so I guessed they must be getting their money's worth.

By the time my first traffic sked came round, I hadn't heard anything from the mysterious broadcaster, and I tuned to our traffic frequency with more disappointment than I wanted to admit. There was nothing for us, but as I had a reply from Brother James to send back to Zetland, I checked the Station Schedule Chart to see when I needed to call them. Due to all the trans-polar ships that dock there, Zetland handles a lot of traffic, and they listen for calls every ten minutes, so I wouldn't have long to wait, or so I thought. They were having a busy night, and it took me three attempts to raise them because stronger signals squashed my first two calls into the noise.

By the time I'd tapped out Brother James's message and had Zetland's confirmation, my bladder was making its presence known, so I nipped out to the yard for a quick leak.

Scanning the skyline as the relief coursed through my abdomen, I caught sight of the beacon flaring in its brazier on top of the hill overlooking the town and harbour. I couldn't help but wonder if that had something to do with all the encrypted messages that had been arriving in the past few hours— Linsey was mustering the fleet.

— · · — · —

Westport was buzzing in the morning. Farmers and fishermen from the surrounding Parishes were streaming in through the gates, and any apprentices that could be spared joined them in the square outside the Portioners' Hall. Although our own apprentices are drawn from the locality, under the Radio Service covenants they are exempted from community obligations, including military or naval service and taxes, or tithing in the case of Linsey.

The gathering men coalesced into groups around the coxswains, who led them away down the hill towards the harbour once they were satisfied with their numbers. It all looked somewhat chaotic, but I could see there was an underlying order, despite the milling around. Evidently the crews were well drilled, and it wasn't long before most of the men had moved out.

I caught sight of one of the grey-robed Councillors standing outside the Portioners' Hall and decided to fish for some news.

"Good morning, Sister," I called.

"Ah, good morning. You're the new radioman, aren't you?" she replied. Of course, one glance at the small, black diamond-shaped badge pinned to my tunic would have told her that, but I thought she did actually recognise me from my various visits to the Hall delivering message slips.

"Yes, been here seven months now," I replied, "But I'm still learning my way round. Just wondering why the fleet's been mustered?"

"I would have thought you'd know about that. After all, the news passed through your hands," she raised a quizzical eyebrow.

"If it was encrypted we'd have no idea what it contained," I explained.

"Well, it's no secret now, I suppose. A big fleet has been spotted off the west coast, and it looks like trouble. We're not sure who they are yet, but they seem to have come up from the south. All the coastal polities are mobilising, just in case."

It was an impressive sight when all the ships filed out of the harbour mouth, oars flashing in unison along each of the sleek hulls. There must have been thirty or more, though I didn't count them out. The lead vessels bided their time in the straits between Linsey Island and the Serpent's Back, the long spit of land that was once part of Linsey before the last Surge flooded the low land in between. The fleet formed up in a wedge formation behind the flagship, and hoisted sails once the ships from the northern Parishes arrived. Only a handful of ships remained in the harbour, including a few Zetlander and Norse merchantmen. For a small island, Linsey can put out a lot of boats, but what with the Arabs and the floods, trade and fishing, the sea is life and death itself.

Somewhere under those waves lies the ancient town where the first Knut was crowned, and I know the Linsey folk say it's been Knuts ever since, but that's not what the mainland historians say. There's been goodness knows how many Royal Houses since the Great Knut, back when all the islands were still one country, before it was eaten up and drowned by the Surges. But it's never a good idea to tell your hosts that their founding myths are bunk, and radiomen aren't supposed to get into that sort of thing anyway. We're just the messengers. We don't have opinions, we don't take sides. That's why we can go anywhere in the isles safely, even when the polities are at war with each other, which I'm glad to say they haven't done in my lifetime. That's a good part of the reason why they could all set sail together to meet this unknown fleet.

It was late in the morning by the time the fleet was properly under way, well past my bedtime, so I hurried back towards the radio station and my bed. As I passed the workshop, I was surprised to hear Rachel and Robyn bickering at each other, so I stuck my head around the door to see what was up.

"What's the matter with you two?" I asked, and they both went quiet as soon as they realised I was there. Rachel looked away, a slight colour washing over her face, and Robyn leapt into the silence.

"She's spoiling my practice!" he complained. "Saying the letters out loud before I can write them down."

"Well, he's so slow," she quipped. "He's not getting half of it."

I usually gave Rachel a lot of leeway, but I was annoyed at this, star pupil or not.

"Rachel, you're really not helping," I snapped. "I asked Robyn to take extra practice, not you. If you can't offer any practical help, you don't need to be in here."

At least she had the good grace to apologise, and not just to me but to Robyn, too. I picked up Robyn's notes and had a look through at what he had copied down. Despite what Rachel had said, he had been getting more than half of it, though not much more. Except for the final section.

"What happened here, Robyn? Looks like you totally lost it. Even what you did get looks like gibberish."

Robyn shrugged, but Rachel, in a suddenly conciliatory tone, added "That's because it was. There were characters in it I didn't even recognise. That's not Robyn's fault."

"What characters? Were they procedurals?" I asked.

Rachel screwed up her face in concentration, her eyes gazing into the distance over my shoulder as she recalled the unfamiliar rhythms she had picked out.

"Umm. There was dah-dah-dah-dah. Like it was halfway between 'O' and zero. Also dah-dah-dah-dit, like 'J' but backwards. And di-di-dah-di-dit. I mean, what's that supposed to be? EL, FE, UI, ID? They're not procedurals are they?"

She was right; they weren't procedural shorthand like BK for 'break' or SK for 'end of transmission', and they weren't regular characters, either. To be honest, I had no more idea than the apprentices had, so I jotted them down and went to the shack to ask the Old Man if he knew.

Barely glancing at the paper, Marko simply stated "Cyrillic. That Rosh ship in the harbour must have a Marconi on board."

— · · · — · —

Whilst I was asleep disaster struck. One of the tubes, a pentode, in the station receiver had popped. When I arrived in the shack to begin my watch, I found Marko and Robyn had hefted the spare regenerative receiver on to the bench. The lidless superheterodyne stood to one side, and I could see the empty socket where the burnt-out valve had been removed. "Not a good watch, then?" I asked, and Marko just grunted, as though he didn't trust his vocabulary with anything more. "Just as well we have separates," I added. "If that had been a transceiver we'd be silent key."

"That's right, so you better treat that re-gen right or Lindsey will be signing off for the duration," he growled, saying, without saying, that he didn't approve of me listening around of an evening. Needless to say, it's not good for a field station like ours to be forced to go silent key. Even as second operator, it still wouldn't reflect well on me or my prospects with the Service, although it would be the Old Man who'd really be in the firing line, of course. Like he'd care, he had his feet well under the bench and would be happy to serve out his time here just running the Linsey field station. He'd managed to get this posting back to his home patch, and seemed to have given up any idea of going for his Master's certificate. Me, well, I might not have settled on my speciality yet, and won't until I get back to the Tower to sit for the full ticket, but I didn't want to remain stuck in a remote outpost for my whole life.

"I'll get a new tube ordered tomorrow," Marko stated.

"I can call up the Tower tonight," I offered, but he waved it away.

"No need. I've got my regular report to send tomorrow, I'll do it all together. We can manage on the re-gen for a few days."

The regenerative receiver was a little harder to tune than the super-het, but with a little tweaking it could be every bit as sensitive. It wasn't quite so easy to mesh with the transmitter, but it with care it would be fine. What bothered me most was that Robyn wouldn't be able to get in his extra practice, but another thought crossed my mind, too.

It took some wheedling, but I finally convinced the Old Man to let Robyn sit in on my night watch. Strictly, it was a bit early in his apprenticeship to be sitting in, but I reminded Marko that Robyn needed some extra help with his Morse, which was true enough, though not the true reason I wanted him there.

The Old Man headed off to the living quarters and I pulled up an extra chair for Robyn. I couldn't be entirely sure of the frequency calibration between the two receivers, but I found the carrier from our transmitter where I expected so it all seemed good. Then I dialled up the frequency of the American broadcaster, willing the white noise to burst into something more exciting. I could have sworn there was something weak, so weak, deep down in the static. It can get you like that sometimes. Listen hard enough you can always hear voices in the noise, as if the wishing makes it true. More likely something in your head just fires off and turns the random sounds into an illusion just beyond perception. Or maybe there really are voices of long-dead radiomen echoing eternally through the ether, whispering secrets the living can never grasp.

I tapped my finger on the dial, and Robyn took the hint. He scribbled down a few numbers and started working his slide rule. Before long he had filled half the scratch pad with calculations. Conscientiously, he returned to the beginning, reworked the numbers and came out with the same answer, and only then did he nod to himself in satisfaction.

"I think we have enough to do it," he offered.

"Can you get started tomorrow? When the OM is busy?" I asked.

He flashed me an impish, conspiratorial grin. "Better than that. I can get it finished tomorrow, too."

I doubt my grin was quite so impish, but it was every bit as wide as Robyn's had been, nonetheless.

— · · · — · —

We had, of course, been over-optimistic. Without interruptions, all would have gone well, but a flurry of encrypts poured in the following morning, and the Old Man roused all the apprentices and had them running urgent messages back and forth to the the Portioners' Hall. Seeing as all the commotion had already woken me, I headed down to the shack myself.

It was a grey autumnal day, and the wind was beginning to bluster menacingly as ragged clouds chased away the remains of the fine weather of the preceding weeks. As I headed across the yard towards the shack, I nearly collided with a deputation from the Portioners' Hall. Their grey robes flapping in the squally breeze and their faces drawn, the Councillors squeezed into the cramped space of the shack, and I soon heard Marko grumbling at the intrusion.

"No, you can't work in here! Now shush, I need to concentrate if you don't want your messages garbled," I heard, and the Councillors started to back out of the doorway once more.

"Can I help you?" I offered. I wasn't sure who was the senior member of the party so I addressed an older Sister who was clutching a large, leather-bound book with pages marked by numerous coloured ribbons.

"Thank you, yes. Is there a room we can use? Your poor apprentices are worn out, and we need to turn the messages round faster. We thought if we could work on the decryption here, it would help all round."

"Of course. You can use the workshop. There's a workbench there, but I'm afraid we don't have seats for you all." I set our poor, worn-out apprentices to the task of clearing a space for the books and papers, and Robyn passed me a rueful glance, no doubt disappointed about the interruption to his project.

I was eager to see how the decryption system worked, but was gently but firmly invited to leave the room. All I saw was a table of figures and letters on the first page of the large book, and that wasn't really enough to satisfy my curiosity. Although I could hear muffled voices through the wooden door to the workshop, interspersed with occasional outbursts, I could get no sense of what was causing all the fuss. Message slips were passed in and out of the room, and now they no longer had to run to the Portioners' Hall and back, only one apprentice was required at each room to ferry the messages. All the outgoing messages were being sent all the way down to New Dumnonia, in the far south west, and it didn't take a great leap of imagination to link them to the recently departed fleet. However, the blocks of random-looking digits were as mute to me as they were portentous to the Councillors.

I left the twins running the messages between the two rooms, and sent Rachel and Robyn off to get some rest. Before I returned to my own bunk, I saw Robyn slip out into the yard, a coil of wire nonchalantly draped over his shoulder.

— · · · — · —

By the time I returned for the evening watch, the OM had a

drained look about him.

"Good shift?" I asked, though not in any expectation of a positive reply.

"Mayhem," he moaned. "It's calmed down now, though. The grey-robes have gone back to their Hall. I doubt it'll be so busy tonight, but you should keep one of the apprentices with you, just in case. How was Robyn last night, sitting in?"

"Good, we made some progress," I conceded, careful not to specify what the progress had been.

"Fine. He can sit in again. I'll send him in after I've eaten."

"You had time to order a new pentode?" I asked.

"Yes, but it will take a while. They've got no stock at the Tower, so we'll have to wait on the next convoy from Nuwinga."

"But that could take weeks!"

"We'll just have to make do. Now I'm having an early night, my ears are ringing like a brothel's doorbell."

There were no slips on the spike, so either the Old Man had kept on top of everything, or more likely, there just hadn't been any other traffic during the day besides the encrypts. I settled into the operating seat, and sat quietly listening to white noise whilst I waited for Robyn or the first string of di-di-di-dahs to emerge. The receiver won the race, and I took down the details of the next transshipment for Brother James as the Zetland station's night operator tapped out the details in that familiar Caledonian lilt of his.

I hadn't noticed Robyn slipping into the shack, but once I put my pencil down and spiked Brother James's slip I caught sight of him sitting beside me, sporting a grin as wide as the Umber.

"What?" I asked.

104

"Don't you want to try it out, then?"

"It's up?" I could barely contain my own excitement as the young apprentice nodded.

"Just hoisted it up the lanyard, and the feeder's ready to pull in through the hatch."

In two minutes we had unscrewed the feeder from the main aerial and connected the new one, which was tuned to the American broadcaster's frequency. It wouldn't make a huge difference, but it could be just enough. A bit of directivity, a little bit of gain, and the new sloper could just be capable of dragging that elusive signal out of the noise and the static crashes.

We barely breathed for the next few minutes as we listened, willing the voices to appear and whisper their far flung secrets once more. It could have been my imagination, but I was sure the lightning crashes were less intrusive. Outside, the sky turned red as the sun sank below the horizon, then finally, with just a couple minutes left before our next sked time, the speaker crackled to life.

At first there was a barely detectable change in the noise, then the signal surged. I didn't know whether to laugh or cry as stirring music echoed pompously through the static. Drums and horns marched out of the speaker. It was a signal, but music could come from anywhere and it didn't help me identify the station. The gods of the ionosphere were playing with me, teasing and taunting my hopes, yet somehow I felt sure it was the same station I'd heard before. I just couldn't prove it. The tune seemed to be coming to some sort of a triumphant conclusion but our time was up, it was sked time. I couldn't pull the plug, though, the traffic would have to wait.

"Just one more minute," I whispered to Robyn, as though there was any danger of us being overheard. The music crescendoed to an abrupt halt, and a heavily accented voice finally announced:

"This is Sisnaddi station..."

What with Robyn's whoop of joy, my own astonishment and the phasing distortion caused by the fading, I didn't take in another word, but that didn't matter. I knew.

But duty called. Robyn quickly switched the aerials back, whilst I retuned the receiver. We were a couple of minutes late, and of course there was traffic waiting for us. I tapped out the all clear, grabbed my pencil, and I can't remember the message I jotted down next. It seemed to drag on forever in my eagerness to tune back to the broadcaster, but eventually the traffic concluded. I signed off, spiked the slip, and sat back in my chair, still stunned.

Robyn leapt into action and swapped the aerials once again, but by the time we had the receiver back to the right spot, the signal had gone, not even a whisper in the background any more. The cloud that shouldn't have been there had gone away again. But it was true. The impossible was possible, even if only for a few minutes.

— · · · — · —

The storm brewing out at sea was as nothing compared to the fury that was unleashed in the shack come morning.

"What the blazes is that thing on the mast?" bellowed the Old Man. "And how did it get there without my say-so?"

"It's just a dipole," I ventured, but that seemed to enrage him even further.

"Do you think I can't see that, Denny?" His face flushed an alarming shade of crimson and his eyes flashed with rage as they bore into me.

Robyn seemed to shrink into himself, trying to make himself invisible. It didn't work, and Marko turned to the apprentice. "Get those slips delivered, I'll deal with you later."

There was a tense silence as Robyn pulled the slips off the spike and rushed out of the door. The onslaught continued as soon as Marko and I were alone.

"I want an explanation! What do you think you're playing at? Who runs this station, Denny, you or me?"

I was taken aback by the scale of Marko's anger. I had realised he wouldn't be pleased, but hadn't expected this outburst.

"Sorry, Marko, you're the First Operator," I said quietly.

"Yes, Denny! I am the First Operator, and nothing goes on that mast unless I put it there, do you understand?"

I nodded.

"Tell me you're not still chasing this silly idea about signals from America," he rumbled, and my silence proved my guilt. "Oh, you stupid fool! Not only have you gone behind my back, and used Radio Service resources without permission, you've also compromised the station's efficiency. That thing of yours will detune the main antenna, who knows what traffic you've missed? Did you think of that?"

"The doublet still loads up fine," I explained.

"Not good enough, Denny. It might still match, but that's no guarantee it still radiates so well. You should know this by now. Get out of my sight! Take it down now, and consider yourself confined to quarters until I decide what to do with you."

— · · · — · —

It didn't take the Old Man very long to decide what to do

with me. It was like a whirlwind, and I had barely enough time to think or say my goodbyes before he hustled me down to the harbour and aboard a hastily arranged transit back to the mainland, destined for the Tower. Robyn was distraught as he helped lug my bags down to the waterfront.

"I can't believe he's doing this, Denny," he whispered, for what seemed like the hundredth time since we'd left the station. "What am I going to do?"

"Just keep your head down and your nose clean. He's already got another Second coming over, he told me. I just wish I could meet her beforehand, let her know how good you are."

"What's going to happen to you, though?" he asked.

"I really don't know. There'll be a disciplinary hearing. He's filed his report, and I won't know what he's told them until I get there and have to answer his charges. For now, I want you to keep practising your Morse, get Rachel to help you if you can. It won't be long before both of you are eligible to come to the Tower for your Second's exam, and hopefully I'll see you both there."

Robyn stood disconsolately on the quay watching my ship ease out into the channel, the careful strokes of the oarsmen steering the small, clinker-built ship into the waves. The crossing was rough, and by the time we'd reached the Serpent's Head Gap I was truly thankful that my breakfast had been light. The ship's navigator joined me at the stern when he saw me clutching the rail.

"You'll be right as rain once we're through the gap," he said.

"Good to know," I replied, my throat dry despite my mouth watering unpleasantly.

"That won't be long, we have the tide with us." He gestured with one hand towards the water streaming through the Gap. The stumpy ruins emerging from the water here formed the Serpent's horns, as seen from Lindsey island. I could just make out the lookout post perched atop one of the crumbled stone towers that had once belonged to an ancient temple, long stripped of its valuable metals.

The navigator's prognosis was correct, and once we entered the Trent Straits and the familiar coastline of home loomed on the southern horizon, my stomach was settled. I returned to the bench, determined to enjoy the rest of the journey, but I couldn't stop my mind churning over the ordeal that was bound to be waiting for me at the Tower.

— · · · — · —

When I had left the Tower all those months before, with my freshly-signed Second Operator's Certificate tucked into my pocket, I had had to walk the few miles to the port to take ship to Linsey. On my return, I was shocked to find my old instructor waiting for me on the quay, a pony and trap beside her.

"Emily! I wasn't expecting anyone to meet me," I said.

"The Council didn't want you to take all day getting up the hill," she explained as I boosted my bags into the waiting vehicle. "Welcome back, though I wish the circumstances might have been different."

My heart sank at this recognition of my shameful return. "Same here. I suppose I'm in bit of a spot, huh?"

"I'm not supposed to discuss that with you, Denny, not until you've been before the Panel."

That didn't sound good. I had some idea, but still wasn't sure exactly what Marko had reported when he'd sent me away.

"How did you like Linsey?" Emily asked, saving me the trouble of changing the subject.

"It's a strange place," I admitted, "and I won't miss all the fish."

"And Marko?"

"I got the impression he just wants a quiet life, hiding away in the backwaters."

"It's hardly surprising."

"How do you mean?"

"After his previous posting. He was with the Paris delegation."

I hadn't heard all the details, but the stories I had heard sent a shiver down my spine. The negotiations had gone well enough, the promise of trade and mutual aid between the islands and the Emirate had capitalised on the rifts between the continental powers. Paris wanted more influence over its neighbours, the islands wanted the Arab pirates cleared from their southern shores. Common cause forged an uneasy friendship between these enemies of mutual enemies. The deal was done, the delegation set off to return home, but the pirates hadn't been cleared from the Channel in time to save them.

"So Marko was one of the survivors?"

Emily nodded. "Yes. But his wife wasn't."

"He never told me any of this. Not that I blame him for that." I could even understand his lack of enthusiasm, his going through the motions. Letting me carry most of the responsibilities at the station. Until I hoisted a sloper to chase dreams and ionised clouds across the sky.

The conversation faltered after that, because we couldn't talk about those things uppermost in both our minds. I quietly

110

watched the familiar landscape rolling past at a pony's pace. We skirted the farms and woodlots, heaths and scattered villages that stretched out along the gravelled roadway as we headed ever upwards into the hills. Finally the tips of the masts pierced the skyline one by one, but the filigree of wires strung between them remained obscured by distance. Then the Tower itself peeked over the brow of the hill, silhouetted against pink sunset clouds in a darkening sky. Ten storeys of ancient concrete loomed over the landscape, ringed at its base by a cluster of more recent buildings added over the centuries to accommodate the extra workshops and student quarters that became necessary as the Service regrouped and gathered together those driven individuals dedicated to preserving and rediscovering the ancient arts of the radiomen.

Our trap rolled between the buildings and pulled up before the wide doorway at the base of the Tower. We jumped down and were greeted by two burly stewards, who led me away to one of the accommodation blocks, as Emily warned me to be ready for the Disciplinary Panel first thing in the morning.

— · · · — · —

In a single day the whole Earth turns about its axis, yet we are often surprised at how much can change in that short time.

When I awoke in the once-familiar surroundings of the Tower's student accommodation, I had my first proper breakfast in months, and I savoured the eggs and coarse, filling bread. I was ready to face almost anything, except a disciplinary hearing.

I was led into the boardroom where the Grandmaster and

two other Master Radiomen were waiting for me, sitting behind a long wooden table. An empty, hard-backed chair stood in the centre of the room, and a nod from the Grandmaster indicated that I should seat myself there. The chair was low, and I felt at a disadvantage looking up into the expressionless faces of my superiors.

Emily settled into another chair at one end of the table, pencil and notebook before her, to take minutes, I guessed.

The Grandmaster cleared her throat before speaking. "Denzil Ronson, you have been brought before this Disciplinary Panel to answer charges of..." She paused to glance down at the papers before her. "Charges of sabotage, insubordination and dereliction of duty at the Linsey Field Station. How do you plead?"

"What!?" I cried, despite myself.

"Guilty or not guilty will suffice, radioman."

"Not guilty, of course. It's ridiculous."

The Grandmaster peered seriously over the top of her heavy, half-moon eyeglasses, then slipped her gaze back behind the lenses to scan the papers before her once more.

"Do you deny then that you repeatedly neglected to monitor the traffic frequency according to the prescribed Station Schedule Chart?"

"I was slightly late, but only twice," I countered.

"So you don't deny the charge, then. Do you deny interfering with the station configuration without the First Operator's permission and compromising the efficiency of the station antenna system?"

"Yes! Well, no, not exactly. It wasn't like that," I replied, damning myself with my own words.

One of the other Master Radiomen chimed in to the questioning.

"How was it then? Exactly."

"I had heard an anomalous signal, a broadcaster that sounded American." That caught their attention, surprise clear on every face. My three inquisitors huddled together and whispered amongst themselves for a while.

"What made you think it might be American?" asked the Grandmaster.

"The accent. It was really difficult. And this." I reached into my pocket to retrieve the message slip that I had guarded since the strange voice had emerged from the noise. The Grandmaster took it from me and peered at the words through thick glass then passed it to each of her colleagues in turn.

"It's hardly conclusive," one of them commented.

"No, it's not," I conceded. "That's why I had to find out more. I listened as long as I could, waiting for some station identification. By the time I tuned back to the traffic frequency I was late for the sked, I'm afraid."

The Grandmaster frowned at this. "You were using the main receiver, not the back-up?"

"Yes, originally, but it was the back-up after the main receiver went down."

"I'm sorry. I don't understand. Do you mean you were using your back-up for traffic?"

"Yes, we had to once the tube blew, but the First Operator had requested a new pentode for the super-het."

There was more muttering between the Masters, and the one to the left of the Grandmaster shook his head vigorously before speaking.

"I can assure you that he has done no such thing."

I couldn't believe what I was hearing. "But he told me that it was on order, that you couldn't send one on because a shipment hadn't arrived."

"Why would we need to wait for a shipment when we have ample stocks here?" he replied. "We run a tighter ship than that. If Marko had sent a request he would have had a replacement within days."

The Grandmaster made a few notes, but there was a look of disquiet on her face now.

"Well, moving on," she said. "Why did you sabotage the antenna?"

"We didn't!"

"We?"

I cursed myself. I hadn't meant to reveal Robyn's role, but it was too late now.

"I had one of the apprentices run a sloper up the mast, to see if I could improve reception on the broadcaster, but it was entirely on my initiative. Marko saw it in the morning and flew off the handle, said it would detune the main antenna, if that's what he means by sabotage. Anyway, it worked."

"How so?"

"We heard the broadcaster again, and this time I got a firm identification."

"You realise this should have been reported to the Propagation Study Group. Why wasn't it?"

"I had told the Old...the First Operator. But he wasn't interested, wouldn't believe me, so I doubt he'd bother to report it. And he sent me here almost straight away."

Something in the room changed then. The questions turned from my culpability to the subject of the signals I had heard. Could I remember the date and time? What was the fading like? What was the firm identification? How long were the openings? What was the exact frequency?

The Grandmaster turned to Emily then, saying "Could

114

you find Master Gerard, and ask him to come through?"

I sat in an uncomfortable silence for a short while, feeling my buttocks going numb on the hard seat, but Master Gerard soon appeared and looked over the details the Grandmaster had noted down. Their conversation was muted and I strained to hear what they were saying.

"Well, the times match, Grandmaster," Gerard said, standing up straight to stretch his cricked back. "And the locations would be consistent. Do we have charts in here? I can sketch it out for you."

The Grandmaster sent Emily out of the room again and this time she returned with with a sheaf of maps and other papers. The conversation was soon flying high above my head, with talk about soundings and critical frequencies and scatter points. This was obviously something Masters study that I hadn't learnt yet. All I could follow was the sense of excitement flowing between the older radiomen. I sat back and watched whilst they worked. They pored over the tables, pumped slide rules energetically, and began drawing elegant curves over the maps before them. The activity came to an abrupt end, and the Grandmaster spun one of the charts around to face me.

"Denzil," she said. "I am minded to dismiss the charges that have been brought against you, given the value of your observation which has confirmed some other anomalous data over the past week or two. You, young man, have made the first confirmed observation of transatlantic propagation in over two hundred years."

"I have?"

"You have. And in my book, that adds up to significant self-training rather than sabotage, insubordination and dereliction of duty. Your instinct was correct in following this up, and you have made a significant contribution to our knowledge."

So that was the verdict recorded by the Disciplinary Panel and I felt the tension drain from me.

"Now, Denny," she continued, finally dropping my formal name, "What is the core ethic of the Radio Service?"

"Confidentiality," I replied without hesitation.

"Exactly. This knowledge doesn't leave this room, understood?"

I nodded.

— · · · — · —

We paused for lunch, and I was more than happy to wrap myself around a steaming bowl of stew with some excellent stodgy dumplings. Just the sort of food I had missed so much in Linsey, and just the thing for the shortening autumn days. Even better, it was accompanied by some proper ale instead of the thin acidic wine that was so popular on the island. Everyone from the hearing was seated at one of the long refectory tables, and I was chatting with Emily about my time in Linsey when the Grandmaster's ear picked up on our conversation.

"You were teaching the Morse classes for the apprentices at Linsey?" she asked, incredulously.

I nodded, wondering where this was leading.

"Why was that?"

"Marko said he didn't want to pass on his bad habits."

"Hmm. You realise he's one of our best Morse operatives?" She shook her head in disbelief. "I'm beginning to think we recalled the wrong operator. What other duties did he pass off on to you?"

I was torn between my lingering loyalty to a man who had mentored me, however reluctantly, for those few months, and my resentment at having been subjected to my first and only taste of disciplinary action. I chewed slowly on my dumpling as I thought, then admitted to writing up verbatims for him, too. The Grandmaster didn't look pleased, but she didn't follow up.

Master Gerard, who I had discovered headed the Propagation Study Group, pointed his spoon in my direction and asked whether there were any other anomalous signals I'd observed that he should know about.

"No, there's nothing else that stands out. The only other thing out of the ordinary was a Rosh ship that was in harbour," I replied.

Gerard suddenly laughed out loud, and his mirth seemed to affect the other Masters, too.

"Now, I bet Marko let you handle the courtesy visit! Vashe zdorovye!" he cried, and suddenly gulped down his cup of ale for no apparent reason.

My confusion must have been written on my face.

"What? No courtesy call?" he asked. "The Rosh are sticklers for that. They always check in with the local station when they're in port."

"I don't recall any visit," I replied, still a bit baffled.

"It's not something you'd forget. You know when a Rosh Marconi turns up at your door with a bottle of vodka and won't leave until it's empty, believe me."

Before we could delve into the mystery of the shy Marconi, our lunch interrupted by rapid footsteps which came to a halt in the middle of the refectory. One of the stewards looked around the room before spotting the Grandmaster.

"Grandmaster, the observers have been picking up a lot of distress calls, can you come to the listening post?"

— · · · — · —

The scene in the listening post was chaotic. Banks of super-heterodyne receivers were lined up in cubicles and a team of six operators were jotting down messages and passing them along to the clerks at the far end of the room. The space was warm with the heat of glowing valves, and it was strangely quiet, for all of the listeners were wearing headphones. Master Gerard had obviously taken a shine to me, for he had dragged me along with the party headed for the tenth floor.

The equipment in this room looked far more sophisticated than any I had used or trained on before, and I would have loved to get my hands on it and put it through its paces. Yet it was clear from the rack-mounted chassis and battery stacks that they would be far too bulky and complex for field use. I eyed all the pre-selectors, variable beat oscillators and fine-tuning dials with a rueful covetousness, and knew the basic super-heterodyne and regenerative receivers issued to field stations would forever feel crude and clunky.

It soon became clear that Arab pirates had raided almost the entire length of the east coast, and polities from the Fowker Islands to Umbra and beyond were exchanging heated communiques, accusation and counter-accusation flying back and forth. How could the raiders, normally so wary, have known the fleets were reduced to skeleton strength, their main force deployed to the west coast, too distant to respond? People and livestock had been spirited away, fishing vessels scuttled and farmsteads burnt to the ground. Amidst all the acrimony, it was proving impossible for the polities to mount a combined response and were being picked off one at a time.

As I pieced together the tragedy that was unfolding, I realised that one station was absent from the roster. Nothing had come in from Linsey. I thought of Robyn and Rachel, Matt and Freja, imagined them... no, I couldn't imagine, refused to imagine what might have befallen them if Westport had been overrun.

I turned to Master Gerard. "There's nothing from Linsey. What if..." I couldn't go on.

He shook his head. "Westport's well defended, you know that. The walls, the spit. Pirates couldn't get in past the batteries." He was right, of course. It didn't depend on the fleet alone. The harbour was well sheltered, at the head of a narrow channel overlooked on either side by brass cannon. It was the east coast that was most vulnerable. Even so, I wasn't comfortable having heard nothing.

The first positive news that arrived was from Zetland, which the pirates had not reached. A Rosh flotilla had set sail, heading southwards to escort a convoy from the entrepôt. It must have been the same convoy that was scheduled to bring the consignment for Brother James. I just hoped he was still alive to receive it, for Eastport was not as secure as Westport. If the pirates were still heading up the coast they would turn tail at the first sight of the heavy Rosh warships, I was sure.

Still there was no news from Linsey, and as the clock approached the top of the hour, I could bear the silence no longer. "Master Gerard, I'm really worried about Linsey. Can we call them?"

"Come with me," he replied, and led me out of the listening post, and down to another room a couple of floors below.

I was seated with the station key in my hand just as the hour struck, and I had the strange experience of calling the station callsign I had been using for the past few months. There was no reply, and I called once more. As I waited for a signal to come back, I smiled wryly, thinking of the time I had kept the Zetland operator waiting as I was transfixed by the American broadcast.

I called again. This time there was a signal, but the Morse was painfully slow, hesitant almost. The exchange of callsigns dragged on for what seemed an age. It clearly wasn't Marko's fist. I got the all clear, finally, and when I replied I slowed down my own sending to match speed with the unknown operator on the far end. I asked the first question on my mind.

- Who is that?
- Robyn
- This is Denny. Where is Marko?
- Missing
- Where is OP2?
- Not here yet
- What is happening?
- Nothing
- No pirates?
- No
- Warn grey robes pirates coming. Find Marko. OK?
- OK

When I signed off, I could feel cold sweat trickling between my shoulder blades, and my hand was shaking on the key.

"I think we'd better speak to the Grandmaster," Gerard said behind me. I agreed.

"Perhaps he's gone to help his family?" Emily suggested. "He is from Linsey, after all."

"I don't believe he'd abandon his post," the Grandmaster insisted once more. "And as Denny told us, there's no sign or news of pirates in Westport."

"Yet," I cautioned. "Meanwhile, we have a field station manned entirely by apprentices. I should get back there. Someone should, anyway."

"Yes, but I don't want to risk another ship right now. Not until we know where Grettir has got to. With pirates on the prowl, anything could have happened. We don't want to lose you, too, Denny. There's far too many operators going missing."

The group fell silent. We were going round in circles, and still nothing was decided.

"Oh, ye gods!" one of the Masters suddenly exclaimed, as though struck by a sudden insight. "Denny, you remember that Rosh ship we were talking about?"

"Yes? What about it?"

"They never skip the courtesy call. Never. Can you recall the Cyrillic characters your apprentices heard?"

I could, and recited them for him. Dah-dah-dah-dah, di-di-dah-di-dit, dah-dah-dah-dit.

"And it was Marko who told you it was Cyrillic, I suppose? You realise those Morse characters are also used in Arabic?"

"What are you suggesting?" the Grandmaster asked, pulling her glasses off and scrutinising the other Master closely.

"I'm not sure. But I'm wondering why Marko only mentioned Cyrillic to Denny. Remember why he was chosen for the Paris mission?"

Ashen-faced, the Grandmaster whispered, "He was the interpreter."

— · · · — · —

For the second time in as many days, I found myself hastily bundled on to a ship, this time crossing back towards Linsey. Shortly before I departed on my return journey, Grettir had arrived at the field station and reported back to the Tower, having been delayed by a long detour around the Serpent's Back to evade a roving pirate. Marko was still missing, but Robyn had successfully repaired the super-het receiver after finding the perfectly serviceable pentode that Marko had hidden in his own quarters.

I had barely had time to meet Grettir and greet the apprentices once more before the grey robes appeared at the station. I was bone tired from the crossing, but my journey wasn't over.

"We think Marko has been found," one of the Brothers told me.

"Where is he?"

"A fishing village a couple of kilometres south of Eastport."

We rode in a cloud of silence, and a small huddle of villagers and militiamen were waiting for us at the water's edge. We dismounted and picked out a route across the mudflat, keeping to the tracks left by the locals. The bodies had both had their throats slit so deeply the heads were nearly severed.

"That's Marko," I said, and turned to the woman's body beside his. Although she was dressed in a heavily blood-stained Arab shawl, her complexion was the same as Marko's.

"And that's his wife," the Brother beside me added.

"So she hadn't been dead. That's the hold they had on him. She's the only one he didn't betray."

Back at the station, I had to report the news to the Tower: MARKO HENDERS OP1 GLNSI SK

Silent key.

End of transmission.

. . . — · —

JOURNEY TO THE NORTH

MATTHEW GRIFFITHS

Dust

Novice Tian huddled under his robes in a small cave carved from the brown soil of the hillside. Outside the frenzied wind swept vast clouds of dust over the barren landscape, entraining the light soil of north China, parched and baked dry over two hundred years of drought.

Beside him he heard the chant of *"Nan mo ah mi tuo fo"*, repeated over and over again in Master Shi's low voice. Master Shi coughed.

While his own lips silently repeated the same chant, Tian fingered the string of rough wooden beads in his hand. Master Shi coughed again. "Master, you must see a doctor in Wutaishan."

Master Shi stopped his chanting. "I have breathed rock chips all my life, a little dust storm will not harm me."

Tian pulled his robe tighter around him. It seemed to Tian like a lifetime had passed since he left the monastery in Sichuan with his teacher, Master Shi, to visit the great stone Buddhas of north China and make copies of their designs. He sometimes feared that that they would never return and the project to build the largest stone Buddha in China would never be completed.

During the night, Tian dreamed of a small house surrounded by fields and hills. He could see the vivid colours of rhododendron flowers, the bamboo that stretched several times his height into the sky, the birds chirping as they flitted among the trees. Then came the image that recurred often in his dreams: a farm with crops ripening in the sunshine, a woman's voice singing, a sense of peace and happiness. He felt himself being drawn to it, looking for the people that dwelled there. But he couldn't find them. He often awoke with an agitation in his legs, an urge to get up and walk as if to physically reach the place in his dream.

When they had finally left Haishenwai in the far north east and began the trip back south Tian felt a weight lift from his shoulders. With each day now home was getting closer. The monastery north of Chengdu, the capital of the Kingdom of Sichuan in west China, was the only home had known since he was six years old after his parents died in an earthquake. A small bare room was not much, but for him it was adequate. The monastery provided all his needs and filled his days with chanting and ceremonies and, under Master Shi, he learned the skills of stone carving.

Master Shi told him often: "You will have the opportunity to create a great work in the name of the Buddha. You are very fortunate." Tian glowed at the thought, yet the lure of his strange recurring dream refused to fade.

In the morning, the storm had blown itself out. They shouldered their packs and hiked south once more through the dull brown landscape covered in fine brown powder. Tian walked slowly alongside Master Shi. "My dream came again last night, Master. I think I miss the monastery."

Master Shi shook his head. "Don't be too quick to rush back." Tian glanced at him. Shi looked at him with a sly smile. "It is good to explore new places and see the wonderful sights of the world. We should make the most of this opportunity."

In the late afternoon their weary legs hauled them to the top of a low ridge. In the distance, glowing white in the sun, was the tall Tibetan style stupa of the temple in the centre of the valley, nestled among the five rounded peaks. They had reached Wutaishan, one of the four holy Buddhist mountains of China and home to over a hundred monasteries and temples representing of all branches of Buddhism.

They walked down into the small town in the valley and found a residence for visiting monks. Master Shi rested while Tian went out to fetch food from a monastery dining hall.

Tian carried their bowls in a small bag over his shoulder. He wandered across a paved courtyard and then began to cross an arched stone bridge that spanned a trickle of a stream. A shadow fell across the worn cobble stones in front of him. He looked up and saw a nun walking towards him. She was young, perhaps a novice like him, and wore long grey robes and brown cloth shoes. Her shaved head was like a ripe peach, her ears small and delicate. But it was not those that clutched at his chest. It was her smile. Her red lips curled up at each end, framing her small, even, white teeth. It was a vision that reminded him of Guanyin, the Goddess of Mercy, herself.

"Good evening brother," Novice Dai nodded to him, hands pressed together in front of her.

Tian stared, his mouth hung open in slack silence. Then with great effort, he blinked.

Her eyes sparkled with amusement. "I see you are dusty from your travels. Have you come far?"

He closed his mouth and nodded. His face blushed crimson. He raised his hands in front of his chest, palms together, then raised them to his forehead. "My apologies sister," he stammered, bowing his head. "I am not used to talking to..." He raised his eyes to hers then lowered them again. "My master and I have just arrived from the Yungang caves to the north. We were caught in a dust storm."

"I have always wanted to visit Yungang. I've heard it is magnificent. Have you eaten?" she asked.

"I am fetching food now for my master. He is not well and I'm worried about him. I hope he will agree to stay here and recover before we continue our journey home." He blushed again. "Forgive me for talking so much. I..." he spluttered.

"Not at all." She smiled again. "The monk's dining hall is that way." She turned and pointed. "I hope your master's health improves."

"Thank you sister." He bowed deeply.

He gazed at her retreating back as she descended the bridge and walked toward a cluster of tile roofed buildings in the distance. His heart pounded in his chest. Master Shi was right. One could see many wondrous sights while traveling. Perhaps he should not be in such a hurry to go home after all.

Tea

The abbot perched stiffly on the edge of an ornate wooden chair. 'Ming Dynasty' their host had said waving a silk clad arm over the furniture in the elegant inner hall of the residence, preserved from long before the *wei ji shi*, the period of crisis.

Many countries had suffered during the *wei ji shi*, not just China. The end of the *Hong Chao* in China, the Red Dynasty, had come about like many others before it, through economic decline, environmental degradation, political infighting and expensive wars.

Beside the abbot sat Master Shi and then Tian. The abbot of the monastery had decided that the monastery would create the biggest stone Buddha in China, bigger than the seventy one meeda tall rock carving at Le Shan to the south of Chengdu. It would a great achievement and something Tian could devote his energy to for years. But such a project required more than just skilled sculptors, it required labour, equipment and money. And so they had come to the home of Jia Shenyi to ask for a donation, a very large donation, to fund the first years of work until word of its magnificence spread and donations began to flow in from the population.

Jia was a merchant who made his fortune from trading cotton, silk and tea from the south and east and even products from overseas borne on ships of sail. He was also a collector of furniture, old books and statues, which he displayed with pride. The abbot gently chided him on his collection, reminding him he could not take it with him to his next life. The merchant had laughed heartily and said he could give it all up in a moment. Tian smiled, but at the same time saw a strange look in the man's eyes. He was not sure whether it was mirth, true disdain for the things he had surrounded himself with, or, as Tian suspected, a deep and growing fear for his fate in the afterlife.

An attendant refilled their tea cups and Jia Shenyi spoke. "I am honoured by your visit venerable masters. Business is challenging these days. The silk road to the west is sometimes beset with brigands and thieves and sailing boats on the ocean are subject to the whims of the winds, and even travel within the six kingdoms of China is not without its complications. He rose and took them into a walled garden and showed them a roofed grotto reached through an arbour overhung by fruiting vines. "Master Shi, I would like to place a statue of Buddha here in my garden to protect…to honour his benevolence and show my family's reverence."

Tian was not surprised. Master Shi had been asked to do such carvings many times by wealthy families eager to improve their fortunes in this life and the next. The abbot and Master Shi exchanged glances as they walked back to the house to resume their conversation. When they sat down again the abbot explained the grand project for which they sought a commensurate donation. Of course he added, for such generosity the donor would attract great merit in this and future lives. He also mentioned that Master Shi and his prentice planned to visit the great stone Buddhas of China to study their designs in preparation.

Jia Shenyi sipped his tea and thought for some time. "Venerable Abbot your visit has been most timely. Since my thoughts have recently been given to statues of the Buddha, and your monastery has a plan which needs support, I invite you to come with me now and I will show you something. I have a proposal that I think may be agreeable to all of us."

Gold

Tian's dream came again. The same farm, stone house, crops in the fields. This time he also became aware of himself. He was a grown up. This was not a dream from his childhood as his monk teachers suggested. He heard the woman singing and was spellbound by the sound. But yet again he could not see the source of the voice.

He awoke early but Master Shi did not stir for morning prayers. When Tian brought him breakfast he did not eat. He left him resting and rushed out to find a doctor.

When he returned Master Shi began to tell him about the golden Buddha in south China. Of course Tian already knew of the Donglin Temple, for it was there that their Pure Land sect had originated over two thousand years before, in the year 386 in the old time calendar.

The golden Buddha was famous in all the six kingdoms as the biggest bronze Buddha in China, a 48-metre tall statue of Amitabha, gilded with many kilograms of pure gold. It was constructed in the time of the *Hong Chao*, with donations from many thousands of people, including from the drowned cities of Hong Kong and Shanghai. Their largess had not saved their cities from the sea but the result, his master enthused, was a sight to behold. "I have never been there but I believe the Golden Buddha is the most wondrous thing in the world."

Tian wondered why Master Shi was telling him about this now. He tried to quiet him and asked him to rest until the doctor came. A senior medical monk and an assistant entered their small room and asked him some questions. The monk took Master Shi's pulses on both wrists and made notes. They talked briefly to Master Shi then left. Tian tried to judge from their words and expressions how serious it was but they both remained encouraging but vague. Tian accompanied them back to the doctor's dispensary and waited until the medicine was ready. He carried back a pungent brew and slowly spooned it into his master's mouth. Master Shi screwed up his face at the bitter taste but took it all. Then he settled back on his bed and closed his eyes.

Tian sat with him for a time until he seemed to drift off to sleep, then he ventured out. He looked to the west and the small town that served the valley and its many pilgrims, and then to the east. His eyes were drawn to the hill nearby and followed the stone stairs leading up to the ancient temple at the top. There were one thousand and eighty steps, ten times the sacred number of beads of his rosary.

He walked to the base of the hill and began to climb. He enjoyed the feel of his legs pushing against the stones. Up ahead he glimpsed a familiar grey robed figure. He sped up and came alongside her.

Dai saw him and turned. "Good morning brother." She bowed slightly.

Tian bowed low. He felt his face flush again and fought to control his laboured breathing. "Good morning sister." He looked up at her again and his face broke into a grin. "I am pleased to see you. I wanted to thank for your assistance yesterday." He looked up the hill. "Perhaps we can climb together?"

She nodded with a trace of a smile. "Is your master feeling better?" Dai asked, as they slowly climbed the steps up the hill to the temple, careful to keep a distance between them.

Tian shrugged. "The doctor has given him some medicine and he is resting. I hope he will recover his strength soon."

"Have your enjoyed your trip?" she asked.

"We have visited many places and seen some of the large stone Buddhas. Our monastery plans to build the biggest in China. It will be a great monument to Buddha and to the dedication of our monastery in honouring his wisdom. Hopefully it will inspire people to follow the Buddha's path. At Yungang we made drawings and notes on their designs and construction methods. After Master Shi recovers we will go south to Meng Shan, there is sixty three meeda high Buddha there."

"Yes, we stopped there on our way," said Dai.

Tian nodded, "And then we will go to Luoyang to view more stone Buddhas on our way back to Sichuan. Are you here on a pilgrimage?" asked Tian.

Dai shook her head. "No. I am here with the abbess of my order and several others. She has an important meeting this afternoon. We are assisting her."

"Oh." Tian continued to climb beside her until they reached the top. They lit incense in the temple and bowed to the statues of the five Manjusri Bodhisattvas there, revered for their wisdom. They strolled to a terrace overlooking the valley. "This is a beautiful place."

"Yes." After a few minutes they began the climb down. At the bottom Tian stopped and turned to Dai.

"I hope your meeting goes well, sister." He bowed his head.

"Thank you, brother." She returned the bow and smiled.

He watched her grey robes glide away across the cobbles. He felt a lightness that made him giddy.

Silk

Jia Shenyi took the abbot, Master Shi and Tian by carriage to the industrial district on the south side of Chengdu. The carriage stopped in front of an imposing warehouse located next the Jinjiang River that ran through the city. He motioned them through a large side door and into a huge space stacked to the ceiling with bales of silk cloth and wooden crates of tea. A team of workers was busy wrapping the bales in layers of cotton and jute to protect them for shipping.

A man strutted among the labourers and barked instructions. He looked over as Jia and the monks entered the warehouse. Jia motioned him to join them. "This is Kong Que." The man bowed the monks. "He is my right hand man. He speaks fluent Rosh, a skill for which he is richly rewarded." He smiled.

"I am honoured to assist you Master, as always." Kong bowed low to Jia and held the positon just a little longer than necessary. Tian stared at his embroidered silk jacket, bright red decorated with peacock feathers, and even more magnificent than Jia's.

Jia turned to the face the merchandise. "This silk and tea is destined for export. In two days the shipment will depart on barges down the river to the Yangtze and then all the way downstream to Yangzhou. From there it will travel north up the Grand Canal to Beijing then overland to the coast. Then it will sail on a coaster north east to the port of Haishenwai. There it will be transferred to a Rosh vessel equipped to sail across the northern ocean all the way to Genda."

"Genda, really? Such a large shipment and so far." said the abbot.

"Yes." Jia moved closer to a pile of silk. "The Rosh tell

134

us the foreigners in Genda and Meriga have strange tastes. They prefer plain colours—reds, yellows, blues and greens, not like the intricate brocades our looms can produce for our robes, dresses, and jackets. The foreigners too have wares to sell but on this occasion Rosh silver is more convenient. This one shipment will fund both your project and my household for a number of years."

Master Shi nodded and gazed over the bales with wonder. "Such trade must entail considerable risk," he said.

"Indeed Master Shi. Kong will accompany it until it departs on the Rosh ship. But for this shipment I have in mind an additional safeguard."

Kong's eyes narrowed. "Master?"

Jia raised his hand and Kong held his tongue. "If your abbot is agreeable I would like you and your prentice to accompany it."

Master Shi's cast a glance at the abbot and Tian. "What use are an old monk and a boy?"

Jia waved away the comment. "You bring with you the protection of a higher power." He turned to the abbot. "Provide an escort for my shipment and the donation will be in your account the day it leaves port for Genda."

The abbot studied him briefly. "Since Master Shi already plans to tour the stone Buddhas in the north a small diversion would be no inconvenience. Isn't that right Master Shi?"

Master Shi licked his lips meditatively. "Yes, Venerable Master."

Wood

Tian again dreamed of the farm in the country, the green of bamboo and the sound of birds and crickets. The singing came again and this time when he looked for it he found the source. It was Dai. She stood in the courtyard of the small stone house and he smiled as he listened to her voice as they worked together winnowing grain.

He awoke in the darkness and fingered his prayer beads. His dream was becoming more real with each passing day. He trembled with excitement as he began to contemplate what it meant.

He was interrupted by Master Shi's coughing. Tian leaned close, his face creased with worry. Master Shi's voice lacked its normal strength. He gripped his hand. "Don't worry. I'll be fine."

Tian nodded. "Yes, Master."

"I have made a decision. When I am well again we will go south from Luoyang instead of west. We will visit the Golden Buddha at the Donglin Temple. All my life I have dreamed of seeing it and this will be my only chance."

Tian's eyebrows quivered on his forehead. "But master, we promised the abbot we would return as soon as possible. He wants to complete the plans for the giant stone Buddha this year and start work next spring."

Master Shi nodded. "Yes. And we can still do that. It will not take long and the sight of such a miraculous statue will inspire us in our work when we return home."

Tian again fetched the medicine then sat with Master Shi until he slept again. Then he quietly slipped out of the room and strode quickly to the steps at the bottom of the hill. Soon he saw Dai approaching. He stood and bowed. "Good morning sister."

"Good morning brother," Dai answered with a nod, but no smile accompanied her greeting.

"Is something wrong?" Tian asked.

At first she did not reply. He matched her step for step slowly up the hill. Finally she relented. "The meeting did not go well," said Dai, casting a wary glance around her.

Tian frowned. She stopped and looked at him. Then her eyes flickered to the forest that clothed the hillside and a narrow dirt path that wound among the trees. "Let's walk among the trees today." Tian followed her at a distance until they were out of sight of the steps.

"The abbess is most disappointed," said Dai once they were away from the steps.

Tian nodded solemnly.

Dai took a deep breath. "Some time ago a wealthy woman, a friend of our order in the east, left a large bequest to the temple in her will, to further our work in the community." She walked a while in silence. Tian watched her face keenly, seeing her jaws clench and unclench.

"The bequest was a quantity of precious jewels. The hierarchy of our Chan sect heard about the matter and brought the jewels here, for 'safe keeping'. Now they will not return them. They have decided that the jewels should be sold and the money used to construct new temples and statues of Buddha instead. They say this is more important than our work."

Tian saw her eyes moisten. "I can see your work is very important to you sister."

Dai nodded. "We help families still affected by the radiation sickness. And one day we hope to cleanse the land of the poisons."

"The poison from the explosions?"

"Yes, the ancient power plants. The war with Japan and the *wei ji shi* affected China as well."

Tian nodded. He had heard a story of the Japanese Empress flying over the ocean on a giant silver bird toward the

137

rising sun.

"My dream when I am ordained is to travel to Japan to learn from our Zen colleagues about the fungi and plants that can absorb the poisons and remove them from the soil. They have experience with these things." She bit her lip. "My ancestors were among those poisoned many centuries ago. The survivors vowed that one person from every generation would become a monk or a nun for one thousand generations until the poisons have dissipated." A tear ran down her cheek. "A long penance wouldn't you say?"

Tian fought an urge to grasp her hand. Instead he fingered his rosary and murmured a prayer.

"I hope that my work might shorten that time and make a better life for my family and others in the future. The jewels will pay for the trip and for us grow the plants and distribute them for many years to come."

Tian rubbed his shaven head and groped for words that could ease her suffering. "Will you have further meetings? Perhaps they will change their minds."

Dai nodded. "Yes we will meet them again today. But I do not believe they will change their decision." She shook her head. "I never dreamed when I became a nun that there would be such...politics."

They reached a small clearing where they could see the valley spread out below them. Dai stared at the view for a minute them looked around for a seat. She spied the remains of a fallen tree beside the path, brushed dirt and leaves from the surface and sat down. Tian joined her on the log. Dai absently traced the creases and knots in the surface of the wood. Beside the log a small seedling stretched skyward. She pointed to it. "The cycle of life, death and rebirth is everywhere."

Tian nodded.

Dai slid her fingers into a knot hole. "Oh, it's hollow," she said. She stood and crouched by the end of the log. She brushed away some leaves and looked inside. "The soul has flown," she said with a faint smile.

She swept the leaves back into place and sat down again. She twisted her prayer beads in her hands and mouthed a prayer. Tian watched her silently. Eventually she stopped and looked at him with a smile. "Thank you for your company. I feel better now."

Tian blushed and nodded. "I…" he started, then stopped.

She raised her eyebrows.

"I have a dream too. A real dream that comes to me often in the night."

Dai nodded for him to continue.

"I see a farm in the country, a house, crops in the fields, trees all around. And I hear a woman singing." He looked at her for a moment. She returned his gaze calmly. "I feel it is a sign for me to leave the monastery. I went there as an orphan and I'm not sure it is the life that I…" He paused to take a deep breath. "Last night I had the dream again, the woman was singing and I saw her face for the first time. It was you."

Dai gasped and clasped her hands together.

Tian continued quickly. "I believe we were meant to meet here, and we can have a wonderful life together."

Dai opened to mouth to speak, the closed it again. Finally she whispered. "Where would we live? How would we support ourselves?"

"We will have a farm in Sichuan and grow crops. And I will plant trees for fire wood and timber. And in the winter when the farm work is quiet I will carve statues and you can meditate. We will choose a village away from the earthquake fault lines, the monastery has a big map from the *Hong Chao* that shows them all."

"Such a long way from my home. What if you became sick? How will we support ourselves, without family nearby?"

Tian recalled the meeting with Mister Jia. "There are wealthy people who would appreciate a Buddha statue in their courtyard." Tian declared. "I will find special stones and carve beautiful statues. I know where to look. We can bury money in a safe place to support us if anything happens and surround the house with high walls."

Dai thought for a while, then spoke. "You have given this much thought, but I am not sure any walls could keep us safe. The community in the temples is our best security brother." She smiled and the sparkle in her eyes returned. "Are you sure you can sell so many statues? Perhaps you overestimate your skills?"

Tian leapt up and searched among the trees and returned with a broken piece of a branch. "Give me a few days, I will show you what I can do."

Dai laughed. "And I will think about your words." She patted the log between them. "You have helped me a lot this morning brother, more than you know." She stood up. "I should go now."

Tian stood and they exchanged bows. He watched Dai walk along the path, a smile on his face, then sat down, pulled a knife from his bag and began to carve the wood.

Jewels

The next morning Tian sat at the base of the hill again. He waited for an hour and began to pace backwards and forwards around the bottom of the steps. He was just about to return to sit beside Master Shi's bed when he saw Dai limping towards him. He leapt up and strode towards her.

"Are you all right sister? What happened?"

"Nothing serious. I turned my ankle." She gave him rueful smile. "It will be fine in a few days. I was a gymnast in school before I joined the order. I'm used to it." She sat slowly on a bench. "I don't think I should climb the steps today."

Tian sat down beside her and nodded. "Did you hear? The jewels you spoke about were stolen. Monks came early this morning to search our room and our bags."

"Yes. They searched ours too. My abbess has been arrested."

"Surely she did not steal them?"

Dai shook her head. "Of course not."

"They will search every building in Wutaishan before the day is out." said Tian.

"Yes. But I doubt they will find them."

Tian looked at her with a frown, then slowly nodded. "Do you think so?"

Dai shrugged.

"How was your meeting yesterday?"

"Same as the day before."

Tian pursed his lips. "So what will become of the radiation project?"

Dai exhaled slowly. "We will find a way."

"I don't think you should do it. The nuclear poison is dangerous. Do you not fear the hair falling out disease?"

She smiled. "They wear special metal clothing when they go into the poisoned areas. They have learned a lot about dealing with these matters themselves and from other countries. My abbess is a scientist. She believes their techniques can be successful in the eastern kingdom too."

Tian gazed at her face. Finally he could restrain himself no more. "Sister. Have you thought about my...my proposal from yesterday?"

Dai stared down at the uneven cobbles beneath their feet. "I need more time to mediate on it. What you are asking is a very big decision. For years I have dedicated my life to the order and achieving enlightenment through meditation and service. I have grown used to being with my sisters and serving the community. I fear trying to survive alone in the country away from others as you suggest would be very difficult for me. Wouldn't you miss your monastery too? Are you sure you want to leave that, and the giant Buddha project?"

Tian nodded slowly. "I will miss it a little, but I'm sure we can do it sister. Sichuan is fertile and the rain is sufficient. And I promise you will have time to meditate. We don't have to be in monastery to achieve the Buddha's Pure Land."

She nodded. "I don't doubt your sincerity brother." She gazed out at the hills that surrounded the valley. Finally she spoke again. "Is your master better?"

Tian shook his head. "His recovery is very slow." He tried to push aside the guilty feeling that crept up on him that if his master passed away it would make leaving the monastery much easier.

Dai nodded and stood gingerly. "I should go now. It is better if we are not seen together too much."

Tian leapt to his feet and bowed. "I hope your leg is better tomorrow." She nodded and shuffled away. Tian strode quickly back to the sit beside Master Shi. Master Shi coughed violently, doubling over. Beads of sweat broke out on his forehead but his hands felt cold.

"I will get the doctor." Tian began to stand up.

"Wait." The master's voice was weak and his breathing

laboured. Tian leant close to him. "There is something I want to tell you. I think perhaps it is time for me to go to the Pure Land. If I leave this world I want you to go to Donglin Temple and finish your training with the master there. Then return to our monastery to build the giant stone Buddha."

"Don't say that Master. You will be fine." Tian dropped his eyes.

"Go to Donglin. Do you hear me?" Master Shi whispered.

"I hear you Master." Tian nodded reflexively but his mind flew to Dai.

He rose and ran to the doctors rooms. He returned with them after a few minutes and found Master Shi still struggling to breathe. The doctor felt his pulses and gave him some medicine. The lines on Shi's face relaxed. He sat with the doctor and his assistant for some time but no one spoke. Tian sensed from the frown on the doctor's face that maybe there was little more even he could do.

Master Shi opened his eyes. He coughed again then settled back. His breath came in wheezy gasps but he smiled. "I can see it, the Pure Land, bright lights and beautiful music. Buddha is coming to welcome me!" He turned his head slightly to Tian. "Remember what I said."

Tian nodded as a tightness gripped his chest. Master Shi settled back and closed his eyes. Tian saw the small round burn marks on his shaved scalp from his initiation many decades ago fade from brown to white. The doctor grasped his wrist and felt for his pulse. He looked up at Tian and shook his head.

Tian's eyes were instantly field with tears. He took his rosary in both hands and began to chant. He and other monks would chant for three days until the soul had departed his master's body to ensure his passage to the Buddha's Pure Land was smooth.

Silver

The coaster tied up at the dock in Haishenwai just after noon. Master Shi heaved a sigh of relief and stopped his chanting. A large dark haired Rosh man stood on the dock observing the deck hands. Once the gangplank was in place Kong strode down it and extended his arms. "*Gospodin* Polzin. *Kak zhizn?*"

"Very good my friend. And you?"

"Very good. *Gospodin* Jia sends his warmest greetings."

They hugged and Kong turned to the monks. "These monks accompanied the shipment all the way from Sichuan. Mister Jia wanted to make sure it arrived undamaged."

"Very thoughtful of him." Polzin smiled and spoke in passable Chinese. "Welcome to Haishenwai, or I should say, 'Vladivostok'. We Rosh have long memories you know." He bowed and the monks bowed in return.

Kong laughed. "Chinese memories are equally long, *tovarisch.* Rosh took this land many centuries ago and we merely took it back."

Polzin shrugged and turned, pointing. "That is my ship. We will start loading right away. It should be finished this afternoon and we can complete our transaction. The northern ocean is now free of ice all the way to Genda. It should be plain sailing."

He began talking in Rosh to Kong. Tian heard only a jumble of exotic sounds except for *shelk,* and *chay* which seemed to come up often in the conversation. A gang of Chinese dockers assembled next to the coaster. Kong talked with the foreman who began issuing instructions. The gang sprang into action and the goods began the short trip from one ship to the other.

The monks walked to a monastery on a small hill north of the docks to rest. In the afternoon they returned to watch the last of the goods loaded into the hold of the Rosh vessel. Polzin had not yet returned but Kong Que was on board and Tian heard his strident voice ordering the dockers to move the cargo here and there in the hold of the ship, rearranging it to suit his whims, then a few minutes later he would change his mind and demand another reshuffle.

It was past dusk before the loading was completed. Polzin had arrived to check the load and he and Kong emerged from the hold deep in conversation. Kong strode over to them. "I have discussed the situation with *Gospardin* Polzin. It is too late to go to the bank now. We will go before lunch tomorrow. Then we shall eat with our friend and depart on the coaster in the afternoon."

Master Shi nodded slowly. "Very well Mister Kong. We will see you tomorrow."

Kong rushed off. Master Shi and Tian wandered towards the monastery. They stopped in at a Sichuan restaurant for rice and spicy vegetables. Afterwards, back on the street they were surrounded by a throng of merchants, street peddlers and passers-by in the dim glow of street lamps. In the half-light Tian thought he recognised Kong wearing Rosh clothes hurrying out of a building and across the street. He saw him walk up the steps into a garish building, its windows covered with brightly coloured curtains.

As he disappeared through the doors, another man came out, a middle aged Rosh man with long brown hair and beard, fine clothes encasing his rotund belly. On his arm was a young Chinese woman. She glanced at the monks as they walked past, whispered to the man and laughed loudly as they climbed into a horse drawn carriage. Tian flushed and dropped his eyes. The carriage door closed and a clopping of hooves on the cobbles bore the couple away.

Ashes

When the third day of chanting was over monks removed Master Shi's body to prepare it for cremation. Tian sat in his room and packed the plans of the stone Buddha statues they had visited into his bag along with his few possessions. Then he worked on completing the little wooden statue he had promised Dai, half convinced that the quality of his work would persuade to accompany him, half aware that to even ask such a question was unreasonable, and in the eyes of his former master, unforgiveable.

The next morning he attended prayers and then slipped the little wooden statue into his small bag and strode to the bottom of the steps up the hill. He saw Dai walking across the cobbles slowly towards the steps, still with a slight limp. She kept her eyes down and began to climb the stairs holding the rail for support as she went. Tian waited half a minute then began to follow her. Eventually he drew abreast on the opposite side the steps. He looked ahead and behind to make sure no one was within earshot.

"Good morning sister. Your ankle is better."

"Good morning brother. Yes, thank you. Much better." She stole a quick glance at him. "I have not seen you for several days. Is everything all right?"

Tian shook his head. "My master passed away. I have been chanting for him."

146

Dai nodded.

Tian reached into his bag. "I have something for you." She looked behind them and momentarily stepped closer. Tian handed her the wooden caving he had made. "It is the Bodhisattva Guanyin."

Dai looked it over. "You are skilled brother. I should never have doubted you."

Tian smiled. Dai focussed on the face of the carving. "Something looks different though."

Tian nodded. "I changed it slightly. Her face is yours. At least a little."

Dai's cheeks coloured. She continued to climb the steps. "My abbess was released yesterday. The jewels have not been found but there is no evidence that she had anything to do with it." She paused and let go a deep breath. "We will leave for the east tomorrow."

"Then we must go early in the morning." Tian whispered. "How can we travel together?"

"You can dress as a monk. I will get you some clothes. We can go north to the Yungang caves and then west."

Dai's face twisted. "I…I am not sure brother."

Tian heart pounded. "I believe we can have a good life together."

Dai stopped climbing. "I think I should not go any further today. My ankle is still a little sore. I will spend today in meditation and I will meet you at dawn tomorrow on the bridge."

Tian stared at her, searching for her meaning.

Dai pressed her hands together in front of her. "I will be there, I promise." She bowed her head and began to walk down.

In the afternoon a monk came to Tian with an urn. He

accepted it with both hands and nodded in silence. It felt heavy in his grasp. He put it down and stared at it before going to a temple to chant until dusk. He went to bed early but slept little. He could think only of tomorrow.

Air

The monks returned to the dock late in the morning. Master Shi had enjoyed a longer than usual sleep. Tian looked around for Kong but there was no sign of him. They walked over to the Rosh ship. The crew were on deck busy preparing to set sail. Polzin appeared and greeted them in Chinese. "Where is Kong?"

Master Shi shook his head. "We have not seen him."

They chatted in a stilted fashion for a while before Polzin began to get concerned. Tian whispered to Master Shi. Shi's eyebrows rose and then he nodded. Tian looked at Polzin. "Mister Polzin," the unfamiliar sounds of the name rolled awkwardly off his tongue, "I think I saw Mister Kong last night dressed in Rosh clothes."

Polzin's bushy eyebrows rose. "Please show me where." Tian guided them back up the street that had walked the night before and stopped outside the building he had seen Kong come out of.

Polzin pointed to a sign, written in both Rosh and Chinese. "This is a bank. A Rosh bank. Mister Jia uses a Chinese bank. Come with me." They followed him to his office and used a radio set to contact Mister Jia in Chengdu. After several messages had passed to and fro it was clear no money had been received at Jia's bank and there had been no communication from Kong.

Polzin lead them to a hotel where Kong usually stayed.

Polzin spoke rapidly to the hotel receptionist. Polzin turned to the monks. "He has gone. But no ships have left port this morning so he must still be somewhere in the city."

Tian looked at him and then at Master Shi. He blushed. "I think I might know where he is."

Light

Tian rose early in the morning and filed through the darkness to a temple with dozens of other monks.

He emerged as a pale grey light began to creep into the edges of the sky, returned to his room, picked up his bags and walked slowly out of the building toward the bridge. He climbed the gentle arch of stone and stopped in the centre. Small dots of light showed in the windows of the shadowy buildings around him.

What if she didn't come? A dull ache in his stomach nagged at him. What good was a dream with no-one else in it?

"Brother?" Dai walked slowly up the bridge carrying a bag over her shoulder.

His heart leapt into his throat. "You came."

She smiled. "Good morning."

Her features were soft in the half light, more beautiful than ever. He thanked the shadows for hiding the flush of heat in his face. He fought his urge to hold her.

"Are you ready to go?"

She paused and then shook her head. His expression froze, his smile dying slowly as he tried to comprehend her gesture. He recited the name of Buddha in his mind to calm his racing thoughts. Please let this be just a small delay.

She took a breath. "Brother, we are both dedicated to

149

achieving nirvana in our own ways. We cannot change that. You know the saying: 'A broken mirror never reflects again; fallen flowers never go back to the old branches.' We would be foolish to think we can leave our communities and create some promised land of our own."

Tian's face fell. He tried to speak but his throat was dry and his voice refused to obey his command.

She lifted an object from her bag. "I have something for you."

Dai held out a silk swathed bundle. Tian took it and slowly unwrapped the cloth. Inside lay the wooden statue of Guanyin he had given her the day before. In its abdomen rested a ruby-red stone. The jewel glinted in the first thread of light that crept over the mist shrouded peak behind her. "We cannot escape our fate brother. We can only do what we are called to do and trust that we and others will benefit from our efforts."

Tian still could not utter a word.

Dai placed her hands on his. "Safe travels, wherever your path takes you. You have helped me in my journey brother. I thank you for that. Remember to leave me here. Don't carry me with you." She smiled. "May Guanyin protect you..." she glanced down at the statue, "and provide for you always." She let go his hands and took several steps back.

The sun broke over the ridge behind her and blinded him. He looked away then angled his head to look at her once more. In the bright orange glow she seemed to float on the bridge in a shimmering ball of light. She raised one hand in a wave. He looked away, his eyes full of leaping stars. He blinked and lifted his head once more to look back over the bridge.

She was gone.

Tian closed his eyes again to dispel the lights still flashing in his vision. The sun's glow warmed his face. He breathed slowly, recited the name of the Buddha and counted off the prayer beads in his hand. Finally he opened his eyes and smiled as he descended the bridge and turned south.

ELWUS HAS LEFT
THE BUILDING

CATHERINE MCGUIRE

Luri wriggled on the ox cart seat; he was too excited to sit, but too tired to walk alongside. After eight years as an elwus, he was finally heading into Memfis! And not just that, but he was gonna spend the rains at the elwus gathering, polishing his craft and maybe—that was always the hope— learning a new song or move that would make him a little finer than the other wandering elwuses. Of course, there was always the danger—which had kept him away for long enough—that his presentation would be rejected and he would be busted down to a plain old actor-singer, no longer allowed to put on the black wig and white costume. He swallowed hard to force the lump out of his throat. Eight years on the road practicing, entertaining town after town, making more than enough to live on—certainly that proved something?

He glanced over at his motor—his second cousin Gordo. The two of them had held out against the entire family on joining the family shoe trade. Ever since they were six, the two of them had been putting on shows, making people laugh and sing along—that's all he'd ever wanted to do. Granted, it was not respectable, nor in any way a guaranteed living, but at least he wasn't a ruinman or a lumberman! The fact that his family's well-known clogs depended on the lumberman for wood and the ruinmen for the antique metal buckles did not change the scorn in which *they* were held. But actors and singers were not much higher, according to his father. Luri hadn't seen him these last five years, even though his traveling took him within a klom or two of the house several times. What was said could not be unsaid, and unless Luri won some high honor, there was not much that was going to convince his family. He shook his head, clearing the discouraging thoughts. Here he was, on the threshold of the best four months of his life! Focus on that!

Memfis was so big it defied description. Luri had heard it was the biggest city in Meriga, but that had given him no sense of size. Now, as the oxen rested at the top of one of the small hills outside of town, he gazed down, stupefied. The houses, warehouses and markets stretched all the way down to the wide Banroo Bay, and the Misipi River that ran the west side of the city dwarfed the riverboats and fishing boats that crammed its waters. And the ruins of what had been the old city went even farther in every direction, except where the swamp encroached from the southwest. Luri strained to see the showmen's section, the one that held their main shrine, the Land of Grace, where he and every other elwus made pilgrimage eventually. Not a ruin like most of the other old world buildings, it held the relics of the man who started it all—and occasionally surprises still turned up in the dirt of the large walled community.

"Are yer comin', or not?"

The carter's voice was like gravel tumbling in the river. The old man had given them a ride from Duca, in exchange for help getting the cartwheels out of occasional mud puddles. This year there had been an unexpected rainstorm in advance of the season, and those who were hurrying to their rain accommodations had been caught unaware. The voice held urgency, and Luri glanced at the mass of dark clouds on the horizon; they were indeed cutting it close. With a sigh, he turned and got onto the cart, shutting his eyes to hold that first glimpse of the city, impress it on his memory.

As they rumbled into Memfis, the old man warned him, "Remember I told yer—this place has 15 sections, and they're really picky about who goes where. Now I'm not saying entertainers aren't welcome, but yer gotta know when and where. Go into the wrong alley, and yer'll never come out again."

"Thanks, Mick," Gordo said. "Can you give us directions to the Land of Grace?"

"Yer goin' there? Of course y'are." The old man looked over; Luri couldn't tell if it was scorn or pity. "I'm stopping at the grain merchants hall. From there, y'take Shrimpers Way about ten blocks, and just where the big open seafood market sits next to the ironmonger's guild, go left about five blocks. Usually there's a couple of weird—I mean, dressed-up guys at the gate. This time o' year, y'can't miss it."

Old man Mick was right. Before Luri and Gordo had walked halfway from the grain merchant guild to the seafood market, they were aware of many others with leather bags, knapsacks, and those boxes that were such a giveaway—the

155

mechanical music boxes of an elwus assistant. Luri's nerves started to flutter again as he glanced sideways at these others, their different sizes and shapes, but all with that peculiar lope that elwuses seemed to fall into after learning the peculiar dances required for the performance. He could tell Gordo was looking at his compatriots, eyeing their decorated boxes, wondering perhaps what songs were hidden within. The magic that had created the old world music was long dead, but some ancient secrets had been preserved and now the famous elwus music existed on special leather rolls that had been cut with tiny rectangles, attached to a metal contraption where little wooden hammers tapped metal strips that sounded different notes—a hurty-birdy. Definitely a lot more birdlike and tinny than the live sound that a drum and banjo could produce, but since elwus music was so well known, and audiences sang along, even a suggestion of the tune was enough. And it was the performance that mattered.

"Keep yer eye on the whirlin' chickens!"

A reedy voice pierced the clamor and Luri glanced over. A boy of 14 in a red and yellow patched outfit was juggling what looked like plucked hens, but far too flexible. They tumbled through the air in a circle over his head. Luri realized they were half-stuffed fabric, with embroidered eyes and beaks. "First I do two, then I do three, then I do four!!" The boy shrilled, looking up at his odd juggling bags.

Ma'am Gaia would not be happy with him pretending to abuse an animal—what kind of *place* was this? Even if it was only pretend…And right on cue, the first handfuls of mud and ripe fruit were flung at the boy, slamming into his motley costume, knocking one of the chickens out of the air.

"G'wan outta here, chicken fondler!" "Take your deviance elsewhere!"

156

The crowd quickly chased the boy down the street. But there were other jugglers—this was the Street of Flying Balls, and Luri could see brightly colored wooden spheres, knives, sticks, even a rope mop whirling in the air, as practitioners showed off. He watched one tall gangly fellow take bites from the apples he was juggling, managing to stuff them in his mouth as they spun by.

"That looks as hard as elwus dancing," he commented. Gordo nodded.

They followed the crowd up another street, where buildings were draped in colorful banners, and poles in doorways dangled glittery glass and metal baubles, though many of them were being taken in before the rains. This was the famous Street of Players, where they said you could get costumes like nowhere else, and thin booklets with act-able stories from before the old world died. Thinking of that brought Luri to mind of the jennels and cunnels who had passed them on the long road to Memfis. Some were saying another Civil War could happen soon. With Presden Sheren dying, and no heir, no one knew who would be in charge. And if war came to this area, how would *any* of the wandering entertainers live?

Luri wanted to stop and browse the trays of trinkets and beads, as some elwuses were doing, but with this many applicants, he might not get a space at the gathering. So they pushed on, ignoring the tantalizing odor of fried spiced bread, goat chunks on skewers and fruit drinks that were being hollered on both sides of the street. He caught sight of a three-story red brick structure, old and gracious, with real black shingles—that must be it! And in a moment, he saw the banner—white letters stitched to a sun-yellow cloth: Land of Grace.

"That's it! That's it!" Gordo squeaked and punched his arm. "Can you believe it?? We're going to Grace Land."

"No. I can't." Luri had no more words; he let his feet take him slowly down the lane. The entrance queue stretched halfway down the block so he had time to look. High walls of mortared concrete spread to both sides of a large gate—he had heard there was enough room in the compound for 100 at one time! With a garden for King Elwus' bones and a ceremonial Crying Chapel and even things he had touched! Now that he was so close, Luri almost panicked. What if all that was just a story? What if it wasn't much at all??

He shoved away such thoughts. All around him, elwuses were murmuring and chatting: "They say he invented music." "What—*all* music??" "Yeah, well, maybe not that really wobbly beet-oven stuff. But the dance music." "Makes sense—he was a king of swing." "Not swing, doofus—Rock and Billy."

Luri looked at the part of the house that peeked over the wall—the windows had glass and fancy wooden frames, and he could see scarlet curtains—the most expensive dye! As they got closer, he saw the metal gates were formed like a page of music (he had seen two such pages and learned some of the note letters)—and there was a silhouette of an elwus!

"They're original—*he* touched those gates," someone sighed.

"That's a lot of metal," someone answered. "I'm surprised they didn't get scrapped."

"They tried. The king's army stopped the marauders, though they got the grave plaques. Battle of the Brassy Buggers, it was."

There wasn't a lot of intact pre-war buildings in Meriga anymore—what was left after war had been renovated to be

158

useful. So this was a doubly special place, defended during the Civil Wars and now guarded by the Bouncers, a brigade who had spring-heeled shoes, the better to chase any scoffers.

A small group appeared around the corner, carrying white painted wood on poles, with the words "Don't Be Cruel". They all had the approved elwus wig, but were dressed entirely in black, and had no sideburns nor dark glasses.

"Blasphemy!" "Lost souls!" The shouting came from the line waiting to get in. Luri looked around in confusion. Gordo elbowed him.

"I know what they are—they're the heretic elwuses! They insist he wore black!"

"Ridiculous! Don't we even have some old costumes of the King?"

Gordo shrugged. "Some people just like to be different."

* * *

Keri gripped the rail of the riverboat; the muddy Misipi was taking its last curve into the city of Memfis, into her last chance. Boats all around her were speeding towards various landings, as the black clouds gathering on the horizon were warning all and sundry to take cover before the rains. *If this doesn't work, I will be stuck here for four months.* Four months in a strange city, with uncertain opportunities for work, unless she cared to become a harlot. She knew a few failed scholars who had, but it wasn't to her taste. No, she was hoping to get a job at one of the digs that would be planned just after the rains, and hoping against hope that she might be given a small advance or at least a cheap place to stay where she could pay them back once the work began. It had taken much longer to come down the Misipi than she thought, and it taken most of her last coins to do so. She was just passed her 20, with two stillbirths and no chance anymore at the Circle, though possibly one of the priestess shrines would take her. But that, too, went against the grain. She had studied the ancient arts at Versty, and could not imagine spending her life on incantations and incense. Lady Gaia needed all the prayers she could get of course, but surely they should be heartfelt prayers? *Ma'm* Gaia—she must remember to use the local term. Would these Southerners accept someone from as far north as Anarba? The one thing priestesses had taught her was that everything was part of the one Circle; that everything in the world had its natural place and should not try to be where it doesn't belong. That went for humans too. And so Keri was trying, with her last few coins, to find the place where she was supposed to be.

When the *Jennel Mornay* tied up at a landing north of the city, Keri had a moment of panic. Dare she ask anyone where the ruinmen were? It was not a place where women normally went. She stood on the landing, buffeted by roustabouts who staggered under huge bales of cotton, sides of salted beef and corded crates of lom wool clothing down from Genda. She grabbed her two carpetbags and hurried to a safe space, craning to look for any sign of the odd kind of building that her friend Mina had told her to look for.

"Ruinmen are always found outside a city," Mina said, over their last breakfast together, "and for whatever reason, their buildings are always strange."

Keri had smiled to herself, touched by her friend's eagerness to help. As if she didn't know about ruinmen! They were all over Meriga, and everywhere acted the same. Of course she didn't know *much* about them, because of the stigma—but now that she was a failed scholar, how could she possibly hold *them* in contempt?

After a moment, she breathed a sigh of relief, catching sight of the leathers and work belt that indicated a member of the ruinmen guild. She grabbed the curved wooden handles of her bags and tottered after him, not too close, but always keeping him in sight as she joined the crowd pushing its way towards the northern gates of the city. There was a city outside the city, dirty and crammed with taverns and shops and crowds of grubby people—so far from the calm order of the Versty that she almost turned and ran back to the ship. She gulped a couple of times and forced herself to keep going. And when she got to the ruinmen's hall, she gasped. Mina had been right. It was the strangest monstrosity: a huge dome made of triangles, most of them metal but some looked like glass windows. It sat a little higher than the low warehouses and the canted, sagging inns that surrounded it. Keri noticed what looked like a water line about a foot up from the walls as she passed. She wondered what this area would be like when the rains came, and made a note to find a second or third-floor room.

Now that the time came to knock on the door, she was terrified. She stood near a blank wall, close enough to see the main door and the men and boys going in and out, willing herself to have the courage to knock. *If I can't ask, I'm not going to get,* she told herself fiercely. She waited until traffic ceased, hurried up to the door and rapped her knuckles against it.

The young man who half-opened the door looked startled, and she wondered if there was another way it was supposed to be done. Before her courage broke, she stammered "I'm a... scholar... And was hoping you might have… a job?"

He still looked puzzled, but in a different way, and he hopped from one foot to another uncomfortably, finally saying, "You can't come in." Seeing her look, he bit his lip, pointed over her shoulder and said "Go to that tavern—I can send… someone. In a minute." He looked at her with real pity and closed the door.

Well, that's that, she thought as she staggered away. *Messed that up completely, and now I'm going to sit in a tavern hoping someone comes up to me? Maybe this is where I start my new career—as harlot.* She felt hot tears welling and bit her lip hard to push them back. There was a tavern in front of her, and it didn't look as sinister as some she had passed. She was too tired to walk much further, so she decided to go in, have a seat and a beer, and then decide what was next.

It looked like a typical drinking hole: a chest-high bar running the length of the room, a couple of bottles on the shelf behind, and a keg or two off to the side. The windows along the opposite wall had been washed sometime in the last month. The tables and benches had seen better days, but they were mostly clean, and the men and women sitting there might have been shopkeepers or craftsmen; they didn't give her a second glance. Relieved, Keri went to an empty table where she could see the door, placed her bags under it and sat. A boy of perhaps 11, wearing a white cotton apron, hurried up and took her order. Afraid the beer would be too much by itself, she asked for some bread and butter.

"We have peanut butter," the boy said with evident pride.

"I've never had that," she replied, "okay—bread and peanut butter."

When it arrived, the tan goop was the consistency of

thick porridge, but smelled like the oil used to propel the riverboat. Somewhat alarmed, she bit into it, and discovered she really liked the taste. It was thick and filling, though it didn't quite go with the taste of the beer. She focused on finishing every last crumb, trying not to think about why she was sitting there alone.

"Are you the scholar?"

The deep voice startled her; she jolted upright. In front of her was a black haired, hawk nosed man about twice her age, clean-shaven and in well-kept leathers. She swallowed and nodded, not trusting her voice.

"I am Mister Corwin." Since he obviously expected something, she waved him to the seat opposite. She hadn't actually thought this far ahead.

"Sir and Mister," she said, using the standard title, "I am Keridwen darra Elina, recently from Versty in Melumi."

"Looking for work?" He glanced at the bar, and Keri blushed. Where were her manners?

"Yes, and please, let me buy you a beer." She felt for the coins in her pocket, desperately hoping they would last. How much would things cost in such a huge city?

He looked surprised, then smiled slowly and nodded. He signaled to the boy who came over with a mug. "Most people wouldn't do that," he said.

"Most people aren't looking for work."

He laughed; a rich, fruity chuckle. "True enough. But the rains are coming—you know we don't work then."

She glanced down, clenching her hands to keep them from trembling. "Yes. But I was hoping to get a contract, so that I knew—and before someone else—" how pitiful she sounded! Reduced to camping out with the untouchables, on the off-chance they found something scholarly or needed

163

copies.

"Ah," his tone of voice changed. She didn't dare glance up, she suspected he understood far more than she'd said. "In that case, there *are* a couple digs we are planning where would be nice to know a scholar is handy." He paused.

This was when she had to ask—*this* was when she had to humble herself, because if not she would starve long before the dig was started. But she couldn't find her voice. She reached for her mug, needing two hands to keep it from shaking.

"And in the meantime—" he continued, as if reading her thoughts. She glanced up in surprise. The smile on his face was fatherly, and another part of her relaxed. "During the rains, we have a lot of feasts, and that takes a lot of putting on. I know that they could use a hand down at the market where we set up. If you'd be interested."

She nodded, again not trusting her voice. That wouldn't be so bad—to work through the rains, end up not in debt, and with a job on the other end. "Yes—yes, thank you," she said finally.

"And you're new here?" He didn't wait for her answer, "Two doors down is a decent inn. You'd be a block from the market and it's safer than many rooms you could rent." He smiled again, nodded and stood. "So that is settled. The inn has a green door; ask for Ronnie. The market is at the end of the block the other side of our hall—the second largest building around here." Another brief smile. "Ask for Marna – she's my sister. And when the rains stop, I'll send a prentice round and we can talk contracts." With a slight bow, he turned and quickly left.

Keri sat there, slightly stunned. *Well—that worked, didn't it?* She felt numb, and the names and directions he just gave her were in danger of sliding out the back of her head. The boy showed up at her elbow and she risked another coin for another beer. Maybe it was early to celebrate, but maybe not. And she needed something to steady her nerves.

That evening she sat in the little room she had rented, fingering the last two coins in her pocket, watching out the tiny grubby window as the sunset flooded the sky with orange. She was here. Tomorrow she would start work as a server—Marna had told her it would be set-up for the next couple days, until the rain finally arrived. Then it would be wild: parties daily and the first week or so the wildest of all. She would even get time off to celebrate, since it was tradition that everyone rejoice in Ma'am Gaia's generosity. Alone again for the first time since she had been sent away from the Versty, she tried to take in all that had happened to her in the past month. One thing was for certain—she was beginning a life unlike anything she had known.

* * *

Luri was dazed by the size and the richness of the main hall—walls hung with red drapes, with row after row of benches and a stage at the front, and overhead thin wires from which dangled silver stars like the small ones on their costumes. They spun and glittered in the light from high windows. He couldn't keep from glancing up at them, though he knew it marked him as a rube. They had passed by strange rooms that had been kept exactly as the King had them—long benches totally cushioned in shiny satin, thick oval rugs like spotted animal skins, colored glass room dividers, and large fireplaces with golden statues and gold-framed pictures on the mantle. It was a jumble of colors and styles,

165

disconcerting. Those rooms were off-limits, with red velvet ropes across the doorways.

A short, thin elwus walked out on stage, waving his hands as if receiving applause; a couple of the nervous newcomers did clap, but stopped immediately when others chuckled.

"Welcome, all you hound dawgs, welcome to the Land of Grace!" He said in a deep elwus voice. They did clap then, Luri so hard his palms hurt. "This is a special time for us all, and I would like to begin with an invocation: Oh great King, love me tender, don't be cruel to a fool such as I. I'm all shook up at the wonder of you. I need your love tonight. Please forget the past, the future is bright ahead. Teach these new hound dawgs we can't go on together with suspicious minds. It's now or never, please light my morning with a hunk o' burning love."

In a different voice, he announced that classes would start as soon as the rains began. Before that the elwuses were free to walk around town, but they should check with senior members as to where was safe. To pay for lessons, they would all be expected to help with cleaning and food preparation. He blew air kisses, bowed and left the stage, and senior elwuses came up to the benches and gestured for the newcomers to follow them. Luri walked in a daze.

The student accommodations were meager, a cot and room to walk around it, and a box under the cot for belongings—but the thatched roof would be dry, and a big central fire pit allowed for drying clothes. Luri was proud to own three shirts and three trousers besides his costume – he could afford to hang one and still have a backup. Some people walked around wet all season, but Luri hated that. It wrinkled his skin. The floor was spread with dry hay, the better to absorb the damp. Otherwise a dorm for 30 would start to reek quickly.

After the evening banquet, the visiting elwuses were given a tour of the inner rooms.

"Y'all realize that this is part of our guild secret," the tour guide said sternly. "What is seen here is ours alone. The power of the King imbues us, but any hound dawg who spreads this gold to the public will be cast out." With that, he turned on his heel and led the way into the central courtyard. There were four concrete slabs in a half circle, each with a small polished brass plaque at the foot.

"Here sleeps the King, his parents, and his Grammy." They all stared in reverent silence. "We know they used to bury people—they did not know better back then. So we honor his wishes."

In a room off the courtyard was the recording studio: a windowless, mostly empty square space with something strange like pitted cardboard on the walls, a wood desk painted silver like metal, with several mostly rectangular boxes also painted silver and the word "recording machines" painted on them.

"The actual machines were taken away as contraband or scrap, but we have the basic idea what they looked like," the tour guide said. Luri noticed there were circles and small squares painted in rows. He had once seen a radio set up; it looked something like that. There was also a short metal pole with a knob on the end—it looked like a fancy version of their singing stick, and it turns out that's exactly what it was.

"This actually once connected to the machines, and elwus sang into it and somehow it stuck in the machine," the tour guide explained. "Legend said we once had recordings of his actual voice, but during the many wars, they were stored secretly somewhere—and we've never found them. A great loss." Beside him, Gordo sighed.

He then led them into another room, where clear glass boxes sat in rows. The contents resembled the kind of scrap one might find in an open market, but laid out as if each was gold. As they shuffled by, the tour guide recited, "his white scarf...one of his frayed shoes...the actual kitchen grocery list...a Bill Yard ball, part of a game he played...a couple of coins from his pocket...his pocket...a comb he once used..." They came to the end of the row, and on the wall in front of them was a gold-framed red velvet square on which was pinned two scraps of white satin.

"This was an original costume," the tour guide murmured, reaching up slowly to touch one piece. "It has almost worn away, but we still allow y'all to touch—this brings the best luck an elwus ever gets." He stepped aside and allowed the group to pass one by one to touch the cloth.

Luri was confused: he loved entertaining and thought elwus music the best, but—adoration? It almost felt like prayers to Ma'am Gaia! Even a king was only a person... He shifted uncomfortably, held back as the other elwuses stepped up to touch the white satin fragments. Gordo hesitated, then stroked the fabric. Further ahead Luri saw others stroking a huge pink metal shape with two round glass eyes that looked nothing like a cart or caddy, but had carried the King, so they said.

He followed the others into a room that held a table with a recessed top padded with green cloth, with holes in the corners and other places on the rim. There were a handful of wooden balls scattered on the top and some long spears crisscrossed.

"This is the table that Bill Yard made for the king. They

would take turns hitting the balls into the holes," the tour guide explained.

"I had heard that the king's house had burnt down during the second civil war—was it rebuilt?"

The tour guide whirled toward the speaker. "It's a lie! This house was protected by loyal bouncers—they never touched it! You could be banned for saying that."

The young elwus shut up in a hurry, but Luri was even more troubled. Why did that upset him so? Something wasn't right.

* * *

Reporting for work, Keri again had to catch her breath— the indoor market for the rain parties was almost the size of a small town! Currently, it still had all its vendors, though some had started to pack up in anticipation. There had been thunder this morning but still the dark black clouds hung on the horizon, like bullies waiting to pounce. Inside, the heat was stifling, and the smells mingled to make something indescribable: oranges, bananas, pineapples along with rubber and oilcloth, resins and old beer, the sour pong of some sharp metallic chemical and the tang of fresh pine. She wondered how the vendors managed day in and day out— perhaps, like the riverboat crews, they lost their sense of smell. And the sights were as vivid and confused as the smells. Piles of golden fruit and crates of live chickens and ducks. Giant barrels holding outlandish aquatic creatures that she had never seen before. Cloth banners hanging from the ceiling, with appliquéd pictures showing the wares. The chemist guild tables were full of lidded wooden boxes, and she watched as one of the guild members carefully scooped some black powder into a leather bag on a scale as a ruinman looked on. This wasn't a clothing or furniture market, but anything you wanted to eat, drink or use as tools was definitely here.

And the crowds were as varied as the goods. Lots of ruinmen of course, and the chemists in their dusty black tunics with the heavy full front gray aprons. Some of the fruit vendors looked like they might be from Meyco—not just slightly reddish tint to their skin, but their shirts had cuffs with chevron embroidery and their pants were a woven plaid, which was not common, where she came from at least. She saw a few more woven plaids and stripes down here, and a strange pattern that at first she thought might have been chemists splashing the wrong chemical on their clothes, but which she finally realize was a method of dyeing cloth that left splotches or wobbly concentric circles of color. There was more color in general down here, and it lifted her spirits. *I must get myself one of those bright blue oilcloth jackets*, she thought. Then she recognized the doorway that led to the back of the market and hurried to work.

That day was a busy blur of washing and drying crates of bowls and plates in preparation, sorting utensils into wooden trays, and bringing in whatever food could be prepped ahead of time, when no one knew the timing of the first downpour. Most of the supplies would be brought in by the prentices once the downpour started in earnest, but Marna said anything that could be done to reduce the chaos was a good thing. Keri was bone tired when she got back to her room, and she was dripping sweat. The heavy lom wool tunic she wore was entirely too hot for this climate. So despite heavy legs, she dragged herself downstairs and asked her way to a clothing vendor. Marna had been kind enough to give her the first week's wages, knowing she have to get set up before the rains. At the outdoor market, the vendors had signs indicating a discount, wanting to sell out before they had to close up and go inside. So Keri got a cotton dress—lovely blue that the seller guaranteed would not run in the rain. She found a pair of light cotton trousers, and although it was very expensive, an oilcloth cap with a brim that would keep some of the rain out of her face. She eyed the oilcloth jackets longingly, but they cost the equivalent of a whole barrel of crabs—at least a month's wages.

On the way back, she was forced to stand in a doorway as the street was suddenly filled with an army—first the jennel and his officers on horseback, then at least 50 foot soldiers, all of them looking arrogant and dangerous. The people around her were quiet, their expressions deliberately blank, no one glancing directly at the soldiers. Surely, there wasn't war already?? That would have spread around the market as fast as fruit flies. She tried not to look either, but the menace embodied in all of those marching men was frightening. Once they passed, she hurried back to her room, determined to ask Marna tomorrow what that had been about.

But the next day, the rains came, like someone poured a giant bucket on the city. Keri ran outside that morning like the others, to celebrate—and spluttered, struggling to breathe. She had once stood under a waterfall—it was like that. Everyone was squealing and shouting and dancing; some were gathering handfuls of water and throwing it at each other, though there was no way to tell if anything landed. Feeling a bit wimpy, she stepped back under an eave to catch her breath. Water was pouring off thatched and slate roofs alike, running into metal or wood gutters and spewing out of the pipes at the bottom. The street was already a river—bits of wood, a scrap of brown cloth, broken flowers and a small basket floated quickly by. One of the groups started a circle dance, almost filling the street from side to side as they linked arms and sidestepped, hooting and singing *Ma'am Gaia's Tears*. It was traditional, but the sad song was so out of place with all of this raucous celebration. Well, the market party would start this afternoon, which meant she would have daily work for the next several months. Even feeling as out of place and homesick as she did, Keri smiled.

* * *

First day of lessons! They shuffled onto backless benches facing the low stage in the big room. Today Luri noticed the stage curtain: an aqua sailcloth patched with silver stars. The silver was probably from Meyco—unless they were original, too. Luri wondered what Gordo was learning—the motors had their own classes and competitions. Then a hefty man with black hair cut Elwus style—not a wig—dark glasses and the shiniest white costume Luri had ever seen, stepped out from between the curtains onto the stage. Swirls of glittering spangles, a wide belt of glass and brass, and chains looped at his hip jangled as he moseyed in practiced elwus style to the front.

"All right, you hound dawgs—listen up!" he snapped, "this is how it runs—each week, we go over—in order—voice, posture, gyrating, costume and content. First the big lesson here, then after lunch, small group practice. We have senior elwii for consultation and every Friday is a contest. You can also sign up to entertain around Memfis—we have lists of those who want elwii for their parties. Any questions?"

172

They were all too awed for questions. And so Luri's training began, becoming more complicated each week. For example, gyrating class began with three elwuses walking onto the low stage behind Master Hips.

"Listen up, hound dawgs—we're going to divide this into four parts: arms, hips, knees and ankles. Each one of them does something different, but they all have to combine in a total effect. It's harder than rubbing your belly and patting your head at the same time."

Luri surreptitiously tried to pat and rub, and noticed others were doing the same.

"Pay attention! Let's start with the ankle: heel doesn't touch the ground, toe turned outward—bounce, bounce, bounce." He demonstrated. "It's gotta look like you're barely standin'on 'em, and you get extra points for not falling over. And of course, with the ankle, you gotta swing those knees—in/out, in/out—like this." He gestured and the onstage elwuses quickly did a flawless elwus shuffle in unison and the audience gasped. Master Hips grinned, knowing how good they were. "And knees gotta turn out at a 45 degree angle, unless you're twistin' 'em. Can you remember that?"

Variations on *yes* were mumbled or shouted. Privately, Luri wasn't sure.

"Okay, now the knee wobble alone—point those toes, stand on the tips, and back-and-forth—" he demonstrated, and Luri noticed his elbows thrust outward; it had to be for balance. "You practice each of these pieces until you don't have to think about them—*then* you put them together. Otherwise, it's a mishmash."

And the singing, which Luri felt he was skilled at, was even more difficult. One weekday, they were put through the paces of emotive singing. The morning session left them all cowed—each of the master elwii sounded *exactly* alike. And that's what they would be expected to do. After lunch, Luri stepped to the center of the circle nervously. He assumed the starting position: left hip jutting forward, right knee slightly bent, shoulders hunched over the wooden singing stick. Dropping into his lowest register, he began, "I'm just hunker hunker borning love, yah. I'm—"

"No, no!" The instructor broke in. "It's not hunker—sing it like you're coughing up a gob! *Hhhhunnka...*" he demonstrated, sounding like he had the rains cough. Luri tried to imitate, feeling it rasp his throat. After four tries, he did it well enough to win approval.

After two weeks of intense practice, feeling the need to get out into the public to get a little bit of appreciation for his skills instead of constant correction, Luri headed to the board that listed gigs. He nudged Gordo and pointed.

"They need an elwus down at a market just outside the south gate."

"You don't want to go there—that's where all the ruinmen hang out," a thin, pimply elwus warned.

"But—they're actually paying!"

"They have to—or they won't get anyone."

Luri's funds were low enough that he decided to take the gig. Besides, he knew what it was like to be looked down on.

* * *

Keri got off work at dusk that day. It had been a wild two weeks, as Memfis shared its bounty with everyone. She had been overwhelmed by the amount of free food, drink and the wild parties—there was nothing like that either at Versty or her hometown, that was for sure! Now she was standing in the crowd, still feeling a stranger, but recognizing one or two of the prentices and misters who partied almost every night. She had grown to like the exotic music and dances, and looked forward to doing some dancing tonight. But first they were going to have an elwus performance. She watched the stage as a tall slim elwus swaggered on to it. She couldn't see his eyes under the dark glasses and of course his wig was black, but his face was attractive and he looked very nervous. *He probably isn't going to get an attentive audience in this party,* she thought, and wondered if he'd be able to sing loud enough. She needn't have worried – his first song bounced off the back wall: "Weeellll, since ma baby lef' me...." he hollered, and the live band slammed into their version of *Heartbroken Hotel.* Since this was one of the Memfis bands, she expected that strange rhythm and bounce, but they did it straight, exactly as she'd heard it years ago. And the elwus strutted and swaggered and got the audience yelling and singing along with him. Keri didn't know most of the words, but she sang the choruses when they came around, as he segued from one song to another: *Too Frayed Shoes, Hound Dawg, Return to Sander* —all the old favorites. By the fifth song, his voice had just about given out and he was dripping sweat. Finally, he bowed, threw air kisses at the audience, and left the stage to loud applause. Then the band shifted into the complicated, raucous music that some called sideeko. She danced a bit, feeling the room swaying after that last glass of beer, then threaded her way to the buffet, where she watched a girl of ten serving out the jambalaya and corn grits, feeling half an expert herself after two weeks' work.

"Could I have some extra crayfish?"

The voice behind her was harsh and raspy. She glanced back and realized with a jolt that the elwus was behind her in line. Of course he was not in costume, but he was so sweaty and his voice so ruined that she had no doubt. Impulsively, she said, "that was a really good show, elwus."

He looked startled, then smiled. His eyes were green and his natural hair a light brown, and he was just as attractive close up. "Thank you. And I'm Luri." He reached for the proffered plate, and gave a startled smile at the large pile of strange shellfish.

"I like elwuses—and you were good," the little girl said. "Do you want cra-fis', too, lady?"

"No thanks—I've got what I need."

Luri gestured with his plate towards the eating area, and Keri followed him to a pair of seats at one end of a long table. Someone set two mugs of beer in front of them, then hurried away.

"I just arrived," he said, with half a mouthful, "what are good places to see here?"

She giggled, which embarrassed her. "I'm afraid I'm new also. Down from Anarba. And I'm Keri."

He blushed and choked down his mouthful. "I apologize—I'm not being very—I'm…" He sighed. "It's just that I'm used to being on the stage, not with the audience so much."

The noise level of the party had gotten loud enough that they were having to shout, and Luri's voice was so bad she was lipreading. "Let's finish our food and go outside," she shouted, gesturing towards the door. He nodded and they both ate more quickly, then grabbed their mugs and headed toward the door.

The rains were still so drenching that they couldn't stand in the street and finish the beers, but there was a narrow protected area under the building eaves. Keri tried to ignore the people howling and splashing like they had gone mad. "If this isn't one of your usual performance stops, can I ask why?"

Luri smiled and gestured with his mug, accidentally moving it past the eaves and getting it half filled with rainwater. He laughed loudly, and she grinned. "This is where the king—the first elwus—was born. All of us want to come here at some point. Now I have the whole rainy season to learn and practice. And you?"

Keri turned toward a server going by with tankards, and grabbed two to cover her embarrassment. "The one you have is pretty soggy," she joked, and then drank a bit faster, hoping to make it easier. "I—well, to be honest, I'm a failed scholar. There's only room for a certain number at Versty and well, they didn't have a spot for me."

"I knew a failed scholar once—she was one of the best singers I've ever met. She went around playing Juliet in West Side Story. She used to tell me a bit about plants and trees." Luri looked wistful, and Keri wondered if they had been lovers. At least he didn't sneer at failed scholars. "Have you decided what you will do now?"

That, at least she could be hopeful about. "Yes, I have a contract with—to go on a dig once the rains stop. And until then, I've been helping out at these gatherings. I have time off because they say everyone should be celebrating Lady Gaia's generosity. I mean Ma'am."

"Do they talk different up north?" He was leaning against the building, inclining a bit closer to her and she felt a shiver of excitement. She smiled and winked saucily.

"I don't know—you tell me. Do I sound different?"

He leaned slightly closer. "Do they *kiss* different up north?" he asked with an impish smile. Well, it *was* the rain festival. She leaned forward and gave him a sample, and happily he was an excellent kisser.

They ended up back at her room less than an hour later, drenched of course, but eventually Keri made a small fire on the hearth, adding to the steamy atmosphere, and hung their clothes on the drying rack that folded down from the wall. Luri watched her from the bed, and she glanced back now and then, admiring his muscled torso. Elwii came in all shapes and sizes, but this one obviously practiced those energetic dances. He had grabbed his costume from the back of the stage, bending over it to keep it dry as they'd raced down the block. It was draped over the room's only chair, white and spangly, as odd a piece of clothing as she'd ever seen.

"Why do elwii always wear white?" She asked as she slipped back into bed. For a while they were too busy for him to answer, but eventually he remembered the question.

"That's what the king wore, they tell us. Although last week I saw some elwuses dressed all in black—apparently there's a whole heretical sect of them. I'd never seen one before."

"Heretical? That sounds like religion."

She could feel his blush rather than see it. "Yeah, I—I'm not sure about that. The people here are really, really in awe of the King. I mean, I knew when I came to his shrine that I would find the real faithful—I just didn't realize...quite how...faithful."

"He has a shrine? I thought you were just entertainers. I mean—I don't mean just—"

He stroked her hair. "No—I know what you mean. And I agree. I thought we were just entertainers too. But—" he was silent for a long time. "I can't actually tell you, because that's part of it—they want us to keep the—special parts—secret."

She could tell he was uncomfortable about that.

"Well, you don't have to tell me anything."

They enjoyed each other a bit more, and when finally they were tired, she talked about what it was like as a scholar, describing the libraries and the various subjects.

"Toward the end, just before the old world died, the art became so weird and indecipherable that scholars think the environmental toxins got to the artists first somehow," she explained. "Or perhaps everyone was that crazy, but they didn't all paint. "

In any case, she told him, art was one of the least important items in the ensuing chaos, so very few paintings survived. In fact, more of the art was preserved in books—large wonderful books in color-than survived in real life. Large paintings had been used as tarps, door curtains or roof covers. The stone sculptures had an even worse fate, since stone was so useful.

"So that's why I keep seeing a bit of a nose or eye sticking out of a wall," Luri commented.

"Yes—the best I've seen was a pretty rectangle of white marble cherub faces in a red brick shopfront. Unfortunately it was spoiled by some art critic giving them black mustaches." They both chuckled.

"But once I realized I wasn't going to be able to—that I was coming down here, I decided to copy out a map that I found in the Versty library," she explained. She went to her books on the table and unfolded a large piece of heavy paper, brought it back to the bed. "It's the old city and of course I couldn't copy *all* of it, but I got the main streets and some of the important buildings and places. Like this—" she pointed to a large rectangular area "—that was where they flew their planes in and out of."

179

Luri leaned over her shoulder, resting his chin. Then he sat bolt upright. "That—what does that say?!?" He jabbed his finger on a place just to the left of the plane grounds.

She squinted. "Looks like it says Grace… Land."

"No! That's not—where are we now??"

"I've been trying to figure that out. You know a quarter of the city is swamp now, but I figure we are just about—here." she pointed. "If I had known what was swamp, I wouldn't have bothered to draw it."

"Land of Grace, Grace Land—could there possibly have been two of them?"

Keri shrugged. "I have no idea. Is it a big problem?"

"*Something's* not right here." He studied the map as if his life depended on it, then put it back down with a sigh. "I don't know. It might be really big." He squinted, thinking hard. "I don't think it's telling secrets just to tell you where our building is—that's common knowledge. It's supposed to be the King's house – but why would they lie?"

Her eyes widened as she suddenly understood. "Oh—if the *real* place was underwater, but they wanted… a shrine…" She stared at him. And no one's mentioned there's any other place?"

He shook his head. "I've seen the graves—oops. I don't know if that's secret."

"I won't tell anybody." She nestled against his chest. "It's intriguing. I wonder if it's possible to get to this old place."

"I'm guessing it's not possible to go anywhere on water during the rains. But I'm gonna find out eventually."

* * *

But that would have to wait. During the months of rain,

he and Keri met at least once a week, mostly curling up in her bed, but occasionally splashing around the city. As an entertainer, Luri had been told where he could safely travel, and Keri was making notes on her map, trying to figure out what groups controlled which areas. As far as they could determine, it was mostly guild-based, but because many trades were passed down, it also became family-based. Next to the ruinmen and chemists area outside the city, the burners and smelters had a section all to themselves. Due east of the entertainers' section were the guilds of spinners, weavers, sailcloth makers and tailors—anything fabric related; northwest of there was the metal arts guilds which also included the weapon makers, and not surprisingly the next sector over belonged to particularly large, wealthy jennel's family and his troops. Down along the southern edge, where swamplands ate up the old streets and Banroo Bay touched the city, the sailors and boat makers and the related trades had their section. The forbidden areas were mostly deep in the sections, and so the boundaries became the trading streets, the areas where the guilds could mingle and overlap. Those main streets were generally considered neutral and safe. And of course if one had business in a section, one could pass the guards safely, but usually it required a chit or password. The night that Luri was hired to entertain the jennel and his soldiers, he was really praying that he had the correct password.

The chance to sing there came as a lucky break—only later, Luri wasn't so sure. Had most of the locals declared their humility to avoid an unwelcome gig? In any case, when word came that the jennel's aide wanted to look over the available elwuses, a surprising number of them professed to having other engagements or to feeling completely too amateur for such a important event. Luri was nervous, but he had won several Friday contests by then and was excited to be able to play in front of one of the area's wealthiest men.

They lined up in full costume along the stage in the big room, and the aide paced in front of them scrutinizing each in turn. Finally, he pointed at Luri.

"This one will do. We'll have a band ready."

Band? Luri looked anxiously at Gordo—was he going to miss *his* big chance? Gordo shrugged and looked anxious.

"Excuse me, Sir and Cunnel," Luri said tentatively. "Does that mean my motor can't...assist me?"

The man glared at him and Master Hips cleared his throat with a warning frown at Luri. Finally the aide answered, "He can *assist* you, but we don't need him to play. We have one of the best bands in the area. All you have to do is sing along. And dance."

Luri glanced over at Gordo, who nodded emphatically *yes*, so Luri accepted. It would be an honor, and it wasn't for him to tell the jennel his business.

Jennel Belknap and his family lived in a huge stone building, almost a castle, in the hilly Northeast area, where there was no danger of flooding, and he had access to the Wuf River that meandered east from the Misipi. The walk took Luri and Gordo almost an hour, passing through the metalworking areas escorted by a blacksmith's prentice, then being handed off to a large, muscled soldier wearing a pale green uniform, a wide leather belt from which hung a small triangular holster and a pearl-handled pistol. He had red ribbons sewn to his shoulders and above the pocket in his shirt, so Luri guessed he held some rank above ordinary soldiers. He said nothing at all to them, and his stiff movements suggested they were beneath his notice, so they kept quiet and followed him meekly. It was getting dark by then, and of course with the rains there was no chance to carry a lantern, but the electric light from the various party inns was enough to guide them through the streets. Luri's costume was kept dry inside a tarped box; Gordo had left his music box under his cot. They were both drenched, but would be arriving in time to towel off. The soldier stalked down the road as if there was no such thing as rain.

Buildings gave way to wide open areas where large tents—big enough for 20—were pitched and where roofed gazebos allowed dry space for the bonfires where drenched soldiers partied with ladies from the town. It was noisy, but Luri could see guards posted here and there, watching to make sure it didn't get out of hand. After the tents, there were small cabins and the parties inside were obviously officers and more exclusive guests. And finally, the top of a long slope, the jennel's home.

Unlike the brick of the Land of Grace, this building was dressed limestone blocks, as solid as a cliff and just about as gray. In the circular drive before the large double doors, a dozen horses and two large carriages were parked. The carriages were unusual because the wheels were huge, wide and rubber-covered. Most of the mud had been rained off, but it seemed just possible these vehicles could actually move through the muck outside the main cobbled streets. Luri had a glimpse of jewel-toned dresses and dark green suits through the windows before they were guided around the back to the trades entrance.

There they were given a tiny room to get ready. It had a basin and pitcher of clean water, a stack of large towels of soft cotton, and two chairs. There was also a drying rack unfolded at an angle from the back wall. Luri and Gordo gratefully stripped and toweled dry. Once the wet clothes were safely hung, they unpacked the dry costume and Gordo's clothes. Luri concentrated on getting himself into an elwus mood. Would he have the co-hones to strut his stuff in front of all these fine people?? Without a mirror, Gordo had to double check the details and be sure the wig and glasses and wide lapels all sat just right.

"I think that's it," he said nervously, and Luri tapped on the door.

A servant, a boy of 10, immediately opened it and guided them towards a staircase. "You'll be fed after the performance—just come down here after you get off stage. No talking to the guests."

That didn't surprise Luri at all; he nodded in agreement and followed the boy upstairs. At the threshold, he put on the elwus swagger, letting the character take him over, pushing the fear deep inside.

The room was even more elegant than the King's rooms, if that were possible. Long pale blue drapes at the tall windows, thick green rugs on the floors, and all the furniture carved as if they were trying to make it sculpture. As he loped across, blowing air kisses, Luri caught a glimpse of a long dining table full of crystal and china just beyond this party room. Twenty or thirty people, all dressed how he imagined kings and queens would dress, stood or sat around the room, chatting and laughing softly. So much more refined than the rain parties in the city below! Luri felt panic welling up. What could he sing that was appropriate, that would impress these fancy folk? He should definitely avoid the racy "Don't Want To Leave Your Teddy Bare."

At that moment, a young woman with cocoa-hued hair and brown eyes came up and asked, "Will you do Jailhouse

Rock? It's my favorite." He nodded in surprise. So maybe even the wealthy enjoyed the King. Slightly buoyed, he went to the low temporary stage in the corner. The band awaited: four musicians—banjo player, drummer, mouth organist and a guy holding a curvy stringed instrument like a woman's torso that Luri now knew was a geetar. They were dressed in shiny sky blue shirts and black trousers, and two singers had green shirts and black trousers. All had their hair combed back like his elwus wig, but not black. His second thoughts began to have second thoughts. They hadn't even rehearsed! *Come on*, he told himself, *you've done this on the road —and where you met Keri. Whenever there's musicians, it's been great.*

Gordo hurried to shift a few chairs and metal music stands so there would be plenty of space up front for his gyrations. He looked at Luri for approval, then sat down at the edge of the stage. Luri nodded to the band, murmured "Jailhouse," turned and started his act.

"Well, thank y'all fur cummin' ta' see me," he drawled. "I'd like to open with a request." Then as the band led with the classic intro, he belted out "Jailhouse Rock", putting his heart and soul in it.

In a pause between songs, some of the conversations—one in particular—blared across the room.

"Jeez Christmas, Jennel—Cobey's too smart to—" The speaker obviously realized his voice was carrying too far. He looked around and dropped it.

Luri hurried on with his routine, picking "Too Frayed Shoes" because it was loud and boisterous. He noticed the band started playing louder, too. He was heartened when some of the audience sang along, "you can chew anything, but lay offa my too frayed shoes…"

185

Even as he singing, though, he was watching the group around the jennel. They had their heads together, and there was no laughter or partying there. The jennel was a tall rangy man with salt-and-pepper hair, a face that looked chiseled in stone and a perpetual scowl. A young soldier hurried in at one point, gave a quick message to the group and started away, only to be grabbed by the jennel, who whispered in his ear and pushed him off. The boy's expression was half panic, half eagerness. *What if it was war?* Luri thought, then realized his gyrations were faltering, so he shoved the thought aside and threw himself back into the routine.

At the end, he got more enthusiastic applause than he expected and the elation almost floated him off the stage. But as they passed the jennel's group, he overheard, "...silos of AKs near zoopark..." The officer speaking glanced up, met Luri's gaze and glared. Luri hurriedly followed Gordo and the band across the room and down the stairs.

They were well fed in a small room off the kitchen—a big bowl of spicy shrimp and rice they called payyeeya, big mugs of excellent beer and fresh bread. Luri thanked the band repeatedly, telling them he had never heard better.

"When he picked me, he said they had the best band going, and he was right!"

The banjo player, Warne, grinned and nodded. "I think we do a decent job, if I may say so myself. I'm glad he picked an elwus to match."

"Never thought we'd be playing this gig, though," the drummer commented.

"Why not?" Luri asked.

The band exchanged uneasy glances. No one seemed to want to talk first. Finally Warne said, "well—there'd been rumors... like some folks said if the jennel doesn't like you,

186

you kinda—disappear."

"Not that bad, not that bad," the drummer said. "But maybe you get roughed up a bit—he doesn't like it when his guests have a bad time."

Luri exchanged glances with Gordo. Maybe they should leave quickly? But they were stuck, without an escort. "I guess the people are happy such a strong jennel is around to protect them."

"Not sure who will protect them against the jennel," one of the singers muttered. He got an elbow and took a deep gulp of his beer.

Luri thought about what he'd heard upstairs and wondered if the city would be smack in the middle of the war, and where—if anywhere—would be safe.

To Luri's surprise, they were escorted back by one of the jennel's inner group—the very one Luri had overheard. He was just as stiff as the first escort, but kept glancing over at Luri, who was feeling both exhausted and beaten down by the rain, which was bucketing as usual. Finally the man said, "Ya'll are new here, so I'll give ya'll some advice. Loose lips sink ships."

Luri stared up in confusion. Pretty much *any* ship would sink in this rain. Had he misheard? He could barely see the man in the downpour, but he looked menacing, even though his words were nonsense.

"Yessir, Sir and Cunnel," he replied, praying that the rank was close.

"The best players around here are blind and deaf," the man continued. Luri knew better than to question, but the man was raving. Maybe it was too much Genda whiskey speaking. Fortunately, they were at the border and the man gestured them toward a waiting prentice. "Mum's the word," he said in parting.

After a block, Luri asked Gordo, "did any of that make sense to you?"

"Not a word—except it was really clear he wanted us to not say anything about the party."

"That's what I thought, too." *But why?* Luri knew that was going to bother him.

* * *

Maybe it was just nerves, but Luri swore he saw that same soldier several times in the next few weeks, when he and Keri browsed the indoor markets, or worked on their mapping. Luri would glance up and see the soldier standing off to the side, apparently busy, but Luri's shoulder blades twitched. Could it just be coincidence? After the fourth time, he was sure it wasn't, but he couldn't tell whether or not he was being watched—or if it was something worse. He finally pointed the man out to Keri, both to warn her and to ask her advice.

"I don't know exactly what I heard, but whatever it was, it's dangerous, and I don't know what to do." They were back in the room, drying out after the latest expedition, where Luri was sure the soldier had been creeping up on them. Worse than that, there were soldiers all through the city, and now Luri didn't trust a single one of them. "I'm afraid I'm putting you in danger, too."

"Can you remember what the exact words were?"

"They were letters—AK, I think. At that point that soldier looked up, saw me and if a look could kill someone, I'd be dead now."

Keri was silent and thoughtful moment. "Unfortunately, I

was a student of arts, not science or military."

"Do they have students of military?"

She shifted uncomfortably. "There aren't many, but there's some who want to know if there's any way peace could be made more permanent, so they had to study the wars of history, to see where they went wrong."

"I know where they went wrong—they kept trying to take somebody else's things!"

She chuckled and cuffed his shoulder. "That's true enough, but I think they were looking for ways to prevent the need for war from building up."

"Building! Yes, he said something about a silo on the zoo grounds."

She looked serious. "If they are storing things, and they don't want us to know about them—that could be good or really bad. I think we should talk to a priestess."

"If we're wrong, or if the priestesses can't protect us, you know we'll be in deep farm muck."

"Then we should probably wait until the rains let up enough that we can get away." She sighed.

We. Luri felt a warm glow as he realized what she had said.

* * *

Finally the rains began to taper, and it was possible to walk down the street without squelching. Luri's classes were winding up, and Keri had told him she was in the middle of signing contracts for the upcoming dig. As he held her that evening, the sadness of parting warred with a frantic impatience.

"I feel like I'm gonna go crazy if I wait any longer," he

told her. "I'm going tomorrow—can I borrow your map?"

"I'll do better—I'll go with you," she replied. "Since I opened this basket of snakes, the least I can do is help resolve it."

He smiled and pulled her into a tight hug. "Even if this elwus thing goes bad, I'll never regret coming down here this season."

The next day, the rains eased enough to show bits of blue sky, though the southern roads where they set out were still awash in muddy brown runoff. They had already determined that they could take a main trading road down to where the swampland started—not as near as they wished, but they wouldn't need a pass. But they *would* need a boat. It took more than a half an hour for the fisherman to pole his flat bottom boat to the small hillock poking out of the water, the one they tentatively identified as near the area called Graceland. As Luri stepped out of the boat, his legs felt like pudding, as if he had practiced elwus moves for hours. This was it—was he crazy or was there something going on?

The fisherman sat in the boat, eating bread and dried fish as Luri and Keri wandered the hillock. It was ringed by large oaks, one of them toppled with its crown in the water. There were obvious ruins of buildings, as well as the posts of wooden fences. The thick jungle plants of a swamp were encroaching on all sides, vining up out of the water.

"I don't see any metal—could the ruinmen have come and gone?" he asked.

"I doubt they would've left all the nice stone, but maybe," she replied. They poked around the outlines of a large building, then wandered along a flat area nearby. Rains had slashed at the bare ground, washing soil away from several rectangular concrete bases. They looked disturbingly

190

familiar. Luri bent down and brushed away more soil. He found holes that could have held screws, and a narrow brass trim. He stood up quickly.

"Gaia's bright green underthings!" He gripped Keri's elbow. "I think these are the *real* graves. Someone told me they stole the brass plaques off, and the ones at—at Land of Grace are arranged in the same pattern. I know it's not much but…"

He started hunting around more seriously, overturning large stones to look underneath, poking in between tree roots. Some flattened ornate iron fences convinced them it had never been dug. Keri offered him a metal trowel, and he looked at her in surprise.

"I borrowed this from a prentice," she told him smiling, "I did have to promise to write a love poem for his sweetie."

Half an hour's random digging revealed little, except that there were probably spoils enough here for a small dig. And then Luri came across a jagged half circle of shiny gold, except it wasn't gold; it seemed like that old hard plastic they'd once had. There were words, and he handed it up to Keri.

"In the chapel," she read, then looked at him wide-eyed. "Isn't that a song?"

"Crying in the Chapel, yes—and I know what this *is*." He was dizzy with excitement. "They used to give out prizes for the best song each year and the prizes looked like plates only somehow they put the music on them."

"Oh—records! I know about those."

"You do?? *What* you know?" He held the half gold disc, thin as a cabbage leaf, his hand shaking.

"That's how they recorded music back then, at least one of the ways. There was the little music box that you have,

191

these plates, things that look like solid drain pipes but etched, long spooled brown plastic ribbons, and there were also computers that somehow captured the music. We have a couple samples of each at Versty, but they are fragile and we don't play them. They were made from the fossil fuels that almost killed Ma'am Gaia, so of course they will not be made anymore."

"And what are the chances something like this would be left in this random spot?"

She shook her head slowly. "I think we need to call in the priestesses."

*　*　*

Three days later, they accompanied a priestess to the hill and explained to her what they knew. She walked around solemnly, her long gown occasionally catching on roots and stones. She was tall and elegant, and Luri wondered if they could get in trouble for even suggesting their idea. But she listened to them seriously.

"Do you have any cause to think there's danger buried here?"

"No ma'am," Luri replied, "it would've been the home of a man, so he wouldn't have anything nuclear, and there might not be scrap, as such—"

"But you're saying this might be the original Land of Grace?"

"I copied the map up in Melumi," Keri explained, "without having any idea what it might be, so I'm only recording what the old history shows. It could be some kind of confusion—"

"—But this, this record belongs to the King, I'd bet my

career on it," Luri exclaimed.

"That might be exactly what you're doing," the priestess replied, and Luri caught his breath. But then she smiled. "I was born and raised here, I know the history of the King as much as anyone. If somebody, somehow, has mistaken his place of rest, we'all would want to know that. I think we need a good Mister who could do the dig slowly, knowing what could be under here."

Luri sagged in relief and glanced at Keri. She squeezed his arm and smiled. Then he thought of the soldier and froze.

"Ma'am," he began, "if somebody knew—or thought—that there might be some danger buried somewhere, then that person has the duty to tell, right? Even if they're not sure?"

The priestess glanced at him sharply. "Absolutely. It is every person's solemn duty."

So Luri took a deep breath and told her what he had overheard, and how he would've thought nothing of it, except that then he kept seeing that soldier.

"So it could be nothing except maybe a private army fact that I shouldn't know, but—"

The priestess waved her hand. She was frowning and staring into the distance. "You did right. These are—unsettled times, and not everyone is taking the wise route." She shut her mouth decisively, as if she had said too much, then added, "We will look into it. Discreetly." She smiled at him, but he wasn't completely reassured. Would he survive to find out what might be on this hill?

* * *

And of course it wasn't that easy—there were contracts and paperwork to be completed, supplies and helpers to be gathered in. The priestess had not demured when Keri suggested contacting Mister Corwin, and he was quick enough to realize what the rewards might be. After one scouting expedition, he rearranged his schedule, trading off his original dig and prioritizing this one. Keri was thrilled to be on the spot, and she sent a message up to her teachers, requesting any historical information they had, including building layout and possessions. For obvious reasons, they did not contact those who ran Land of Grace, and the dig was sworn to even more secrecy than usual.

Luri and Gordo canceled their plans to go on the road, entertaining around town, but mostly sitting at one of the cheaper taverns nearby until the evenings when Keri returned to the dock. The small size of the island meant the ruinmen had to camp on the mainland just at the edge of the swamp, though they left a guard on the island each night. One reassuring bit of news was that Jennel Belknap had decided to move his soldiers farther afield—the tavern was full of people chattering about seeing the entire Army moving north, and that the priestesses had been called in to bless an area near the old animal zoo, though no one knew why.

One evening, Keri stepped off the boat, grabbed Luri by the shoulders and danced him around, crying, "We found it— we definitely found it!"

He felt his chest contract and it took a moment to force out the words, "You opened the—grave?"

"No of course not! We found a small room full of trophies. Many of are gold. One's from his Grammy, and one says Music Hall of Fame. I researched that—that was the whole country's best musicians! And there's a couple of plain black plates that I'm almost certain are records—real recordings of the king's voice! And there's most of a small airplane under one of the mounds—the name on the side is Hound Dawg Eye Eye!! Eye Eye means two. A lot of that plane might have to go to pay the ruinmen, but some could stay as a monument."

"Monument? Then, are they thinking of—moving the shrine?"

She nodded emphatically. "The priestess has already talked to Mister Corbin, and gone to the Circle—this is too important to the city to ignore. The Circle will go to Land of Grace tomorrow and inform them. It's gonna take a while, but any real relics will move back to the island. And we'll find more."

"But how will people get there?" Gordo interrupted.

Keri turned and gestured toward the island which was visible from the dock. "The Guild of Boat Makers think they can create a pontoon bridge that will work during the dry season, and might even hold up during the rains. You'll still have your shrine—this time it'll be a real one. And I think they'll ask you to stay."

Luri stared at her for a moment then enveloped her in a passionate hug. "Gaia's green underthings! Me working for the King? And Gordo too??"

"Of course."

"And—what about you?" The future had veered abruptly, but if she wasn't there…!

She looked down, then smiled up at him. "There will still be a lot of work on the island this season, and Mister Corwin was impressed enough to offer me work for the next several seasons. After that—who knows?"

Who knew indeed? But with Jennel Belknap temporarily derailed, perhaps the city could have peace. He pulled Keri closer, leaned her head on his shoulder. Was there a way for

Versty to have scholars studying far away? There might be a lot of history buried here. And maybe—he barely dared think about it—he could restore respect for the King to the balance that Ma'am Gaia decreed for all things. A truly great man, but just one of Ma'am Gaia's children. Perhaps it was an unbalanced pride that caused this deceit to happen in the first place. Maybe there was even room for the heretic elwuses—who knew what the dig might reveal?

His thoughts spun; the future was as opaque as the brown water lapping the dock. Hard to believe his wandering days might be over; they had been such a part of him. But now he definitely understood what the King meant about "burning love." He stroked Keri's hair and wondered who the king's special woman had been; or maybe it was more than one. Or maybe it was even the music itself. He stared at the island; the oaks that ringed the real Land of Grace. Yes, music could certainly be worthy of devotion—there was something magic, something of Ma'am Gaia in the music itself.

OVER THE TOP
OF THE WORLD

BEN JOHNSON

A Warm Summer's 'Eve

Yan shifted uncomfortably on the hard wooden bench and drank deeply from his clay mug. The beer tasted bitter. A sleepy looking elwus strummed at a tar in the corner, and the innkeeper busied himself with rinsing and drying mugs. Yan tried to remember how many pints he had ordered and how much copper he had left in his pocket. Outside, a strong southerly wind moaned through the streets, moving the summer heat from place to place. The candles burned low and flickered as gusts of wind came in through the open windows. A figure opened the door and entered the tavern. He walked deliberately. His light summer cloak swirled around him. He placed a silver piece on the bar. The innkeeper poured two mugs of beer and two shots of rum.

"You want this with sugar and lemon?" the innkeeper asked. The cloaked man nodded. He turned his face to Yan and motioned him over to the bar. Yan briefly saw the black patch over the man's left eye, recognizing him from the failed hunt. Yan pondered running from the inn, but instead dragged his feet one unsteady step at a time towards the bar. The man's lips twitched upward slightly, which Yan took for a smile.

"You are Yan sunna Webb, yes? Yan the hound boy?" the man asked. "I am Jorge, Second Gent of Cunnel Bangor. I was on the hunt today, but I don't think we were introduced. Come have a drink with me, boy."

Yan looked up at the man who stood a good dozen senamees taller. The man had a broader chest and dark hair that fell about his shoulders. The hair was the same shade as the patch over his eye. Yan noticed several knives on the man's belt.

"Have you come to kill me?" he replied. The man's lips pulled back into a full smile, showing two gold teeth.

"I don't buy dead men drinks, boy. Waste of booze. Drink up!" he motioned to the shot glasses and mugs. Yan did as instructed, letting the rum, sugar and lemon mingle on his tongue before swallowing. He chased the rum with the beer, noticing the beer was cool and bubbled on his tongue. Expensive

"Thank you," Yan said.

"The boy has manners," the man said to the innkeeper who nodded.

"I have a proposition for you, young man." The older man pulled off his cloak and hung it on a hook at the end of the bar. He sat on the stool near the end of the bar but kept from turning his back to the door. Yan sat.

"Yan sunna Webb, trainer of hounds. What a mess your dogs made of that boar today. Have you been here drinking since the Cunnel sent you packing?"

Yan nodded, feeling the warmth of the rum overpowering the cool beer.

"Rum, sugar and lemon. Doesn't that mean you are a sailor?" Yan asked.

"I knew you weren't as dumb as the Cunnel said." the corners of the man's lips twitched upwards again. The inn-keeper quietly went back to cleaning mugs. The elwus slid off his chair and grabbed Yan's orphan beer. He slunk back to the far corner of the bar. They both watched him. The man with the eye patch shook his head. "He'll pass out before I'm done explaining my proposition."

"What is your proposition?" Yan stumbled through the question.

"I'm not a sailor boy, but I will be putting to sea. Cunnel Bangor has contracted myself and my p'toon out to Her Grace, Amiral Celya Ban, First Amiral of all Nuwinga. Me and my mureens will be setting to sea with the Amiral over the North Ocean to Rosh. There, we will set about sinking Rabic ships and killing Rabic pirates until either the Presden of Nuwinga tells us to sail home or the Patriarch of all Rosh gets tired of us wooing all their fair maidens, or boys, or even tweens, if you find that enticing. The Amiral told Cappen to scour all the towns and villages of Nuwinga for anything that might give us a tactical edge over the Rabs, or failing that, any able sailors we can coax onto a ship, or failing that, any warm bodies that can learn to hoist a sail. You and your dogs might suffice for the first, or failing that, least the last. So what are your plans after tonight boy?" he picked up his mug.

"Well, I thought I might go home," Yan slowly replied. He took a swig from his mug, too. "The hounds, my bag of clothes, are pretty much all my family gave me when I left. My older sister was always better at hounding. She will take over when my parents are too old to keep the village hunters supplied. I don't know how much a hound sells for here, and I can't imagine settling here as a dog farmer." He shivered at the thought.

"Well, boy, the Rabs are only dog farmers. And that's only the poorest of them. Over there, they have no dogs larger than maybe twenty kilgams. They certainly don't have hounds like yours. They'd run screaming at the sight of just one of yours!" He drank.

"I don't know if my hounds would be useful in a fight. They're hunters, not really fighters. You could probably find fighters if you sailed down to Ammers or maybe Worster. I hear they have fighters there." Yan blinked and drank again.

"I could, but I doubt a bunch of fighting mutts could spend months on a ship. They'd probably all eat each other. Anyway, think on it. I will return in the morning for your answer. You'll be better paid in the service of an Amiral than farming dogs in this town." The man downed his beer, stood, threw his cloak over his shoulder, and strode from the bar.

When he had gone, the innkeeper sidled over to where Yan sat. Nearly whispering, he said, "I'd get you a good price for those dogs. The town doesn't have but one dog farmer. It's a better job then getting drawn by a bunch of Rabs ten thousand kloms from here under someone else's sky."

"My hounds are not for sale," Yan replied.

"Sheath yourself," the innkeeper shrugged. He moved off down the bar. The elwus snored in the corner, cuddled up with his tar. Yan drank the last of his beer and stepped out the back of the inn into the blustery night. He relieved himself in the back alley then walked to the small barn behind the inn. One of the hounds stirred when he entered. Yan followed the sound of thumping tails. He laid out his own olive drab cloak over the hay and laid down next to his hounds. One of them licked the tears off his face. He closed his eyes and dreamed of another failed hunt. Morning came too soon.

In the Hold

Yan leaned back against the hull of the ship. The bottom seemed to fall out again from under it. His stomach crawled around his insides, trying to find a place that it could curl up and die. Yan thought about throwing up again. The light in the hold came only from small ventilation shafts that ran up to the deck. He sat opposite of the kennel in which his hounds slept. They all looked at him forlornly. He shook his head, leaned back again, and tried to sleep.

Sleep only brought dreams … dreams of death and dying …dreams of a man screaming … dreams of howls of pain. He awoke and saw one of the ugliest sailors on board standing over him. Yan thought he was going to poke sticks through the bars of the kennel at his hounds as some of the other sailors had done.

"You need a slop bucket, boy?" the man asked him. The sailor did not seem to notice the heaving waves. He did not lean against the ribs of the hull the way Yan did when he bothered to try walking.

"No, I think I will be okay. I don't have anything left," he croaked out. The sailor smiled a gap-toothed grin.

"Feedmaster has a task for you. Well, for your dogs. They eat rats?" The sailor replied.

"I would think so. I think they are as hungry as me," Yan shrugged. He stood, keeping his left hand on the rib of the hull. "Where are the rats?"

"Grab one that likes close quarters and follow me," the sailor motioned to the kennel. Yan staggered over to the kennel. He knelt down and opened the door. He whistled and called for Dalya, the smallest of his hounds.

"She's really too big for a rat hunt, but we can try," he opened the kennel and Dalya, his short-legged hound came out of the kennel and sat down beside Yan. Like Yan, none of the hounds had eaten much since boarding the ship. He and the hound followed the sailor towards the trap door leading to the hold. The sailor stopped at the post by the door and pulled a lantern off a nail. He handed it to Yan and fished about for a striker and flint. Yan barely maintained his balance holding the lantern for the sailor.

"What's your name again?" he asked. The sailor grunted, pulled the flint and striker from a pouch, and lit the wick. The man opened the trap door and led the way into the darkness of the ship's hold, bending low to avoid hitting their heads on the beams. The sailor stopped and pointed at a large pile of tan hemp canvas. Yan took a knee and whispered his trigger word to the hound. She crouched low and sniffed the air. The sailor stood over them, watching the whole thing. Yan thought he saw the man roll his eyes, but in the blackness, he may have only see a flickering shadow cast from the lantern.

Dalya crouched low, moving forward slowly and purposefully. Her nose twitched faster. Yan thought he could actually hear the rats squeaking through the dank, close air. His heart beat a slow cadence in his ears. The gap between the canvas and the coils of rope barely left enough room of a small boy to squeeze through. Yan had seen several of the midshipmen come out of the hold with rat bites. He did not notice Dalya move up almost to the edge of the canvas. She leapt with a nimbleness he did not know she had and landed on a rat.

Dalya dispatched the rat with a quick shake of her head, then pounced on another. Yan and the sailor knelt, transfixed by the display. Dalya systematically rooted through the folds of the canvas. Occasionally, she would yelp as a rat's claw met her muzzle. Yan hardly moved. Some time later, Dalya trotted back to Yan with a fat brown rat in her mouth. Her haunches wagged with her tail, and she began chewing on the rat. The bones crunched between her jaws.

"How many did she kill?" the sailor asked Yan.

"I lost count. I think I'll take them to feed to the others. We can get a count that way," Yan held onto the posts and fumbled through the folds of canvas, extracting rat carcasses as he went. He asked the sailor for a sack, and the man produced a burlap bag. They both returned to the lights of the lowdeck with a full sack of rats. Yan let Dalya back into the kennel and began throwing rats to the dogs. Only the burly tackle hound Byrd threw a rat back, but promptly scarfed down the corpse. Yan muckraked the kennel and made his way with lurching stomach to the sundeck.

Stiff gusts of wind slapped him in the face. Salt stung his parched lips. The odious smell of sweat and unwashed bodies flew away, replaced by smells of frothy waves capped by streaks of creamy foam. The warmth of the sun refreshed him far more than the heat of the lowdeck. He staggered to the rail and dumped the muck overboard. He set down the pail and looked out at the swelling sea. The fleet spread out around the *Warrior Queen,* rolling over two meeda swells. Sails billowed in the stout southwesterly wind.

Directly to port, the *Hero of Udsen* slid into a trough, riding up to the crest of the next swell in unison with the *Warrior Queen.* The *Udsen* sported two decks of cannon, three full masts and a slender silver smokestack. The men of the fleet spoke in hushed voices about the blood that drenched her decks during the Battle of Lannic Sidi. According to them, the ship herself survived the battle, no thanks to her Cappen, but to a daring young Tenant. Now they all sailed under her banner.

Beyond the *Udsen,* a string of sloops and brigs flounced over the rolling seas. Each sported one or two masts, a single deck of guns, and no smokestacks. The sailors of the *Warrior Queen* would at turns dismiss the crews of the brigs and sloops as simple pirates or sea beggars, or conversely, commend them as the most able of sailors. Beyond them at about a full klom's distance, another line of sloops and brigs perched atop swells before sliding down into troughs.

Directly behind the *Warrior Queen* followed the largest ship of the fleet, the *Amiral of Saint Yan.* All three of her main masts sported four sails each, and each of her decks sported a full dozen guns on each side. Two traversing carronades protruded from her foc'sle. At least a dozen sailors clambered up and down her main masts, trimming a sail here, letting out more canvas there. Her jib seemed like it would drown itself in the back of the next swell; then the massive ship would slip up the back of the wave and perch upon it. On the few occasions he ventured to the sundeck, Yan could not take his eyes off the *Saint Yan.*

"She's a hell of a ship!" Jorge's words startled Yan. He nearly dropped the slop bucket as he turned to the Gent. One of the man's taut smiles tugged at the corners of the lips.

"Why doesn't the Amiral take her as the flagship?" Yan blurted out the question that had been on his mind since the fleet had left the Nuwinga coast. Jorge leaned against the railing.

"Well, the Amiral is a powerful woman, but Cappen of the *Saint Yan* is no middling Cappen on the make. She comes of a family that dates back of the drowning years. If I remember correctly, her family pretty much rebuilt Saint Yan after the floods and led the city through the worst of the century of the sea peoples. They were Amirals of their own and still sail under their own banner. If Cappen of the *Saint Yan* decided to head home with her fleet, Amiral Ban would have trouble stopping her. It might even come to blows."

A number of sailors boiled up from lowdecks. They formed a knot pressing around a rotund older man with a gray streaked beard. The bearded man stepped forward out of the crowd, followed by a girl not much younger than Yan. Having only seen her lowdeck, Yan noticed for the first time how closely she resembled the older man. The man threw a wadded ball of canvas in Yan's face. It bounced off his nose and over the side of the ship.

"What in drowned dell's name have your dog-chops been doing in the hold?" he bellowed. He took another menacing step towards Yan. In his hand, Yan noticed what was probably the biggest sewing needle he'd ever beheld. The young woman stepped forward as well.

"I, I, my hounds?" Yan stuttered. He fixated on the grey and brown streaks in the beard, noticing bits of string tangled up in it.

205

"Yeah, boy! Your damnable whatever you call them! They've been eating canvas down in the hold!" his voice grew shrill as it reached a crescendo.

"No. NO! They were just, well the one, I took her down ratting. One of the idlers told me we needed to go hunt rats," Yan tried to step back, but the rail of the pitching ship hit his upper legs. He nearly sat down. He could hear the greedy Lannic bubbling and sloshing below him. No one on the deck said a word. The sails groaned before the wind. Somewhere in the distance, Yan heard a single set of footfalls on the deck. A figure appeared in his periphery.

"What in the foam dancer's name is happening here?" a woman asked, her voice low but resonant. The sailors all stepped back, and the bearded man backed away from Yan. The threatening needle receded. Yan moved last and found himself looking upward at a pair of almond-colored eyes. Their gaze felt sharper than the bearded sailor's needle. Yan sucked in a belly full of air. Her features came into focus. High cheekbones, skin wrinkled, deeply tanned, tight-curled locks spilling over her tattooed shoulders, the tattoos receding in an inked wave under a bright turquoise tunic. The designs of the tattoos continued across the tunic, embroidered with a dull sulfurous yellow. Yan pulled himself up off the rail.

"Amiral Ban. I'm, um, I'm sorry Amiral Ban, Mam. My hound. I took her down to the hold. We were hunting rats. My hand on a heart-mother tree! We were not trying to damage anything. Just the rats." Yan struggled to speak. The Amiral nodded, and turned to the bearded man.

"Mam Amiral, Queen of the Sea. Mother of the Fleet. This fool and his dog-chop were down in the hold. They wrecked the spare canvas. Had no regard for the health and welfare of the crew!" the round man spoke quickly. Yan saw the sailor he'd met earlier walking quickly across the pitching deck. He said something to the mureen that flanked the Amiral. The mureen barely whispered to her, and she turned to the sailor.

"Amiral, Mam. The dog-boy was down there with me. I brought him down there to hunt out the rats the cooks and quartmisters have been complaining about." The sailor spoke as quickly as the round man. He looked down at the deck. Yan felt the ship roll down the backside of another swell. He braced his right knee against the rail, then straightened his back when the Amiral turned around.

"Gent Jorge, this boy serves at your pleasure. What do you say?" the Amiral looked past Yan.

"Amiral, Mam. The dog-boy knows nothing of the sea nor the drowned dell nor the foam dancer. His people dance 'round trees rather than raise them as proud masts of great ships. If a sailor came to him and told him to find a hot keel scrub, well," Jorge spread his hands for the punchline. The sailors all began elbowing each other and smiling in Yan's general direction. Yan tried to stand a senamee taller. The Amiral nodded.

"Canvasser, your concern is just. But I will not recommend Cappen flog the boy. Those rats were destroying the ship's grain. We will take on more grain than I would like in Greenlun due to the vermin. I will also recommend you, Gent Jorge, keep a closer eye on the boy and his four-legged mureens. The rest of you, get back up on those masts. You look like a pack of Jinya monkeys." the Amiral turned back to the aft of the ship and walked past the sailor that had led Yan to the hold. The mureen followed her. Amongst the dispersing crowds of sailors, Yan heard a shouted joke about why anyone really goes down into the hold.

Greenlun

Dalya and Byrd led the procession, their juniors followed in line. The freshly butchered hog bounced off every rock and root the leather sledge passed over. A padded rope passed over Yan's shoulders, holding up the tail end of sledge and keeping its contents from falling by the wayside. Yan whistled to stop, and the hounds slowed, then sat. Only Byrd and Dalya looked over their shoulders at Yan. The prevailing winds blew off the bay, carrying the smell of cook fires and a faint whiff of sewage. From the ridge, Yan could see the whole fleet. Their masts and yardarms stood still; their hulls barely bobbed. They reminded Yan of white oaks during the depths of winter, their trunks naked, branches exposed before the fierce northern winds.

Yan looked back at the sparse forest behind him with trees that barely stood 10 meedas tall. He hesitated, then whistled to the hounds and headed down the hill. Their pointed ears slicked back in parallel with the movement of their legs. Their noses twitched, and their tongues slapped against their lips at each whiff of the raw meat. In about an hour Yan and the hounds stopped at the edge of the rocky beach. Yan looked again over his shoulder at the rolling forested hills. Just ten more minutes to the docks.

Yan flung the padded rope from his shoulders. He sniffed then picked up a mostly dry piece of driftwood. The hounds yipped at him and looked at the carcasses. Yan wiped his nose, whistled low at them, and pointed to the slope. The hounds bounded off in the direction of his extended finger. Only Dalya ran to his side. Her tail slapped his thigh as she eagerly tugged at the high tide driftwood. He cut the wood into strips just half the width of his little finger. He arranged the strips into a cone, stuck the flint to steel and coaxed a tiny flame with low breaths.

Yan knelt on both knees, kissed the fingers of his left hand, touched his chest above his heart, and then blessed the logs being consumed by the fire. He didn't notice the approaching people until Dalya left his side and ran to the butchered carcasses. Her bark summoned the other hounds. They circled back and forth between Yan, the carcasses, the fire, and the interlopers. Byrd and Merc, another of the large males, stalked towards the closest figure. Their growls swelled from the tips of their tails and toes.

"Call off your mutts, boy!" a familiar voice came from one of the figures. Yan saw a flash of steel near one of the figures. He could make out their green coats in the dull, late-evening light. He stepped around the fire and whistled, pointing at his feet. The hounds all circled around him, ears alert, tails swishing over the pebbles of the rocky beach.

"Are you here to take the hog?" Yan didn't know what else to ask.

"Lords no, hound boy. We heard you were going hunting, but you left as soon as we docked. If you call those hounds off, we'll build a real spit and an actual fire for roasting those piggies. Dell knows if you're nice, we'll hunt with you tomorrow. Maybe get something more respectable, like a full grown boar!" Yan recognized the voice of Jendry, one of the mureens who answered directly to Gent Jorge. The man moved into the light of the fire and held his hands open for Yan to observe.

"I guess the hounds and I weren't going to eat both of them tonight. Maybe you mureens could help?" he motioned with his blade towards the carcass. A number of the mureens guffawed, disappearing into the evening shadows. Jendry kept the fire between himself and the hounds. The fire had burned low.

"Stir that fire up, boy, and I'll slide the hogs over. As soon as you back those hounds off, we'll have some roasted hog," he stripped off his green uniform jacket and laid his rifle on top of it. He plucked a small paper pouch from one of the pockets of his jacket. He emptied the contents into his right hand, crumpled the paper and tossed it into the fire. Grabbing the largest chunk of hog, he began working the herbs into the meat. "We capsized the *Warrior Queen* looking for herbs when we heard you were hunting. Some of the mureens said if you came back with nothing, we could flavor one of the dogs."

"No one is going to eat my hounds!" Yan pointed his blade at Jendry.

"Of course not, boy. I just wanted to make sure you had some fight in you with that last bit. Bring that blade over here and start cutting the ribs away from the spine." Yan walked to the opposite side of the hog. He knelt down and began slicing. Dalya followed him and lay down by his ankle as he worked opposite of the mureen. The other hounds lay down on the far side of the fire. They growled low at the returning mureens.

The mureens set to work building the flames. Shortly, the mureens had a rack constructed over the fire. The seasoned ribs Yan and Jendry had cut away were laid across the rack. Both he and Jendry moved to cutting up and seasoning the haunches of the boar.

Yan heard several of the hounds lick their chops behind him in the darkness. He flicked tendons and meat with too much gristle over his shoulder to one hound at a time. He noticed one of the larger mureens, who stood the farthest away from the hounds, staring as he flipped them pieces of meat. Yan took a thin strip from the bottom of the hog's right leg. He wadded it up into a ball, held it between thumb and palm. He motioned to Teeth, a white tackle hound. The fifty kilgram hound gently worked the meat out of Yan's hand and down its gullet. The big mureen flinched.

"You can feed one of them if you like," Yan grinned and held out a new slice of meat to the soldier. The man took a half step back. Several low giggles went around the fire. A skinny young mureen, a few years old than Yan, approached him.

"Loaf won't even eat dog, much less feed one. I'll give it a try." A long black ponytail fell out from under her leather helmet. She reached out a slender arm and took the slice from Yan. She held the slice between her fingertips and advanced on the hound. Yan grabbed her arm without thinking.

"These hounds have coywolf in them. Command them first, then approach. Say 'Teeth, sit!'" Yan told her. She commanded the hound as instructed. The big animal prompt-ly sat, pulled his lips back to show off two rows of large white teeth, and licked. The female mureen took a step back, looking at Yan for direction. He put his hand behind hers and pushed it towards the hound, saying "Good boy." The hound leaned forward and rooted the meat out from under the mureen's thumb and slurped it down. The other hounds quickly jumped up and moved toward Yan and the mureen. She stepped backwards from the hounds, bumping into Yan as she did so. The hounds formed a semicircle in front of them. Several of the mureens got to their feet. Yan heard sa-bers rattling out of scabbards. He also heard the hammer of a gun cock from across the fire.

"Sit, mutts!" never raising his voice, he commanded the hounds, letting the words resonate from the bottom of his lungs. All seven of the hounds promptly put their furry haunches on the gravel beach. Dalya and Legs, the slender pointer with a long nose and thin blond coat, laid down and slicked their ears back. Yan heard at least one solder behind him let out a sigh. The female mureen took her left hand off the stabbing blade tucked in her waist and relaxed.

"You make them sound so fierce when you call them coywolf. But these two are just looking for their fair share," she stepped away from Yan, took the hunting blade from his left hand, cut another two slices off the feet of the hog, and handed the blade back to Yan. "What do I tell them to do if they are already on their butts?"

"Say their names. Dalya and Legs, then say, belly here," Yan replied with a grin. The two hounds heard him and began scooting towards him. The mureen repeated the command and both hounds turned ninety degrees without lifting off the beach and began slithering towards the mureen. They stopped within arms reach of her, tails wagging back and forth across the gravel. She extended both hands with meat packed under her thumbs. The wagging increased as both of the animals received their rewards. Legs rolled over, sticking her paws in the air and whipping her back from left to right. The female mureen laughed. Two other mureens advanced on the hog carcasses, slicing off strips of meat and asking for the names of the other hounds.

"Pero, belly here." "Mable, belly here." Soon even the large mureen with the tense expression advanced around the fire and stood watching as the rest of the platoon fed boar scraps to the hounds. He occasionally flipped the racks of ribs, while Jendry tended the fire, though he never turned his back to the hounds.

Jendry summoned the mureens for meat and grog. They fell into line, each with a tin cup and slab of bread pulled from their hemp rucksacks. The large mureen pulled one rib off the fire at a time, slapping the meat onto the chunks of bread as each soldier stepped up to him. In turn, they stepped towards Jendry, who filled their tins with water, topped it with a shot of rum, and dropped in a sliver of lemon. Each soldier took a seat around the fire, putting down the tins and squeezing lemon into the grog.

Yan stood at the end of the line with Aliyah, the slender mureen with the long black pony tail. He noticed that no one ate but sat cross-legged with the cup in the left hand the bread and meat in the right hand. Yan received a slab of meat and grog and took a seat near his hounds. After he sat, he realized that his tin cup was in his right hand, so he switched to imitate the mureens.

The large mureen pulled a small brown clay pot from his rucksack. Removing the lid, he pulled a pinch of salt from the pot and moved from soldier to soldier around the circle, sprinkling salt one the rib in each soldier's outstretched hand. Each time, he would intone the words "Fat'r Nautlis, who bears up *Pelagaea* on his swollen back, we venerate you. Mat'r Gaia, giver of life to all who sail with *Pelagaea,* we give ourselves as we receive from you. We thank you for this food, and we will return to the sea and soil whatever we take from it."

The mureens tilted their heads to the sky as the large man spoke the words. Yan knew the words of the consecration as well as the ceremony. In his home village, the priestess would invoke the name of the Mat'r first, then Fat'r of the

213

sea, and their gifts returned to the soil before the sea. He leaned his head back as the blessing was said over his food.

The North Ocean

Lemon yellow sunlight washed the deck with a pale light. Yan had no idea what time it was, but he was sure it was past the sun's bedtime.

Admiral Ban had the crew going through the motions of battle. She divided the fleet into two around mid-morning. *Warrior Queen* and *Amiral of Saint Yan* sailed at the center of two crescent formations of sloops and brigs. The *Hero of the Udsen, Lannic Master* and *Scotia* led their own flotillas in V formations as the 'opposing' fleet. The ships sailed at each other over and over again through the course of the day, still sailing in a vaguely eastern direction, all the while circling each other looking for an opportunity to outflank the other. In the lowdecks, the sailors repeatedly ran guns out through their ports, then ran them back in, going through the motions of reloading and firing the cannons.

Jorge paced back and forth on the deck, cursing at the mureens as they practiced hand-to-hand combat in rhythm with the constant rise and fall of the deck. Yan and the hounds would race from one end of the deck to the other, ducking and dodging around the mureens. When they reached the bow, they would swarm a man-shaped dummy, practicing bite and release. After a minute, they would turn at race back to the stern and attack another boar hide dummy stationed astern. They made sure not to place themselves in the path of Amiral Ban as she moved periodically from the tiller on the command deck over the Amiral's Quarters on the level of the sundeck. Jorge had told Yan that any good

Amiral observes the action firsthand, then confers with her charts and radiomister in the quarters. By that measure, Yan guessed the Amiral was doing a fine job.

He certainly was not. His shoulders could not lift a saber. His stomach would not quit rumbling. His hips struggled to keep his torso over his legs, and his legs burned from the constant racing up and down the sundeck. The hounds, however, did not seem fatigued in the least. They had reduced both dummies to limp, eviscerated sacks. Yan yearned for some grog. Every time he thought of stopping to ask Jorge, the Gent's eye patch would pop in front of his mind's eye, and he would turn the hounds for another run.

An excited shout came from high in the crow's nest. One of the sailors banished to it seemed to fall down the main shrouds towards the deck. The woman was not falling, but her feet lightly touched the ropes as he climbed down to the deck. She raced to the command deck at the stern, excitedly pointing east. The petty officer and Cappen listened to her. Yan tried to concentrate on directing the hounds toward the dummy, but Jorge had positioned it in front of the comm deck. Yan made out the words 'ship' 'foreign' 'before' and 'quarters.' He glanced over at the mureens, who had slowed the pace of their evolutions. Jorge did not even curse them for slowing their pace. When Yan's gaze caught his eye, he motioned the young man over. Yan called a break to his dogs and trudged towards the foc'sle. The ship pitched forward into another trough as Yan reached Jorge. His legs nearly gave out and sent him toppling into the Gent of Mureens. He just caught himself by driving the tip of his saber into the deck.

"You'll need to sharpen the point when we go lowdeck for sleep," he castigated Yan. Yan figured he was getting off easy because the Gent wanted to know what he had over-heard. He pulled the saber out of the deck and stood at attention as best he could. The hounds all sat.

"She said something about a foreign ship, possibly running before the wind, and then the quarters. Not sure about that last bit, Gent." Yan filled in the blanks with words he had missed. Jorge nodded and raised his right arm. The mureens stopped. Yan noticed the clatter of gun carriages slacking off lowdeck. A different petty officer threw open one of the hatches near the foc'sle and marched up into the sunlight. She strode confidently aft.

Amiral Ban emerged from her quarters in the command deck, motioning to the approaching petty officer while conferring with Cappen and a tenant. Yan shook his head as she approached the main mast, dispensing orders all the while. The Cappen dashed to the tiller and the tenant grabbed the petty officer by the shoulder. Both women disappeared back down into the hold. The Amiral reached the mainmast with a different tenant in tow. The mureens all snapped to attention as she passed. Yan's aching back protested greatly as he tried to stand a little straighter in the woman's presence. The breeze blew the ends of her dark curly hair about her shoulders. She was the only woman on the ship allowed to wear her hair loose.

"Gent Jorge, prepare a boarding party, at least ten mureens. Tenant Rob will lead. Have the boy here prepare one of his dogs as well. The rest of the mureens should report to he foc'sle." Jorge snapped the back of his closed fist to his forehead. She returned the salute and continued towards the bow.

Jorge turned to Tenant Rob. The two men conferred briefly and the Tenant departed lowdeck.

"You heard the Amiral, pick one to board with us and kennel the rest," Jorge motioned with his left hand at the hounds. Yan gulped, whistled to the dogs, and headed lowdeck to the kennel. He fed and watered the dogs, then returned to the sundeck with Teeth. The tips of the burly golden hound's pointed ears twitched from side to side. Lowdeck, the sailors spoke softly as Yan and the hound went past. From the snippets of rumor he gleaned, the fleet might be just a few kloms from the Pillars of Mu'ham'd with the Caliph of Rom's mightiest war galleys bearing down on them. When he reached the mainmast, Jorge had ten mureens assembled in full battle dress, toting rifles over their shoulders along with boarding pikes.

Yan looked out to sea. The sloops and brigs clustered round *Warrior Queen* had spread out into a semicircle. Farther east, the rest of the fleet and their flagships continued towards Rosh. Directly ahead, a mast-less gray hull bobbed in the choppy blue waters. The *Warrior Queen* sailed directly at it.

"Gent Jorge, why is the fleet leaving us? And why are we sailing right up to this ship?" Yan inquired.

"The fleet's mission is to get to Rosh and try to cut down on all the piracy in the Balteka and the Nordsee. They can be reached by radio if need be. As for why we are boarding this ship. Well, an Amiral who leads from the fore can sail farther at night than another might in a thousand sunny days. An Amiral that leads from midships probably won't lose a fleet. An Amiral who leads from the stern won't stay Amiral for long," Jorge stared at the approaching wreck the entire time. Yan turned back to observe the approaching mess.

The mast had been blasted off almost at the deck. A number of holes dotted the port side of the hull between the waterline and the railing of the sundeck. Yan could see odd scraps of wood and broken beams scattered across the sundeck. The vessel was wider than most of the military ships, and its foc'sle and stern had been reduced to a pile of lumber that the poorest family in Yan's village might have been ashamed to call home. As *Warrior Queen* came alongside what Yan now thought of as a floating garbage heap, he noticed maroon stains splashed about the sundeck. Sailors tossed ropes tied to grapple hooks onto the wreck, mooring the two ships together. The mureens ran a ladder over the side of the ship onto the deck, which bobbed about two meedas below them.

"How is Teeth going to get over there?" Yan turned to Jorge. The Gent merely nodded above them. Yan looked up and saw two sailors operating the cargo boom attached to the mainmast. Below it, someone had rigged a large burlap bag out of a piece of canvas secured at each corner with hemp rope. They lowered the makeshift hound sling by pulley. The sling landed at his feet. He coaxed Teeth into it then waved his palm upwards to signal to the sailors to hoist the sling. He took hold of the guideline and went over the side of the ship, keeping his eyes on the hound as he worked his way down the rope ladder. He picked Aliyah out of the half dozen mureens standing on the foc'sle by her long black pony ail. She and the others aimed rifles at the deck of the wreck. His bare feet hit the sundeck as Teeth's sling bounced down next to him. The hound leapt out and barked at the contraption. Yan heard laughter from the sundeck of *Warrior Queen*.

Another mureen was already over the side of the ship and moving down the ladder to join him. Next over was Jorge. As soon as the swarthy man had his wing-tipped boots planted on the deck, he drew his boarding knife with his left hand

and his revolver with the right. He pointed it at the gaping hole in the sundeck where the hatch to the main hull must have been.

"Draw your blade and lead the way, boy." Yan did as he was told. He could see a steep ramp leading down into the cratered mess. He walked up to the edge and looked over. Teeth brushed up against his left leg and preceded him down into the hold.

Yan squinted as he advanced. He reached the bottom of the ramp and peered into the languid shadows of the moribund craft. He could only make out vague shapes in the distant corners. The hold of the craft had to be at least four meedas tall, making it at least twice as tall as the hold of the *Warrior Queen*. The splinted remains of the mast split the ramp as it reached the floor of the hold. The air reeked of decomposition and spoiled meat. The acrid stink clawed its way through Yan's wrinkled nostrils, plucking at the back of his throat. He swallowed before he could gag. He moved towards the bow, following his hound.

As his eyes adjusted to the low light of the hold, he began put together identifiable shapes out of the amorphous shadows. To his right lay a pile of tattered canvas. To his left, pushed up against the bulkhead, some bloated form spilled wriggling guts onto the deck. Yan glanced quickly over his shoulder. Above him, the boarding party busied themselves with other tasks on the sundeck. Ahead of him, a canvas door stretched taut over a frame blocked his view of forward section of the hold. Teeth stood motionless at it, his nose pointing to the crude wooden handle. Yan reached forward, grasped the handle and felt slime ooze between his fingers. He jerked the handle towards him. The door collapsed in a salty cloud of canvas dust and splinters. Teeth leapt over the tattered wreck. His head flipped back and forth. Yan barely made out the form of rat hindquarters clinched between the hound's jaws. The hound spat out the dead rat and Yan advanced into the forward cabin.

On the *Warrior Queen*, the same area housed the surgeons' quarters on the gun deck, and apprentices on the lower deck. On this ship, the forward compartment held nothing but a mess of smashed boxes and scattered provisions. Teeth busied himself snuffling around the chaotic clutter. Yan kicked a few of the shattered boxes around, finding nothing of interest. He turned, and the hound followed him. They walked towards the yellowish square of light amidships. Yan squinted, blinded by the glare reflecting off the deck. As they reached the edge of the square, Teeth stopped. His hackles shot up and he snarled. His deep, rumbling growl rolled aft into the darkness. Yan pointed his hunting blade.

A lone figure stumbled out of the shadows, pointing a wooden pole at them. His skin appeared gray to Yan, who counted every splinter buried in the figure's gaunt fingers. The sharpen point of the pole floated through the air towards Yan's face. A screech snaked across the void of the hold.

Teeth leapt at the figure, ducking under the spear. Both paws landed on the gray, cracked skin of the figure's chest. Jaws wrapped around the forearm, dragging the figure to the deck. The spear clattered down with the figure, landing more than three long strides from Yan. The hound released his grip, and the figure rolled away from him. The hound clamped down on the back of the figure's neck, pinning him down. The figure yowled in pain.

He moved forward, towards the thrashing figure.

"Quit fighting my hound!" He yelled. He repeated himself, but the figure continued slapping his hands on the deck.

Yan whistled to Teeth, who relaxed his jaws and backed off. Yan found his foot on the figure's wrist. He shouted for Jorge. Mureens tumbled down the ramp and stairs, surrounding the figure.

Archangel

The sun lurked below the horizon, although the whole southern half of the sky still glowed like an impending dawn. The sailor in the crow's nest cried out that land had been sighted. Sailors boiled up from lowdeck onto the sundeck, leaning over the rails and pointing south. A few even kissed each other, and the tenants said nothing. Yan emptied the hounds' slop bucket over the starboard rail. The sea spread out in all directions with no sight of land. He nudged Anold, the large mureen who always gave the blessing at mess.

"Maybe she just thought she saw land?" He gestured at the expanse of the Northern Ocean.

"Look up," he pointed a fat round finger to the sky. Yan looked upward and saw a flock of seagulls gliding about on an invisible thermal. Yan blinked. He couldn't count the number of days since he'd seen one. Another cry came from the nest at the top of the main mast. Yan followed the pointed fingers to the southern horizon. He could just barely make out billowing sails peeping over the horizon. The fleet had not seen another vessel since finding the wreck east of Greenlun. In a matter of minutes, more sails popped up over the southern horizon. Soon, a veritable wall of canvas sailed into view. They had reunited with the rest of the Nuwinga fleet. Shortly thereafter, a low dark line, barely discernible in the late evening glow, showed itself. They sailed along the coast of northern Rosh for a week.

Stomping feet awoke him. A large female sailor punched him in the shoulder, nearly knocking him out of his hammock. She said Cappen wanted him in his improvised mureen uniform above deck with his hounds. They had reached Archangel.

Yan changed quickly, constantly knocking into the hammocks of the other mureens, which were empty. He had evidently got the message last. He walked into the kennel and fitted the leather vests the mureens had made from the Greenlun boar hides on the hounds. On the deck, he whistled and motioned. The hounds clustered around him.

Along the port side, all the mureens stood at attention in full battle dress in a square formation. They wore green coats with yellow trim, leather helmets and white breeches. Jorge stood with Cappen, the tenants and Amiral Ban at the helm. Nearly half the sailors stood scattered about the sundeck or up in the rigging. Yan wondered where the other half was as he and the hounds took their places with the mureens. On shore, he could see a tiny figure waving a bright red and white triangular flag. Anold nudged him, and Yan saw that every mureen now covered their ears with their hands. He did the same. The sundeck vibrated, and the rigging hummed as the cannons on the upper deck fired a volley, followed by the guns on the lower deck. The mureens and sailors on deck removed their hands from their ears. Yan realized then where the other half of the crew had been. He looked toward the shore.

Archangel spread along a steep shoreline for at least five kloms. Terraced warehouses clung to the massive swell of land, surrounded by row upon row of thatched straw roofs. Yan spotted a series of three towers poking above the crowded city: One red, one blue, and one yellow, each tower topped by golden domes. At either end of the city, guns fired from terraced ramparts to return the salute. Crowds teemed along the waterfront, which itself extended many meedas out into the bay; hundreds of small barges lay docked at its wharves. After the last gun fired, Cappen gave the signal, and the sailors in the rigging unfurled W*arrior Queen*'s main sails. The ship plodded towards the largest jetty that stuck out from the city, the rest of the Nuwinga fleet behind her. After about a half hour, the sailors threw mooring lines to the dockhands, and after two months at sea, the *Warrior Queen* again married the land.

A dozen sailors manhandled a gangplank from the sun-deck to the jetty. Dockhands secured the gangplank. Ashore, a set of minstrels struck up their three-stringed instruments and commenced singing a language Yan could have scarcely imagined. Their round vowels and sharp consonants jelled in his ears. A cluster of a half dozen men stood solemnly on the jetty until the song concluded. The man in the middle wore a gold-trimmed conical hat and some kind of long robe or tunic striped with three thick bands of red, blue and yellow. Two men flanked him. One carried a huge, leather-bound book, and the other a giant glittering cross. Behind them, three men in yellow jackets and brown pantaloons stood at the head of a column of the Rosh soldiers.

Once the song finished, the man in the gold trimmed hat advanced onto the gangplank, scepter in hand. The other men carrying the book and the cross followed. They boarded *Warrior Queen* and stopped in front of the Amiral, Cappen and First Tenant. All three snapped the backs of their fists to their foreheads. At once, the mureens slapped their rifles to their shoulders, and the sailors crossed their hands in front of their waists. Yan signaled with a flick of his wrist to the hounds to lie down on the deck. The Rosh contingent exchanged formalities with the Nuwinga officers through a translator. The Amiral gestured to the foc'sle, and they all walked towards the bow.

The man in the gold-trimmed hat and the Amiral stopped in front of the mureens. The Amiral took three steps in front of the man in the gold-trimmed hat, turned around and gestured at the mureens. She declared loudly, "The children of Pelagaea have come to serve as the point of the spear?? bullet??. They shall fight with valor and bravery and will die if they must to send every Rabic pirate they find to the drowned dell below the waves!"

The mureens let out a bellow and removed their helmets, waving them above their heads. Three of Yan's hounds stood up and barked at the waving mureens. The others shifted their weight from one side to the other. Yan's face burned. He whistled and pointed to the deck. The hounds went down.

The man in the gold-trimmed hat turned towards Yan. He wrinkled his nose, and his face crinkled. He spoke rapidly to the translator. The man spoke to the Amiral with a thick accent, "Patriarch of Archangel, Savior of the Flock, asks why you bring food to show. We have much in city. They are large. Why you do not eat them on North Ocean?"

"Tell His Grace, that these animals are not part of the ship's store. They are our surprise for the Rabs should they get close enough to board *Warrior Queen*," She replied. Yan's chest swelled.

The translator hesitated, turned back to the Amiral, and exchanged a few hushed words. Satisfied, he spoke to the Patriarch. The man gave the hounds a brief, disgusted look.

Ladezh

A glow illuminated the southern horizon. Yan could make out the moon high in the late August sky. Cirrus clouds trolled the northern horizon, covering up the stars. Yan sat on the starboard rail. Cappen allowed the hounds onto the sun-deck after the day's hunt. They chewed contentedly on a reindeer bones. A light breeze occasionally ruffled the top-gallants, but otherwise the night was calm. Ankle-slapping ripples bounced off the hull. Many mureens and sailors were above deck, taking in the fresh air. Along each bank, trios of oxen tugged on lines attached to the each ship's bow, towing the fleet south towards the Balteeka.

Pawel the Rosh translator stalked across the deck toward Yan. He was the only Rosh not skittish of Yan's hounds. Dalya and Mabel looked up as he approached, thumping their tails on the deck. He sidled past them and sat on the rail next to Yan.

"This is pleasant night, no?" Pawel stated.

"It is always nice to be out from lowdecks," Yan agreed. He frowned then asked, "Why are you the only Rosh I've met so far who isn't scared of my hounds?"

Pawel chuckled, "Why Nuwinga not scared of hounds?"

"The sailors on this ship used to be," Yan shrugged.

They sat quietly for a minute. Pawel drew a small bottle from his tunic, pulled the cork, and downed a large gulp. He handed the clear bottle to Yan. Yan took a gulp, and handed the bottle back. Pawel laughed.

"Go ahead. Another drink, I bring to share, not to clean your mouth. There's lemon and rum for that."

Yan took the bottle and tilted the bottom completely ver-tical. The fire of the spirit slammed a door in his throat. He snorted, feeling his nose burn with the vapors of the spirit. He almost dropped the bottle as he choked the rest of it down. Pawel grabbed his tunic and pulled him forward.

"You can't join Mother Rosh just yet! You fall in here, the river byessie will take you," Pawel chortled, grabbing the bottle. Three of the sailors tugging on the lines of the jib chuckled, elbowing one another and shaking their heads. Yan's face turned red.

"That's good stuff." Pawel cast a look over at the sailors tugging on the line to hoist the jib. One of them looked back at him and shook her head.

"It's okay, you will learn to drink sterner stuff soon enough. You might even live through it," he patted Yan's shoulder.

"You Rosh sure talk about dying a lot," Yan finally got out. "That's all I heard about in Archangel. Talk and jokes about dying."

"Of course we do. Everyone dies. It's something we all have in common. Do Nuwinga make jokes?" Pawel petted Mabel. The Genda moose hound curled up between him and Yan. Dalya scooted over to Pawel's knee and stuck her head in Pawel's hands. He began kneading the hound's ears. Yan thought about their conversation out front of a crowded saloon in Archangel.

"There's something to understand about Rosh people," Pawel intoned gravely. "A Rosh, deep down in soul, understands life is quick. You Nuwinga hear that 20,000 souls buried under Ladezh canals and you look so scared. To us, they are souls laid on the altar, before the Patriarch and before the great God, and offered up to glory of all Rosh. How many of you, Nuwinga, die in a gutter, pissed on, unnamed?"

226

Yan thought about it. He stared across the hull at the shadowy birch forest looming up out of the still night. Water slapped at the sides of the ship. He looked back at Pawel, "I suppose some of us die that way. I suppose many of us do not. We live by choice in Nuwinga, and when we die, our bodies are left for Mat'r Gaia to take back what is hers"

"That's what your women priests might say," he gestured broadly, his yellow tunic flapping as he moved. "There's more to a life than just our quick time. There's life and soul of whole land, whole people, and whole church. Our holy Three."

The two sat on the rail for a while. Yan's ears seemed to pick up even more sounds in the night, as the heat from his face moved to his gut. In the canal, silvery fish leapt at unseen insects, splashing back into the water with aplomb. On the bank, the oxen grunted and heaved under the yoke. A lone bird called softly. Another low call came in reply. Pawel handed the bottle back to Yan.

"This is all just bunch of bread. It is some kind of bullshit. I don't know how say in Nuwinga. I was born seeing all colors – yellow and blue and red. I live like this long time. I see red in setting sun. I see blue of marshes and sea. I see yellow yolks. Then, I turn maybe eleven, maybe twelve. It happened sometime then. My head hurt so bad one morning. Like pins behind your eyes when you drink too much. It keeps on like that for days and months. I start dropping things. Everything ends on ground. My friends call me dirt boy because I'm always picking things up off ground. Only day anyone talks to me, day I sing in church. I sing in church, and they all shut up. They tell my dad 'Your boy gonna be one of Three.'

227

"My dad got no time for that. He say to me 'Pawel, you going to fish with brothers just fine.'

"Then come New Year Feast. Sun all gone from sky and whole village crowd into church to sing and dance and praise Three. I talk like a fool all through night, tell stories only old folks know. Major of our village hear me and all through spring he want me talking when he has guests. I tell story like a seagull shits.

"So I grow up, and I have only shriveled old priests for friends. My father keep saying I gonna fish with brothers, but he keep putting me to priests' door. It is cold even at equinox up this far above the crown of world. I think you say Mat'r Gaia's head or something. Anyway, some time there a little dog walk up to me when I sit on steps of church.

"So I sit there wrapped up in a deerskin and my naughty clothes. And up to me walks this little dog, only little because it young and hungry. So I give it bread and some fat and cheese. Dog start to follow me around, even into church. And it smart, so it hide in the dark corners of church when the people there. It shut up and hide when I up front telling story of Three.

"Finally people start to notice my rat, that what they call it, in church, so I gotta put him out back when summer festival happen. And festival, stupid dog shows up and follows me around town while I preach to people. My papa not giving anymore bread to me now, and brothers only take me fishing when they know he does not see. I give the dumb dog a name. I call him Laika. It old name.

"Now days getting really short, and I start to sleep inside church. Keeps me warm. I stay in there with priests. Laika stay with me even when days nice, because priests leave me and dog alone. I tell all old stories on steps of church and all over town—stories from Suffering and Temptation, stories from Volga and Don. You Nuwinga say 'drowning years.' We Rosh say 'time of rushing waters.' All old stories. I stay past equinox of fall. Then snow happens, and I run inside of church. Me and Laika. We lie on benches all night and listen to snow beat on window of church and feel cold wind blow across our faces.

"My eyes get worse, like some bird squeeze it claws in my eyes. I can't see no things. Just to find door or squat pot. No one in village tell me about herb. No body. Then New Year Feast come around again. Priests told to move away benches and whole village come to church to sing and dance. So we do this thing.

"Everybody there. Big man Grushka and his men there. Grushka stand hundred senamees above you. He wide, his hair long, he smell like bitter flower I don't know what to call. His story told in Yarslavl about battle at Poltawa. He sits next to altar and even tells priest what to do. No one in village say no when Grushka say so.

"He sit up there where Three should be for feast. He yells to back of church 'Blessed boy! Come up here and tell us all stories!'

"I walk up there slow, with stick, because all I see are crowded feet on my sides and follow light of feast fire in middle of church. My stupid Laika walk with me and push me away from people stick their feet out to make me fall. I stand there and tell long story about glory of Rosh when patriarchs small and mustache men big.

"I tell story he like, that Grushka. And he sit there and listen whole time. Then, at end he just sit back and say, 'Village is hungry, boy. Let us cook up that meat you have with you.' And everyone in village, everyone praise my singing in

229

church, all close in on me and Laika. That last night I leave village without my dog.

"I forget the wagon ride to Archangel. I wake up in Church of Holy Three there. I learn a dozen language in Archangel. I learn to walk in boats?? like never in my village. I learn about herb in Archangel. I went down past the Mark and up to Greenlun and all over to Katai-on-North-Ocean. I never keep dog, and I never set foot behind priest. I smoked herb, and I can see beyond my hands. Then, I hear about Nuwinga fleet comes to Archangel. I hear Patriarch looking for translators. Now I serve Mother Rosh, not some stupid Grushka, not some two-faced priests."

Pawel paused for a minute. His pronounced lower jaw and scraggly brown beard moved back and forth. Yan could hear him grinding his teeth. His milky eyes squinted, possibly trying to focus on the far shore.

"Someday I go back to village. Someday I travel a thousand kloms just to deliver one slap to that Grushka, and I will endure the beatings." He tapped the bottle and pipe together.

"Try again," he said. Yan took the bottle and took a long pull. Without taking time to inhale, he swallowed the spirits. He did not cough. Pawel took a long pull himself and yelled to the whole sun deck. "Boy drinks like man now!"

A few sailors chuckled. One of the male mureens yelled back across the deck something about hairs and Yan's backside. Some petty officer in the foc'sle yelled at Yan to shut the chattering Rosh up. Pawel stuck out his tongue and gestured rudely with both hands at the foc'sle.

"Petty officer forgot you speak Nuwinga," Yan finally took a breath.

"Petty officer thinks he going make cappen someday," Pawel added.

"Yeah, I know, and he probably will die first. Because that's the joke, right?" Yan spoke with all the sarcasm he could muster with the spirits buzzing in his head.

"Now you talk like man, too!" Pawel grinned.

A few days later, the fleet entered the eastern end of Balteka. Pawel and the other Rosh on board held a small service as the ships left the canal and passed over the drowned city of Peter. Favorable winds propelled them west, south of Suomi. They passed in sight of the Isle of Estee. Fishermen sailed out to the fleet to sell their catch.

The next day, Cappen summoned Pawel to his quarters to listen to a Rabic broadcast. The transmission came in during one of the later larboard watches. Pawel came out of the cabin a little while later. Yan and three mureens had two of the hounds out on the sundeck, teaching them to dodge the points of a boarding pike. Pawel wore a frown.

"How goes it with Cappen?" Yan asked.

"Rabic broadcast, probably from Detch lagoons." Pawel said. "Man on radio says message is from Caliph. In Rom. It's same message tattooed on the back of the gray man you pull off that wreck in North Ocean. Messages says Caliph welcomes fleet from over top of world to Balteka, and to graves of water."

Get Your Hounds

The fleet turned farther south, angling away from Norj and towards the Detch lagoons, which stretched for kolms upon kloms from Polsha to the western end of the continent. No more fishermen plied the waters of the Balteka. Every evening, the Rabic radioman foretold the arrival of the Caliph's fleet. The crew of the *Warrior Queen* placed bets on how many days would pass before seeing an enemy sail. Their answer came four days southwest of Estee.

The sun crept above the eastern horizon, but enemy sails did not come into full view until early morning. The sailor in the crow's nest shouted the warning just before the sailors of starboard watch came up from lowdecks for their first quarter.

Yan rushed to the sundeck as the sun first peaked over the eastern horizon. He watched as shapes began to form out of the ambiguous shadows of the shore. The shapes crawled along the horizon, their hulls barely visible in the distance. Their mast and sail stood out from the trees of the lagoons once Yan learned to differentiate them from the canopies. He counted six galleys. He thought he had taken an accurate count, but then one or two would disappear into the lagoons while another one or two would take their places.

He sidled over to where Jorge and Pawel stood near the mainmast and asked if he should prepare his hounds for battle. Jorge shook his head, telling Yan to wait for Cappen to call general quarters. Cappen did not call quarters that day, and the Amiral never raised the battle flag from the mizzen. The Rabic galleys never left the cover of the lagoons. The two fleets shadowed one another for another two days.

On the third day, a large galleass emerged from the dusk. It stood two decks tall, with a jib and driver sail attached to the mainmast. Gun castles stood at bow and stern, a second pair bulged out from each side of the hull at midship. A second set of flags flew from a flagpole mounted to the stern. Amiral Ban emerged from her quarters and stood on the foc'sle, peering through a spyglass at the new arrival. She turned to the ship's First Tenant and spoke briefly. The man scurried aft, disappearing into the Amiral's quarters. He signaled to the petty officers and mureens stationed by the ladders from the sundeck to the command deck. They sounded general quarters on tin whistles.

Sailors dashed across the sundeck to their stays, reefing main sails and deploying extra jibs, or lowdeck, preparing the guns for battle. The female mureens raced up the stays to firing lofts on the fore, main and mizzenmasts. The male mureens took up stations at the foc'sle carronades and on the sundeck before the comm deck.

"Go get your hounds, boy! Report to the stern!" Jorge shouted at Yan.

Yan dashed lowdecks. He dodged sailors breaking out stores of gunpowder and shot, tying off gun carriages, and readying buckets of sand. All seven hounds sat up in the kennel, watching the bustle of activity.

Byrd barked as Yan approached. Yan pulled the blackened boar hide jackets off their hangers, opened the kennel door, and stepped inside. He fastened the leather to the hounds and let them out. They followed him up the ladders, then once they emerged onto the sundeck, followed him to the stern. He noticed that only two smaller sloops had set full sails and followed the *Warrior Queen* towards the enemy ships. He could just make out the topgallants of the group of sloops clustered around the *Hero of Udsen* many kloms behind them. It appeared to him they might even be striking their sails. He reported to Jorge. The Gent told him to take up positions at the entrance of the Amiral's quarters.

"Why isn't the rest of the fleet joining us?" Yan asked the Jorge.

"Do you show all your cards when you play a hand?" Jorge replied curtly.

"So the sloops lag behind us to mask the movement of the rest of the fleet in case the galleys get past us?" The Gent merely nodded. Yan looked back toward the shore. The galleys had left the cover of the lagoons and pointed their bows straight at the three lead Nuwinga ships. Oars stroked in unison from each side of the sleek hulls. They had struck their sails. Yan felt the deck shudder, but heard no roar of cannon. Jorge nudged him, and Yan followed the Gent's gaze up. The unobtrusive smokestack mounted between the main and mizzen belched black smoke. The smell of burning seed oil filled his nose. The rumble increased, then changed to a gentler hum.

"Cappen just engaged the ship's steam engine," Jorge explained.

A low crack sounded from the port side. Yan looked over as a spout of water splashed in front of the *Ammerst Lad*, which had maneuvered almost a klom ahead of the *Warrior Queen*. The sloop did not fire a shot in reply, instead tacked further from the *Warrior Queen*. The other sloop *Flipping Cod* tacked less than a klom ahead of them. Another shot cracked from the foc'sle of one of the galleys. Another spout of water burst from the water ahead of the lead Nuwinga ship. Yan heard someone say something about another brig from the fleet following *Warrior Queen*.

A deep boom echoed from the shore. An orange flash and billow of slate smoke emanated from the large galleass at the center of the Rabic force. All the mureens took a knee. Jorge pulled Yan's right arm, bringing the young man's knee down to the deck, too. He heard a low whoosh and then a splash to starboard.

"They've ranged us in! You'd better keep your head down for a while," Jorge commanded. Still, the Nuwinga guns remained silent. Yan had not even heard the gun ports open. Suddenly, the ship lurched hard to port. Yan craned his neck. The Rabic galleys and the bow of *Warrior Queen* now pointed straight towards each other. The *Flipping Cod* veered slightly to port, though not nearly as sharply. The whole southern horizon flashed. Cannon fire rippled down the length of the Rabic formation. The early mist had burned away under the morning sun, but the galleys disappeared in a new martial fog. Yan could hear cannonballs ripping through the air overhead. He heard a wet splat, then a splash, as a sailor furling the foresail disappeared from the yardarm. A loud clang sounded from low on the port side. Shards of hot lead hissed up the hull and onto the deck. Yan thanked the Fat'r of the sea for the iron plates bolted just above the water-line. Still the guns of the Nuwigna ship remained silent.

"The Rabs drew first blood! We will draw twice that!" Jorge stood and bellowed across. The mureens kneeling on the foc'sle waved their helmets, the mureens in the lofts whistled and whooped. Even a few of the sailors in the rigging gave out a cheer.

As the galleys reemerged from the gun smoke, they lashed out again at the Nuwinga flagship and the leading sloop. Yan saw over the rail a line of splashes towards the *Flipping Cod.* The whole deck heard the crack and crash as the main mast of the sloop tumbled into the sea. The sloop stopped almost immediately. The Rabs directed another round of fire on the stricken stoop. Yan counted far fewer splashes, but heard a number of crunches and crashes as iron shot hit wooden beams.

The *Warrior Queen* turned hard back to starboard. Now she and the galley at the end of the Rabic line sailed on perpendicular courses. Yan peeped over the port side just as the carronades in the foc'sle sounded off. One by one, from fore to aft, the guns of *Warrior Queen* fired off. Both the upper and lower gun decks fired. In his periphery, Yan noticed smoke billow from the *Ammerst Lad*. The mast of the flanking galley disappeared, and its foc'sle cratered. Yan saw many of the oars hanging limply in the water. He could hear frantic shouts and splintering beams aboard the galley.

Humming under the deck increased as the *Warrior Queen* picked up steam. Even in the stoutest breeze east of Greenlun, the ship had moved only half as fast. The next galley in the Rabic battle line came abreast of the port guns, which sounded off again in succession. The Nuwingan's shot splashed around the galley. The third galley of the Rabic line traversed her carronades from the stricken sloop back towards the *Warrior Queen*. Both rounds punched holes in the studsails of the fore and main masts. The *Warrior Queen* tacked slightly back to port, aiming for a gap forming between the three galleys and the large galleass. The three galleys at the far end of their formation reached the *Flipping Cod,* pouring fire into her. The sloop's guns replied, but without her main mast, she did not move.

Guns fired from the foc'sle, midcastle and stern of the galleass. Shots smashed into the hull of the Nuwinga ship. Screams echoed up from lowdeck. The *Warrior Queen* slid down a low swell, crossing barely a hundred meedas in front of the Rabic galleass. Her guns sounded again, blasting the foc'sle of the Rabic ship. Her oars beat twice as hard as before against the surface of the green sea. The Nuwinga guns on the starboard side sounded off. Yan snapped his attention back towards the three galleys rowing hard towards the stricken sloop.

The starboard guns fired again, only two minutes after the first volley. Yan thought the rounds struck home but he could not be sure, for his attention returned to the port side. A rattle of rifle fire spat from the deck of the galleass. A Nuwinga mureen and two sailors flopped to the deck. One groaned loudly, the other two silent. A thump emanated from near the mast of the galleass. Two thin, dark lines arced through the air towards the Nuwinga ship. Yan could make out what looked to be huge fishhooks at their leading ends. The lines snagged in the rigging near the fore stud sails. Two sailors each clinched large blades between their teeth, worked their way along the yardarms towards the lines to cut the galleass loose. The lines were taut, and only a minute later the prow of the Rabic galley smashed into the port side. The carronades in the foc'sle fired frantically at the deck of the galleass, while high-pitched yipping came from her decks. Nets, lines and a ladder lunged across the scant space between the two ships. The cannon lowdeck bellowed, flinging shot into the oar deck.

The first Rab jumped onto the deck, squarely midship. The man was not much taller than Yan and not much older. He wore a light tan leather jacket tied tightly around his torso, and a leather helmet. He carried a large stabbing sword in his right hand. With his left, he drove a wrought iron spike into the deck and tugged on the line tied to it. Yan did not hear the shot, but the man dropped to the deck.

Two more men descended onto the deck. Yan heard neither the roar of guns nor the crack of rifles nor the splintering of wood. A loud snarling bark whipped his mind back into focus. The hounds were up on their feet, barking loudly. Jorge grabbed his shoulder and pulled him forward as he ran at the dozen Rabs busily fastening the lines from the galleass to the deck. The other mureens charged forward around them. Some fired from the hip; others shrieked like wounded hogs. The hounds followed on Yan's heels. A few of the Rabs fired at the advancing Nuwinga, but most pointed their pikes and rushed towards the stern.

"Hounds, hunt!" The hounds darted forward, around the mureens, closing the distance before they did. Yan rushed by the main mast, running at full sprint towards the large Rab wielding a huge boarding pike. In slow motion, he swung the pike at Yan. His vision narrowed as he focused on the pike.

The flat, spade-shaped blade slashed through the sunlight, then clattered to the deck. The noise broke Yan's concentration. Byrd had clapped his jaws around the man's left forearm. Crimson sloshed and frothed between the hound's teeth. The man let out a wail of fright and pain, slapping at the hound's head. Byrd released the man's arm, put his weigh on his haunches and leapt forward again, this time grabbing the man's left ankle. The hound crouched and pulled the man off balance. He fell to the deck, kicking wildly, as Byrd pulled him away from his comrades. Yan reached the man, not sure what to do next. The man rolled onto his stomach and tried desperately to claw his way back towards the rail. Byrd released his ankle and chomped the man's leg. Yan dropped onto the man's back. He slid the hunting blade between the man's throat and the deck and pulled the blade. The blade ground against bone, the scratching noise reminded Yan of the first hog his father had made him butcher.

Yan sustained a blow to the left side of his head. Pinpoints of blue light blinked into his vision. He fell to the right, off the dying Rab, onto his back. The stink of butchered guts washed over him. His vision faded around the edges. His eyes could only focus on a figure, distant in the loft of the main mast. Green-clad arms cradled wood steel. A bright flash blinked at him from the mast. A shadow blotted the sun. Something heavy, covered in tacky warm ooze, fell on his arm.

The shadow moved, sunlight returned, blinding him. Yan felt hot breath against his left ear and heard a gurgle, a moan and rhythmic thumping. Yan rolled to his left, towards the sound and vomited.

He pushed himself to his knees and saw Byrd crouched in front of him, with jaws clenched around a Rabic man's neck. The man flailed with a blade at the hound. Each time the flat of the blade struck the hound's boar hide jacket Yan heard a slap. The blade had made some progress through the leather. Numbly, he reached over the hound's back, took hold of the man's hand, and removed the blade. The hand went limp and dropped to the deck. Yan surveyed the carnage. Gray smoke floated serenely over piles of bodies. His hounds leapt onto the backs of the Rabs, dragging them to the deck for the mureens to finish off. Lowdecks, the cannons roared, tearing apart the whitewashed hull of the galleass.

Into the Marshes

The fleet sailed west for two days following the battle. One Rabic galley had slipped away, its captain used the wreck of the *Flipping Cod* to hide from the Nuwinga flotilla. Once they had sunk two of the galleys that had boarded the *Flipping Cod,* the third galley sprinted away, first north, then back to the southwest, into the lagoons. Lookouts in the highest crow's nests could spot its mast moving through the mangroves like tree loosed from its roots. By dawn of the third day, the mast had finally put down roots.

Amiral Ban ordered Yan and Yevan, the Rosh gunnery Gent, and Yan's hounds to accompany a contingent of mureens from the *Amiral of Saint Yan* into the marshes. No one had found a working radio on any of the galleys, so the Amiral wanted the crew of the fugitive galley stopped before they could reach friendly territory with word of the size and strength of the Nuwinga fleet.

According to Pawel, the Detch lagoons contained numerous small fishing villages and trading posts. The Rosh, the Rabs, and the Norj all had enemies and allies along the coast. Most villages feared the arrival of any tall mast or group of armed strangers, after centuries of continual warfare and raiding. He added that the Nuwinga should not expect to find friends in the marshes.

Neither shots nor any significant noise disturbed the early morning air as they approached the galley. They found it beached on a dry patch of land. The oars had been neatly stowed on the rowing deck. The slop buckets were empty. None of the carronades remained mounted to their swivel posts, and not a scrap of paper could be found in the officer's quarters in the stern. One of the mureens found a pile of bloody clothing, near the bow. Yan held the tunic to Pero's nose. The hound took the scent and bounded away with it, somehow managing to keep all four paws dry as he rushed off into the marsh. Yan, Teeth and Mabel ran after him.

Nose to the ground, Pero the Meycan blood dog led the contingent along a barely visible trail of dry land. The mangroves stood taller as they moved south. Spanish moss hung from their outstretched branches. Even as the day unfolded and the sun grew brighter in the sky, the stagnant marsh darkened. Periodically, a mureen would curse the drowned god and stab at the water with a bayonet. Yevan punched

Yan in the chest before he stepped over an upthrust cypress knee. They stood at the edge of a wide, open clearing.

The harsh noon sunlight blasted down on the clearing. Mangroves marched away from them on either side. Row upon row of felled logs stretched for three hundred meedas or so to a very slight rise. A line of mangroves had been planted atop the rise. Looking east and west, Yan saw the clearing stretched away from them, bending at right angles and disappearing from view. Yevan pointed a finger at the rise across the clearing. Yan strained his eyes to see what the grizzled Rosh had observed. Finally, a shadow slipped from one trunk to another. Yevan clenched the fabric of Yan's tunic and slowly, walked him to the right, behind the huge tree. Teeth and Mabel sidled with their master, huddling behind the cypress knees. Greedy marshy soil sucked everyone's feet down to the dense roots that spread out from the trunk of the thirsty tree.

Pero remained on the dry patch. She jumped forwards, nose down, following the scent. Yan quickly grabbed the other hounds' collars. He opened his mouth to call to the errant hound, but Yevan pushed his beefy, grimy hand across Yan's mouth and clenched. No one breathed. No breeze stirred the lolling leaves of the trees. Pero moved further into the clearing, sniffing left, then, right. Once, she put a paw on a fallen trunk then lurched backwards. The trunk rolled slightly towards her. A soft splash reached their ears. The two hounds tensed and strained under Yan's grip. Pero now stood two thirds of the way across the clearing. Yan heard a shot.

The hound yelped sharply. She flopped backwards. Her hind legs did not respond. Her front paws disappeared between two trunks. Both trees began slowly rolling towards each other, forcing the hound's paws into the water. She yowled in anguish. She lifted her right paw out of the muck, placing it on one of the rolling logs. The weight rolled the log, dragging her left paw deeper into the mire. Her head disappeared between the logs.

Yan tried to scream. His lungs moved air, but no noise pierced the air. His grip on the collars tightened. His teeth gnashed at the Rosh's hand. Iron and salt mixed on his tongue. The other hounds ceased straining and licked his face. A Nuwinga mureen behind him lifted her eyes to the sky and her lips mouthed a blessing to Mat'r Gaia for the hound.

The Tenant snapped orders. A pair of mureens set up the mortar they had lugged inland. The female mureens spread out, crouching on the knees of the huge mangroves and cypresses, pointing their long sniping rifles across the clearing. The Tenant and Gent dropped their packs, and a dozen of the largest men did the same. They put down their rifles and picked up boarding weapons: axes, machetes, sabers and revolvers. The Gent signaled to the mortar crew, the gun sounded.

A volley of rifles spat a response to the other side of the clearing. Bullets zipped overhead or splashed into the brackish water. The snipers returned fire. Three figures fell out of the reeds and bamboo on the far bank. The mortar round exploded on the top of the embankment. A man screamed.

Yan stood up, pulled the revolver Jorge had given him from its holster and let go of the hounds' collars. The Gent told him to wait for the first three mureens and then to follow him out of the cover of the mangroves. Yevan pulled his saber from its scabbard. The first mureens rushed forward, screaming the name of *Saint Yan*. Rifle fire rang from the far embankment, and the Nuwinga snipers returned fire. The Gent ran after the leading mureens followed by Yan and Yevan. The Tenant and the rest of the mureens followed. The hounds ran alongside Yan, baying and barking and growling. The Rabs on the rise fired again at the Nuwingans. One of the mureens behind the Gent fell forward with barely a grunt. Rounds cracked by Yan through the muggy midday air.

The mureens reached halfway across the clearing. The far embankment seemed to recede with each stride. Behind them, the mortar went off again. Another round exploded on the high ground ahead of him. Another volley of rifle fire. The first mureen in the Nuwinga line dropped to the ground, holding his leg, screaming. Yan jumped over the fallen man. After an eternity, the second mureen reached the far bank, plunging into the two-meeda tall reeds. Polished silver steel flashed in the light. The next mureen fired his revolver at a shape hidden in the reeds to their right. Teeth and Mabel sprinted ahead, snarling, finding an almost invisible game path up the side of the embankment. Their haunches disappeared into the bamboo and reeds. A human cry welled up from among the green stalks. Another surprised shout was heard, with the sound of thrashing and snapping reeds. Yan and Yevan followed the sounds through the walls of bamboo.

They found Mabel, with his jaws locked around a skinny young Rab's throat. On second glance, He looked younger than Yan. Yevan speared the boy with his saber. Yevan disappeared further into the bamboo, searching for the sounds of fighting and the second hound. Yan looked down at the revolver in his hand, then back at the dead boy. His whole body shook. More mureens had reached the base of the embankment. Some fanned out into the bamboo and reeds; others followed Yevan up the side of the embankment. Shouts and the clash of steel on steel rang above the fluffy white tufts of the bamboo. Mabel's nose nudged Yan's empty hand. He patted the hound on the top of the head, then tilted his head back, mouthing words to Mat'r Gaia.

One of the mureens stopped behind Yan and shouted for him to bring his hound up the embankment. Yan looked down at his hound, then, turned and followed the mureen. They met Yevan just below the crest of the embankment. Teeth had followed the Rosh out of the reeds. Someone's blood had splashed across his boar hide vest. Yan shivered again. The mureen said something about a group of Rabs holed up behind a palisade south of them. Yevan's hazel eyes scanned the top of the embankment, never letting his head get much above its crest. He said something over his shoulder to Yan.

Yan and the hounds scooted up next to the big man. The top of the embankment appeared to serve as some kind of the cart path. A narrow rutted road ran up to the gate of the palisade on the right hand, and arced back to the west. Tall mangroves and cypress trees lined each side of the road. Yan saw several black haired heads bobbing around behind the palisade. Behind it, he could see the tops of masts above the thatched roofs of the village.

He looked pointed at them and said to Yevan, "Yhose look like the masts on the galleys."

Yevan frowned, "Rab soldiers. Rab galleys"

The Tenant approached the edge of the path. He and the Gent were deep in conversation about how to work their way down the embankment and scale the village walls. Yan told the Tenant about the masts and Yevan's words. The Tenant snickered at the suggestion, saying these Rabs would break just as quickly on land as on sea. He rallied the mureens. The female snipers and the mortar crew were picking their way across the dry ground of the clearing. Yevan motioned to Yan to get away from the village. Yevan unslung his rifle, aiming it over the embankment. The Nuwinga mureens began working single file through the bamboo, moving southwest down the embankment towards the village. The last green coat disappeared into waving stalks. Yevan stood like a statue, watching the palisade. Two of the female mureens joined him, and Yan moved to the bottom of the embankment. The hounds and he stood by the mureens with the mortar. He looked northeast, seeing only fallen trees floating on the muck of the clearing. He squinted, noticing for the first time that the trunks of the trees lay parallel to each other and the embankment. None of them bore any branches, and their bases all appeared cleanly cut. Yan looked back to the west, seeing nothing but meedas upon meedas of fallen trees.

"This isn't a fishing village. This looks like a loggers clearing. We float cut trees down canals just like this back home," he mused to the gun crew. The woman in charge gave him a long look.

"That would explain why they beached the galley here, rather than keep sailing. They were putting in for repairs." She replied. She plugged her ears.

Yan put his hands over his ears. The gun belched smoke. They all watched the village. The round exploded somewhere behind the walls.

He did not know who spotted it first. Perhaps half a klom down the log jam, a low dun-colored shape stirred. The prow of a galley emerged from the tangled undergrowth past the village. Oars lifted and then sliced the water. In their rush to cross the clearing, none had noticed the open water west of the village. The bow guns of the galley traversed back to the east. Yan saw the gunners pull their lanyards. Silvery smoke puffed form the carronades. Yan and the mureens threw themselves onto the damp earth. The first round struck the embankment three meedas behind him. The other landed just short of them with the sound of a fist striking flesh. In the bamboo and reeds, air rattled out of someone's chest.

"They won't miss that shot again!" a mureen in the gun crew shouted.

Rifle fire barked and rattled from the deck of the galley. Lead rounds thudded into the trunks in the logjam. Much closer, rifles and pistols sounded from the green growth along the embankment. Yevan fired at something, followed quickly by the other snipers. Someone blew a whistle between Yan and the village. The undergrowth itself seemed to resonate with shouts and screams. Gun smoke began to rise slowly, mingling with the white tufts of thrashing stalks

"Run, hound boy!" The woman running the mortar crew shouted at him.

Teeth and Mabel jumped up, barking to follow. Yan looked at Yevan. The tall Rosh man had already slung his rifle over his shoulder and was dragging two mureens away from the embankment with him. Yan stood to run. He saw boarding pikes flashing above the reeds on the embankment. He turned and sprinted north across the clearing.

Looking over his shoulder, past Yevan and two snipers, he saw three other mureens appear from the thick grass, running from the village. The guns on the galley fired again. The ground around the three men erupted in twin gouts of black earth. One of the men seemed to shatter. Yan ran for the marsh. Bullets ripped through the afternoon air. His breath turned ragged. His vision telescoped. The shadows of the mangroves seemed to lengthen, reaching out to him as the trees receded. Mabel's brown haunches bounded ahead of him.

He reached the shadows of the trees. Someone behind him yelled to keep running. Each fresh breath clawed the bottoms of his lungs. He scarcely heard the report from the galley. A mangrove twenty meedas tall groaned and twisted, splashing into the marsh to his left. Bullets zipped overhead. The gun crew exited the anonymity of the shade, screaming at the three mureens waiting with the dinghies. Yan and the mortar commander dashed past the prow of the beached galley, his heartbeat hammering in his ears. Both hounds jumped into the first dinghy past the galley. They landed a split second before the mortar commander, who fell into the bow of the little boat, her legs tangled with the mureen who had been straddling the bow.

Yan grabbed the bow of the boat with both hands, trying to hold it steady as the two fumbled about in the bottom of the boat. One of the female snipers jumped into the dinghy. She knocked both of them over, sending all three of them crashing back to the bottom of the boat. Yan struggled to keep the boat stable.

The other sniper and the rest of the gun crew jumped into the second dinghy and pushed off from land. He looked back at the galley. Two mureens backed away from it, slashing at three Rabs wearing brown breeches and tan leather vests. The Rabs stabbed at them with long boarding pikes. Yevan rounded the prow of the galley and raced past all of them, carrying an injured mureen over his broad shoulders. A few meedas behind him, two more Rabs climbed over the side of the beached galley in pursuit.

The revolver in Yan's right hand lost its weight, floating upward and away from his body. He locked arm, his vision

247

focused on the dot of iron at the tip of the barrel. The onrush-
ing figures of Yevan and the Rabs blurred. He lined the back
sites to each side of the front. His thumb pulled back the
hammer. The yellow blur of Yevan's jacket floated left, the
brown vests came into view. He heard Jorge's voice in his
head, commanding him to exhale and squeeze the trigger.
White smoke jetted way from him. His left hand let go of the
bow of the boat. He fired again. His feet squelched out of the
mud and onto dry land. He turned and stepped towards the
galley. A light breeze blew the smoke towards the marsh. A
green-jacketed form dragged another green jacket away from
the vague shapes clad in brown. Yan fired again and again
until the revolver's hammer only clicked when he squeezed
the trigger. He stood still on dry land.

Yevan tossed the injured mureen into the dinghy. He
reached out, grabbed Yan's shoulder and pulled him back-
ward, nearly lifting him off his feet and tossing him into the
boat. The mortar commander caught him and guided him onto the thwart in the back of the boat. Yan dropped the re-
volved as she shoved the starboard oar into his hands. She sat
down next to him, grabbing the port oar. Yevan pushed the
dinghy's bow away from shore and climbed in.

Yan bent his back churning the water and pushing the little boat away from land. in front of them, Yevan and another
mureen pulled at a second set of oars. A female sniper sat in
the stern of the boat, facing land. Her elbows rested on each
knee, the long barrel of her rifle pointed out over the water.
She fired at the mass of Rabic men that now covered the bow
of the beached galley. Puffs of smoke jumped from their
guns. Bullets splashed around the boat. One bit the wood by
Yan's oarlock. His hounds huddled in the bottom of the boat.

Yan looked north at the other dinghy. They had pushed off as well, also rowing furiously away from land. Another volley from the Rabs thumped into the sides of the boat. A hot spike drove into Yan's left calf. He yelped, clenched the oar and rowed faster. A third volley splashed around the little boat. Finally, a smooth brown trunk of a mangrove slid past Yan and obscured the galley from view. Both boats rowed through the screen of trees, emerging onto the open sea. The first swell lifted the boat and it pitched forward. Yan's weight shifted and blinding pain raced up his leg. He did not remember screaming.

THE HEART OF WINTER

WALT FREITAG

Carver had done what he could; now it was up to the priestess to live or die. It would be a near thing, but perhaps enough warmth had remained in her core, her chest and belly, to keep her in the world. He had removed her sodden and frozen clothing—she would just have to accept that, if she lived—and wrapped her in the lom fur cloak he'd been wearing. The fire was built up as much as the limited draw of the fireplace would permit, turning the air in the shelter into a dense stew of the smells of wet stone, wet wool, and wood smoke. But warm. The layers of green and brown robes and limb wraps she'd been wearing—the ones she hadn't thrown to the wind in the final delirium of cold, anyhow—hung in the small center of the shelter, the only standing room, between them and the stacks of split firewood in the crawl space opposite. The garments were no longer stiff with frozen rain but would stay damp, in these conditions, for days.

The warming had to be slow. Too fast, and her blood could carry poisons from her chilled limbs into her heart all at once, shocking it into stillness. He had placed a skin of warmed water at the small of her back. A potful of ice water hissed and steamed on a grate over the fire.

It would be better to wrap himself up in the fur cloak with her, and warm her with his own body heat. But that, he'd decided, would be going too far, asking too much of her tolerance and his...dignity, perhaps. Reluctance, anyway. It they'd had to huddle in the storm in the open, that would be wood of a different grain, but here in the shelter, the fire would serve.

He shifted the cloak to uncover her head, and reached in to check her pulse at her neck. It was still there, weak but not faltering. Her hair was black and only shoulder length, perhaps abbreviated for the exigencies of travel. Her skin was darker than his—whose wasn't?—and more olive-brown than the Nuwingan red-brown or Gendan tan. That, and the cut of her tunic, made her most likely a Merigan priestess. They came sometimes, once in a great while, to the heart of Nuwinga, for a solstice vigil in view of the sacred Agocho. But this one had met instead a blinding storm of sleet and freezing rain and cold, whipped up to lethality by a merciless wind.

Her expression was serene, which was not a good sign, because her ears, nose, and fingertips would be quite painful when, if, she awoke. The whitened flesh there would feel like burns. Not like burns feel afterward, away from the heat, but burns that were still in the fire burning. He'd have to start attending those soon, to save them if he could, but it was still too soon. He reached under the cloak to her right wrist. No palpable pulse had reached there yet. But there would be time.

He reached past the hanging garments to grab two more splintery pieces of wood that he added to the fire.

* * *

Denna felt herself suffocating. She reached blindly to free her nose and mouth from some damp and heavy covering. Her hands and face were wet and numb and burning all at the same time. Frantically she pawed at the obstruction, some furry creature… no, just fur, and it shifted past her eyes and suddenly she was staring directly at a fire.

"Calm, there," a man's voice said. "You're safe. Lie still."

"Burner," she said to the fire, and was surprised that she'd spoken out loud.

"I brought you to a shelter. You were on the mountain."

She peered into the flickering gloom to find who had spoken. He was right there next to her, gray-haired and gray-bearded, dressed in a plain reddish-brown wool shirt and some sort of lined leather trousers. His skin was pale but his hands and face were streaked where sweat had run through smoke smudges. Those hands were the largest she'd ever seen, and the man's shoulders looked massive too. He looked like he had a pretty hefty belly to match, though it was hard to tell for sure, in the cramped space and shadowed firelight.

"Put your arms down," he said. "Your hands need to be in the warm water, and I only have one pot and one bowl to use."

She tried again to examine her hands but could only see them silhouetted against the firelight on the wall. "It hurts," she said, and at the same time realized that under the furs, she was all but naked. "Oh." Strangely that realization brought some clarity to her mind instead of alarm. The man was treating her. She remembered being in a storm, in a wind colder than she could ever have imagined. She'd been lost, nearly blind, battered by falls and near-falls, barely even to walk or even stand after the cold rain covered the exposed rock under her feet with a layer of ice.

She let the man guide her wrists back toward the containers her hands had been immersed in. The water felt boiling hot. She gasped with pain, but didn't resist.

"Your left hand got the worst of it," he said. "You must have taken that mitten off first."

"I took...?" She remembered warmth, a feeling of passing through an ordeal and arriving at a place of peace and comfort. "Yes, that's right. Mam Gaia came for me."

"You were dying of cold. That's what happens, sometimes. I've seen corpses half undressed, or all the way."

"I was supposed to be reborn. I was ready."

The man stood up, leaving Denna looking at his knees, the leathery trousers covering his legs. His voice came disembodied from the gloom overhead. "Reborn," he said. "Tell me, do you really think that, or is it just something you say to be polite?"

She didn't know how to respond to the impertinent question. After nearly being reborn in the storm, was she still in danger here, from him?

"Where are we?" she asked.

"This is a shelter I set up, high on a shoulder of Whycah Mountain. We're two kloms from where I found you. This part—" he patted the sloping roof and one wall—"is a ruin. It's the foundation for a tower that, I'm told, was once part of a machine that carried people to the top on a cable."

"Ruins? Here?"

"Oh, yes. They're around. Even Agocho had a machine, a railroad, that carried people straight up to the top. It went up a ridge on the far side from here. There are still traces you can find."

Which probably means he's climbed there himself, thought Denna. Maybe nothing at all was sacred to him. That meant she definitely was in danger, alone with him.

Still, he must have carried her here, and hadn't taken advantage of her while she'd been helpless. Even amid her other bruises and scrapes, she would have known, if he had.

"Of course, everyone knows about the ruins on the top of Agocho," he was saying. "You can see them from here, from the ledges below us I mean, across the valley. At the dawn of the old world, they called that part of Agocho, the highest part, Washington, after the first Presden of Meriga.

"Here's a story I heard. They printed papers up there, like pages of an almanac but written a few pages each night, to tell what happened the day before, that they heard by radio. Every morning, boys would take that day's pages and slide down the railroad tracks on wooden boards from the top to the bottom, to sell them to the people living in the towns down there. The boys thought it was great fun, even though sometimes one of them would break his neck coming down."

Denna pulled her hands out of the pot and bowl. Her fingers still tingled but the worst of the burning sensation had passed. She said, "and you believe that story, but not in being reborn?"

"Ah, 'believe.' I believe in stories, which is different from believing they're all true." The man crouched back down on the ground and poked at the fire.

"You priestesses talk about being reborn," he went on, "but I don't remember any other lifetime, or being anyone or anything but myself. So if I get 'reborn' tomorrow, and come back as a baby or, I suppose as a lom, to live a different life without remembering this one, well that's no different from me just being ended and some different baby or lom being born."

"'Ended?'" she repeated. "You're not an old believer, then?" Old believers didn't get reborn, or didn't think they did, but they believed they went somewhere else when they died. Unless they were different in Nuwinga.

"Oh, the old believers have a fine deep story. A resurrected god who forgives, and saves us from the wickedness we're born into. I wish it were so. I could be an old believer, except for the 'believer' part."

"You don't seem to believe in much of anything. What are you?" He was retrieving more wood from the stockpile. "Lumberman?"

"Ha!" he said. "Burner, lumberman, ruinman. Tanner, brewer, hunter, trapper."

"Which guild, though?"

He guffawed derisively. "None. I don't belong to any-one."

A man with no guild was no one to be trusted. She could be in trouble, and might even get reborn after all. But she wouldn't cringe or beg, or mince words.

"In Meriga we'd call you a defiler," she said.

"In Nuwinga too. Just words. I do what I do."

"You cut and burn and hunt and trap without blessing, is what you do."

"'Easier to get forgiveness than permission.' That's the rule in Nuwinga, for dealing with Circle, and with you priestesses too. Been that way since before the old world. Even in the towns. Nuwinga's different from Meriga that way, though they don't admit it. And up here, well, do you see any red hats anywhere around?"

"I'm not talking about Circle. I meant, without Gaia's blessing."

"If by Gaia you mean the world, here it is." He made an all-encompassing gesture. "And here I am. That's all the blessing I need."

"Taking what you want. That's the thinking that brought the old world down," she said. And what, she thought but didn't say, did he want now?

"This wood, this fire, is what *you* needed to keep you born, or however you'd put it. When you let others take what you need, and then you shut them outside the walls for it, call them lumbermen or ruinmen, *that's* when you're re-making the old world. Thinking yourself different, trying to deny that if you *have* lumbermen then you *are* lumbermen."

That, Denna knew, had been a long-running sore point between Temple and Circle. But it seemed he had her on the wrong side of it. "We priestesses know that better than any-one!" she said. "We carry Gaia's blessing to everyone, whether they plant or burn. But we can't stop people from being people. And we can't all live in the wilderness."

"I suppose this place would get crowded," he said.

"And I suppose asking 'what are you' was the wrong question," she said. "*Who* are you?"

"Ha! Got me there. They call me Carver."

*　*　*

"Please hand me my clothes, Carver," the priestess said.

257

She was staring at the fire again. "That thin brown cotton wrap first." Despite the warmth inside the shelter, broken only occasionally by cool drafts as the wind swirled this way and that outside, she was shivering now. That was a good sign, as long as her muscles didn't exhaust themselves.

Carver watched as she passed the fabric carefully through her hands, and produced by some sleight of hand a small cloth packet. She dropped it into the half-full pot of water. "Put this back on the fire to boil," she said.

Without waiting for Carver's reply, she reached under the cloak and pulled out a small knife. Carver wondered where she had carried it. Wherever it had been, he hadn't seen it or felt it while carrying her down the steep icy trail or while stripping her wet outer clothing. She used the knife to slit the edge of the cloth, which she then tore into long narrow strips. The movements of her fingers were stiff and clumsy but she didn't complain of any pain.

She'd be afraid of what he might do, he thought. Or what he might have done, if he were a lot younger still, though she couldn't know that.

He thought about reassuring her, making promises, but that would only give her more cause to fear. Better to pretend that no such idea had ever crossed his mind.

She sorted through her other clothing. It was still damp and smelled of smoke, but most of it was good wool and Carver knew it would still provide protection from the chill outside, where they must soon go.

"If you're leaving, Priestess, I'd suggest waiting for dawn," he said.

"It's not still solstice night." She spoke with certainty, but there was still a question in it.

"The night after. You slept all day. The water in the skin

is drinkable, and fresh water's not far. But I had to leave my tools and pack sledge up near the ridge to go after you. Which means I have no food here. We'll have to move on when it gets light."

Carver fussed with the fire while Denna rested quietly with her eyes closed. After a while, the pot had warmed and a spicy scent mixed with the stale air. She handed him the torn cloth strips and told him to immerse them in the heated mixture.

"Back in Meriga," she said as he put the cloth strips in the pot, "Gaia sent me dreams of Nuwinga. I saw the mountains, but they weren't worn and rounded like here, they were steep and sharp. And there was a cliff with a stone face in it, a bearded old man."

"I heard there are mountains like that all over the world, much bigger than these," he said. "There was a stone face a few days' walk from here, but it crumbled away with the old world. Maybe you saw pictures in an old book."

"I thought there would be something new here, something I'm sent to learn."

"So you didn't just come here to be reborn?"

"I don't know. Perhaps not."

"It seems to me if getting reborn was the idea, there's much easier ways to do it."

When the pot had cooled, Denna pulled out the soaked cloth strips. The two longest ones she wrapped carefully around her hands, finger by finger in a practiced pattern. When she was done the ends were folded inside somehow and each hand and finger was covered. She wrapped another strip in tilted bands around her face above and below her eyes, covering her nose and ears. Then she sat up, pushing the fur aside, covering herself with her heaviest green cloak.

259

From somewhere in the folds of the garment she pulled out another little herb packet. "Put a little water in the pot, and make tea with this," she said. "For both of us. It will give us a little more strength."

* * *

Denna realized she was no longer shivering. Her limbs felt weak but capable. Fortunately her feet were uninjured, well protected from the cold as well as from the rough footing, by heavy leather over-boots lined with wool felt that she'd acquired a weeks' travel inland from Porta. She would be able to walk.

The loss of her mittens was a greater problem. Though Carver had assured her that the worst of the cold was already past, exposing her raw hands to the wind would be excruciating. Carver agreed to sacrifice part of the length of his cloak, and when the small kit of needles and thread from her under-tunic turned up missing, torn away by the wind no doubt, he'd set out using his own belt knife to cut and lace crude lom fur hand-pockets for her using strips of the shaved hide.

She had offered to pay him for these goods when they reached a bethel house. He grunted vague agreement but wouldn't discuss a price. Her own money was lost with her own food and supplies, but her sisters or the people would aid her.

Her misgivings, that there she was entering into some kind of Dell's Bargain with this strange man, had not entirely left her. But she had little choice. If she could get back south to a town or even a farm, she could try to end the bargain and make a new one with someone more trustworthy.

She'd tried to make further conversation.

"Are you alone out here, Carver? Do you have a companion?" she'd asked.

"None," he'd said. "I'm afraid my tastes in… companionship aren't sanctioned here. Or anywhere."

"Really? You don't mean children, I hope."

"No!"

"Well then, I hear Nuwinga is like Meriga, very tolerant of variation. Men, women, tweens, as long as you're both willing."

"Well, there's the problem."

So, he wasn't willing. Asexual, loner, misanthrope maybe. Bad experiences with people. It happened. There would be time to probe more delicately. She was trained to advise in such matters.

Feeling more herself, she looked around the tiny shelter. The roof that had looked like stone was a slab of ancient pitted concrete, stained black with soot and steeply tilted toward the stone fire pit at the lowest end. The smoke from the fire ran along it toward its top edge. Here and there, deeper pits in the concrete exposed some of the metal rods embedded in the slab, from which Carver had hung the horizontal cords on which her clothing had… well, not dried, but gotten well-smoked, at least. The roof joined two side walls, which were more or less vertical. The whole structure had the shape of an open crate held sideways and then tilted up on one edge, but with the bottom partly filled with rubble to make the floor closer to level. The bed she'd lain on was a simple canvas cot stretched between smoothly carved wood poles. The open side of the shelter's concrete "crate" was closed with a roughly stacked wall of un-mortared stone, that stopped just short of the top edge to provide a vent for the smoke. A tunnel-like passage through the wall was closed off by pine boughs trapped behind a lattice of sticks.

Faint light was leaking through the vent, and peering behind the pine-bough door. It was dawn.

Denna began softly singing the observance for the sunrise, the parts she could do while laying down and uncertain of direction. Carver, still busy lacing the crude mittens, made no comment. She had worked most of her clothing back on, leaning close to the fire to bake as much of the moisture out of it as she could.

When she was finished, she declared the tea ready. The pot had cooled to a pleasant warmth and they both drank, she from the bowl and he from the pot. As the light from the openings had brightened, they had allowed the fire to burn low, and Denna watched with mixed feelings as Carver scattered the remains and stomped the embers and wet them into extinction, nearly emptying the water skin.

There wasn't much else to gather up. Denna unwrapped the bandages from her hands. They were still wet, and it would do her hands no good to chill them again. Instead she put on the fur mittens. They were loose, but folded inside so that she could keep them on by grasping them from within. Carver secured his knife, wrapped the cloak around himself, put a small bag of other items inside the pot, and slung the pot and the water skin over his back.

He shifted some stones at the lattice at the entrance and then lifted assembly lifted away, two lattices with fresh pine boughs squeezed between them. Beyond the opening, a passage sloped upward toward daylight.

* * *

The two emerged into gray brilliance and wind. They

were on a shoulder high on the mountain, at the bottom edge of a finger of forest stretching from the shoulder to higher slopes. The trees of the forest were barely few meetas tall, but densely interconnected, impenetrable except along the trail.

In every other direction, the ground dropped away into a white void. The wind-whipped mist exaggerated the heights and depths of the mountainside. Carver knew that there were a few places in these mountains where one might fall a great distance through open air, but there were not many of them, and this was not one of them. What looked like an empty void beneath their feet actually sloped away rather mildly a dozen or so meedas down. Still, a fall that far onto the tumbled boulders below would as likely kill you as not.

From above ground, all that could be seen of the of the shelter was the concrete ruin, a pedestal that had fallen from its footing when boulders below or above it had taken another step on their slow persistent march down the mountainside. There was no sign of the metal tower that had once risen from it, except some rust streaks on the downslope side. Unless one looked closely down the entrance tunnel between the stones, the shelter wall looked like any of hundreds of other piles of jumbled rocks across the mountainside.

"There's no clear path down from here. We have to go up first," he said to the priestess. He led her toward the forest.

In no more than a few dozen steps, they were in what seemed like an ordinary woodland path, except for the diminished height of the trees. The ground was wet from the mist but not frozen. The dense pines to either side blocked their view and cut the wind. The path soon began sloping upward, gently at first and then more steeply, and began switching back and forth across the width of the shoulder. For a few hundred meetas it seemed the land around them was rising more steeply than they were climbing, until what had been a ridge projecting from the main summit had transformed into the bottom of a forested ravine, with steeper slopes all around.

Carver turned around to Denna and pointed upward, toward the top of the ravine wall above them. There was another concrete foundation there, this one upright, as though it had been and would be there forever, still supporting a few upright metal struts.

The path turned along the ravine wall and worked its way up it, first to the left and then doubling back to the right. The slopes that had looked vertical from head-on turned out to be steep but manageable, retreating back the same distance they rose. Near the top, the tops of the trees were barely higher than their heads, and as they climbed past the last trees, the wind returned. The height of the ravine had taken them past a slight gradation of temperature, and the character of the mountainside changed again within a few steps.

Above them and to either side was an open slope of broken rock that seemed, not despite but because of the mist limiting their view, to stretch out without limit. The rocks were limned with ice that seemed to be growing from the stone, forming horizontal spikes of ice on every exposed edge. The spikes pointed directly into the wind that was carrying the mist up the slope from the shrouded valley below.

"This way," said Carver, proceeding to the right, sideways along a slight crease in the slope that made for slightly easier steps. "Easier going up ahead." Compared to the storm two nights previous, the conditions were not all that difficult, and except for grabbing his cloak for balance from time to time, she was keeping pace with little difficulty.

The daylight brightened on the slope to their left and suddenly, within a minute or two, the mist cleared away around them. They could see the valley below, and then the nearer slopes of Agocho, and then the whole central ridge. Agocho was covered in white. Even the ruins at the top, tiny at their distance, sparkled in the pale sunlight, brighter than the piles of gray and black cloud that still shrouded the surrounding hills. The storm had pelted Whycah with sleet, but the higher ridges of Agocho were covered with new snow.

"There she is, Priestess," Carver said. "Might that be what you came to see?"

"They call it the heart of Nuwinga," the priestess said.

"The heart of winter," said Carver. "Winter here comes earlier and deeper now than in my younger days. Old people I talked to then used to see snow once or twice in a few years in *their* younger days. Priestesses traipsing around on the solstice weren't risking their necks so much then."

"It's changed that much? Are you sure?"

"Here's a story I heard. Winter used to live way up in the very north of the world, on a big floating island of ice. It lived there all year round, sleeping through the summer, and in the fall it would stir and begin to prepare. Around the solstice, it would throw itself into the wind and fly around the world, bringing snow and ice and cold. But when the old world fell and the ice island melted, all the world saw any more was a weak shadow of what winter had been. The real winter, deep winter, took refuge right here in Agocho, waiting for the time it could return to its ice island. It's waiting still, but getting restless, like the start of a long long autumn. Give it a few more lifetimes, and it'll be back. The heart of Nuwinga is knowing it's there sleeping, knowing it'll be back."

As if to illustrate Carver's prediction, flows of cloud soon begun spilling over the shoulders of Agocho, veiling them again from view, filling the valley below, and creeping up the lower slopes toward them. They stamped the cold out of their feet and continued toward the path down.

* * *

"How long ago was it," Denna asked, "when winter came later than now? How old are you?"

"Now that's not a very polite question, young priestess."

"It's just, you know a lot of strange stories. I wondered."

"Strange stories are all I know. When I was a tot I learned to talk, and what are words but little stories? Ask what a word means and the answer you get will be a tiny story. Oh, sure, there are some words that you can point to and say, *that's* a tree, and *that's* a mountain, but even those things you don't know unless you know their stories."

"I know all about that."

"I have to come from somewhere, right? So if I didn't get reborn from somebody else, it seems I'm just made out of bits and pieces of old stories instead."

They talked about other stories. The time the old believers say a great flood covered the whole world. The chemist who brought a man made of dead body parts to life. Trey Sunna Gwen and his search for the seven treasures of the old world. The voyages of the living tree-ship *Pelagaea* that planted new forests all along the Nuwinga coasts after the old ones died with the old world. The priestess's own travels down the lower Ussen, up the Lannic coast to Ports, and overland to the mountains.

Their path climbed over a lip of piled rock and then descended into another finger of forest. Almost immediately, it began descending steeply, below the ice level. "We're heading for a camp of mine," said Carver. "Got some supplies there, some food, and a dry shelter."

"Is that where you live?"

"Up here? No, I have a comfortable lodge, up a different valley, where I can do my work."

"Carving?"

"Yep."

"What do you carve?"

"Here's a story you won't believe. I carve toys."

"Toys."

"For children. Dolls and tops and burr puzzles and little loms with wheels for feet."

"Really? Why?"

"Because I can. Well, and because toys are always new. A kid gets a toy and to them it's something new in the world. It's a way to be part of their stories. That's the only way of getting reborn I can accept."

The path rolled on down the hill, one stone after another underfoot for klom after klom. The forest grew taller and denser. The air lost its chill and a few clear patches appeared in the sky, though the trees hid the sun and the surrounding mountains most of the time.

"I said back there that there are bigger mountains," said Carver. "But there aren't any older. Not in the whole world. We can't imagine how old they are, but stand in a place like this and they'll whisper it to you.

"Here's a story I heard. There was a time these mountains were spires going seven kloms into the sky. When they were part of different continents before they split up and moved around to make the continents we have today. The world is old, Priestess. The difference between what we call the old world and today isn't even an eye blink to these mountains.

"Your Mam Gaia, you think of her as something like Circle, but bigger. Making rules, deciding punishments, listening in on your rites. Like she notices us at all. But who was she punishing when she ground these mountains down under two kloms of ice?"

The man's maundering was becoming irritating again. Denna said, "Carver, I don't think you really understand much about Mam Gaia."

"Maybe not. Just stories I heard."

Carver walked in silence for a while, and when he spoke again it was about mundane things. The hours of daylight left, the likely weather, the distances to farms and towns. In much less time than it had taken Denna to climb to the ridge on the solstice eve, the slope had again become gentle, and soon the path they were on joined a more well-beaten one that followed a rushing stream.

Over the sound of the water she heard faint voices, far away and out of sight. Carver heard them too, and took a few quick steps back, and looked around warily.

"People ahead," he whispered. "Don't tell them I helped you, or that you even saw me. You won't need these…" He took the improvised mittens from her hands. Denna didn't resist, but she felt him pull hard enough it wouldn't have mattered if she had.

"They've come looking for you, most likely, and found my camp. I'm sorry I didn't get to give you toys. If you get a chance, there's some in the camp, in a bag under the flat stone by the fire pit, but don't let them see you take them. Give them to children. Goodbye, Priestess."

He hurried away, faster and more furtively than she'd

seen him move before. For all his size, he seemed to blend into the forest and disappear within moments.

She didn't try to question or follow. Instead, she walked on to where the voices sounded clearer.

Easier to get forgiveness than permission, he'd said.

Well, there's the problem, he'd said. After she'd said: "…as long as you're both willing."

I do what I do, he'd said.

A resurrected god who forgives, and saves us from the wickedness we're born into... I wish it were so, he'd said.

What had he done, with what consequence? She could guess, but did she want to hear the story the name "Carver" would unlock?

She followed the voices to a hidden camp a hundred meetas off the path. Two men and a sister robed in green were there, searching.

She called out to them, wondering what she would tell them.

A MERIGAN GLOSSARY

A MERIGAN GLOSSARY

JOHN MICHAEL GREER

The glossary below includes all the place names in my novel *Star's Reach*, giving their modern equivalents, along with certain other terms that may be unfamiliar to readers in the twenty-first century:

Amiral: Admiral, in Nuwinga, the Admiral of a fleet is chosen from among the Cappens that bring the most ships with them

Affiga: the continent of Africa

Aiwa: the former state of Iowa, now a region in Meriga

Altan: town in Meriga, formerly Alton, IL

Ammers: town in Nuwinga, formerly Amherst, MA

Anarba: town in Meriga, formerly Ann Arbor, MI

Arksa: the former state of Arkansas, now a region in Meriga

Balteka: Baltic Sea

Banroo Bay: large, ecologically rich estuary at the mouth of the Misipi River, named after the drowned city of Baton Rouge

Baraboo Sirk: the one circus to survive the end of the old world; for many years based in Baraboo, WI

Baspresden: vice president, a hereditary officer in the Merigan government

Bellem: village in Meriga, formerly Bethlehem, IN

Burners: guild responsible for cremating human remains and safely disposing of the ashes

Burning Land: most of the state of Pennsylvania, which is riddled by subterranean fires due to an untested fossil fuel extraction technology used in the last days of the old world

Cago: city in Meriga, formerly Chicago, IL

Cairline: the former state of North Carolina and the portions of South Carolina still above water, now part of the coastal allegiancies except for a small western portion belonging to Meriga

Caliph: religious and political leader of Rabs in Europe

Cansiddi: city in Meriga, formerly Kansas City, MO; a garrison town, base of the Army of Suri

Cappen: Captain, in Nuwinga, a Cappen of a warship is often a hereditary position, especially Cappens of larger warships

Chicamog: village in Meriga, formerly Chickamauga, GA

Circle: in Meriga, Nuwinga, Genda, and the coastal allegiancies, an organization of women who have had healthy babies; in Meriga and Nuwinga, a major center of political power, closely allied with the priestesses of Mam Gaia

Clums: town in Meriga, formerly Columbus, IN

Coastal allegiancies: independent semi-feudal, semi-anarchic society occupying the eastern seaboard of the former United States from Deesee south to Joja

Conda: village in Meriga, formerly Golconda, IL

Congrus: hereditary advisory body, part of the Merigan government in Sisnaddi

Cunnel: in Meriga, a member of the lower aristocracy; the term descends from "colonel"

Deesee: drowned ruin in the Lannic Ocean, formerly Washington, DC

Dell: an evil spirit in Merigan folklore

Detch lagoons: area of northern Germany and all of Netherlands flooded by rising seas

Duca: town in Meriga, formerly Paducah, KY

Durrem: town in the coastal allegiancies, formerly Durham, NC; site of a battle between Merigan and allegiancy forces

Elcart: town in Meriga, formerly Elkhart, IN

Elwus: Elvis impersonator, a common type of traveling entertainer in Meriga

Ensul: town in Meriga, formerly Evansville, IN

Florda: legendary land drowned beneath the Gulf of Meyco, formerly the state of Florida

Fowain: town in Meriga, formerly Fort Wayne, IN

Fat'r Naulis: Nuwinga deity; male deity representing the wealth and danger of the sea

Genda: formerly Canada, a nation occupying most of the former eastern Canada

Greenlun: formerly Greenland, now a chain of ice-free islands in the Lannic east of Genda

Hiyo: the former state of Ohio, now a region in Meriga

Hudsen Straits: former Hudson River valley, flooded with salt water due to sea level rise

Ilanoy: the former state of Illinois, now a region in Meriga

Interruption of Continuity: program in the last years of the old world to construct computers and other technology that would remain viable for several centuries; abbreviated IOC

IOC: see *Interruption of Continuity*

Ipsee: town in Meriga, formerly Ypsilanti, MI

Isle of Estee: formerly Estonia, was cut off from mainland Europe after the Greenland and Antarctic inundations

Jennel: in Meriga, a member of the upper aristocracy; the term descends from "general"

Jinya: the former state of Virginia, now part of the coastal allegiancies

Jirido: town in Meriga, formerly Cape Girardeau, MO

Joja: the former state of Georgia, divided between Meriga and the coastal allegiancies

Jonsul: town in Meriga, formerly Jonesville, MI

Josbro: town in Meriga, formerly Jonesboro, AR

Keelo: kilogram

Klom: kilometer

Lannic Ocean: the Atlantic Ocean

Lannic Sidi: drowned ruin in Lannic Ocean, formerly Atlantic City, NJ, site of now-famous battle between Amiral Ban's ship Hero of Udsen and fleet of three Jinya pirate brigs

Lebna: town in Meriga, formerly Lebanon, KY

Lebnan: capital city of Nuwinga, formerly Lebanon, NH

Leedo: town in Meriga, formerly Toledo, OH

Leen: village in Meriga, formerly Saline, MI

Lekstun: town in Meriga, formerly Lexington, KY

Lom: llama, the most common livestock in Meriga

lowdeck: Nuwinga nautical term for any deck on a ship below the main deck

Luwul: city in Meriga, formerly Louisville, KY

Madsen: town in Meriga, formerly Madison, IN

Mam: common title of respect for a woman; derived from "ma'am."

Mam Gaia: the deity of the established religion in Meriga, the Earth understood as a goddess

Mat'r Gaia: Nuwinga deity, Mat'r Gaia is equivalent to Mam Gaia in Meriga

Melumi: town in Meriga, formerly Bloomington, IN; see *Versty*.

Memfis: city in Meriga, formerly Memphis, TN

Meriga: formerly America, a nation occupying the midwestern and southern parts of the former United States.

Meyaplis: city in Meriga, formerly Minneapolis, MN; a garrison town, headquarters of the Army of Misota

Meycan Empire: see *Meyco*

Meyco: formerly Mexico, an empire comprising the historic nation of Mexico, the southwestern quarter of the former United States, central America, and portions of northern South America

Mishga: the former state of Michigan, now a region in Meriga

Misipi River: the Mississippi River

Misota: the former state of Minnesota, now a region in Meriga

Mister: common title of respect for a man; also, a fully trained and qualified member of a guild

Mu'ham'd: the prophet Muhammad

Munsa: village in Meriga, formerly Munster, IN

Mureens: marines

Namee: tsunami

Naplis: city in Meriga, formerly Indianapolis, IN

Nardiga: the continent of Antarctica, now ice-free, forested, and inhabited

Nashul: city in Meriga, formerly Nashville, TN

Neeonjin country: the northwestern coastal regions of North America, including parts of the former Washington and Oregon states and the province of British Columbia, settled by refugees from Japan in the 22nd century of the old calendar; "Neeonjin" derives from the Japanese word *Nihonjin*, "Japanese person"

Noksul: city in Meriga, formerly Knoxville, TN; a garrison town, the base of the Army of Tenisi

Nordsee: North Sea

Norj: formerly Norway, one of the few parts of Europe not conquered by the Arabs in the 21st and 22nd centuries of the old calendar

North Ocean: formerly the Arctic Ocean

Nuber: village in Meriga, formerly Newburgh, IN

Nuwabnee: town in Meriga, formerly New Albany, IN

Nuwinga: formerly New England, a nation extending from the Hudsen Straits to the Lannic Ocean

Nyork: the former state of New York, now a region in Meriga

Oggis: the month of August

Old Believer: a Christian, as distinct from a worshipper of Mam Gaia

Old world: in Meriga, the common name for the era of industrial civilization

Orrij: ruin in Meriga, formerly Oak Ridge National Laboratories, TN

pancake, to: in ruinman slang, to collapse vertically, rather than falling over to one side

Patriarch: religious leader in Rosh

Pelagaea: a legendary living tree-ship that sailed the oceans and seeded hardy trees above every shore she visited, her story is a major pillar of Nuwinga faith

Pen: the former state of Pennsylvania, mostly abandoned due to underground fires; see *Burning Land, Wes Pen*

Pickers: guild responsible for sorting through trash for recyclable materials

Pisba: city in Meriga, formerly Pittsburgh, PA; a garrison town, the base of the Army of Wes Pen

Player: in Meriga, an idiomatic term for musician

Polsha: formerly Poland

Poltawa: formerly Poltava, Ukraine

Poyen: village in Meriga, formerly Napoleon, OH

Prentice: apprentice

Presden: president

Proo: town in Meriga, formerly Peru, IL

p'toon: Nuwinga term for platoon, generally twenty to forty mureens, depending on the size of ship, plus officers

Rabs (adj Rabic): descendants of Arabs, (and other groups from North Africa and the Middle East) that conquered most of Europe during the 21st & 22nd centuries

Rocalan: town in Meriga, formerly Rock Island, IL

Rosh: formerly Russia, one of the few parts of Europe not conquered by the Arabs in the 21st and 22nd centuries of the old calendar

Ruinmen: guild responsible for demolishing old world buildings and selling the metal for scrap

Rutlen: town in Nuwinga, location of Nuwinga's Versty, formerly Rutland, VT.

Sanlarun Straits: former Saint Lawrence Seaway, greatly expanded by sea level rise

Sanloo: city in Meriga, formerly Saint Louis, MO

Semba: the month of December

Shanuga: city in Meriga, formerly Chattanooga, TN

Sirk: circus

Sisnaddi: capital city of Meriga, formerly Cincinnati, OH

Skeega: town in Meriga, formerly Muskegon, MI

Sowben: town in Meriga, formerly South Bend, IN

sundeck: deck of a ship open to the elements; Nuwinga term

Suomi: formerly Finland, region that is nominally independent of Rosh

Suri: the former state of Missouri, now a region in Meriga

Suri River: the Missouri River

Tar: guitar

Tenant: Lieutenant, in Nuwinga this rank is only used for officers on a ship

Tenisi: the former state of Tennessee, now a region in Meriga

Toba: the month of October

Tomic River: the Potomac River

Troplis: town in Meriga, formerly Metropolis, IL

Troy: city in Meriga, formerly Detroit, MI

Tucki: the former state of Kentucky, now a region in Meriga

tween: intersexed person, a common genetic mutation in Meriga

twenty: idiomatic for twentieth birthday, the cutoff age for Circle membership

Url: village in Meriga, formerly Earle, AR

Versty: center of higher education; the versty in Meriga islocated in Melumi, the one in Nuwinga is located in Rutlen. See *Melumi, Rutlen*

Wanrij: village in Meriga, formerly Walnut Ridge, AR

Wes Pen: the western quarter of the former state of Pennsylvania, the only inhabitable portion; see *Burning Land*

Wesfa Jinya: the former state of West Virginia, now a region in Meriga

Wobbish River: the Wabash River

Yami: legendary drowned city in the lost land of Florda, formerly Miami, FL

Yarslav: formerly Yaroslavl, Russia, religious center of Rosh

Yoree: town in Meriga, formerly Peoria, IL

CONTRIBUTORS

Al Sevcik experienced childhood in a small river community in rural Hawaii. After graduation from Hilo High School, Al earned degrees in technology and business. He served in the Air Force during the Korean War. His working career took him to Denver, Los Angeles, New York City, and Houston. Retired, Al now lives near the Galveston, Texas, coast.

Grant Canterbury is a naturalist and writer who grew up exploring landscapes wild and settled in Alaska and the American West. His stories have been shaped by both the imaginative sweep of science fiction and the recombinant complexity of the natural world. Currently he is working on a novel of exploration and magic in the Renaissance. He resides near Portland, Oregon, with his family and quirky spaniels. See **canterburia.blogspot.com** for irregular project updates and posts.

Troy Jones III lives in Huntsville, Alabama, where he keeps the computers running, does sign-language interpreting, and makes soap. Not all at the same time, of course.

Tony f. whelKs is the fiction-only pen name of a fifty-something writing living in the East Midlands of England. Initially trained as a pharmacist, he has worked in electronics, communications, and renewable energy, then spent some years as an activist with a variety of environmental NGOs. He is also an amateur radio operator and permaculture gardener. His fiction was first published in the satirical periodical *Guernsey Attic Press* in the 1990s, but writes nonfiction newspaper and magazine articles under his real name.

Matthew Griffiths is a New Zealand engineer and environmental planner who currently lives in Australia working on environmental management. He loves reading and writing, especially about his twin interests: global sustainability and China. At other times he plays guitar with more enthusiasm than skill. He and his wife have two children.

Catherine McGuire is a writer and artist with a deep concern for the earth and the living beings residing there. She uses her creativity to speak to the many deep concerns facing us all today and into the future. Her poetry book, *Elegy for the 21st Century,* was published by FutureCycle in 2016 and her two children's SF novels published by TSR in the 1980's. She lives in Sweet Home, Oregon on a mini homestead, with chickens, rabbits and bees. Her sci-fi novel, *Lifeline*, will be published soon by Founders House Publishing.

Ben Johnson grew up in Tulsa, Oklahoma at the intersection of the Great Plains and Green County. He is a graduate from Booker T. Washington High School and the University of Oklahoma. After college, he moved to Delaware to serve in AmeriCorps and later worked as an EMT and volunteer firefighter, providing aid to those in need. He met and married his wife in Delaware and they relocated to rural Pennsylvania. Currently, they reside in Tulsa with two dogs, one cat, and three chickens.

In his spare time, he gardens, brews beer, and plays the guitar. His literary influences include Mikhail Bulgakov, Issac Babbel, Gorge Luis Borges, and George Orwell among many others.

Walt Freitag is a programmer, lab technician, game designer, DIYer, skeptic, and lifelong SF nerd. His first published work was a text-based computer game about exploring the stars. He's now pursuing more conventional forms of fiction, and more challenging views of the future.

ABOUT THE EDITOR

John Michael Greer is the author of more than thirty books, including four books on peak oil and two science fiction novels as well as the weekly peak oil blog *The Archdruid Report*. A native of the Pacific Northwest, he now lives in an old red brick mill town in the north central Appalachians with his wife Sara.

25894431R00172

Made in the USA
Middletown, DE
27 December 2018